AN
INVITATION
TO MURDER

An absolutely gripping murder mystery full of twists

NORMAN RUSSELL

Oldminster Book 1

Originally published as
Tongued with Fire

JOFFE
BOOKS

Revised edition 2021
Joffe Books, London
www.joffebooks.com

First published by Troubador Publishing in Great Britain
in 2019
as *Tongued with Fire*

© Norman Russell 2019, 2021

Cover art by Dee Dee Book Covers

ISBN: 978-1-80405-037-8

1. 'WILL YOU WALK INTO MY PARLOUR?'

Lord Renfield stood in the great window embrasure in the parlour of Renfield Hall and looked out on to the forecourt, where Jessica's red Mini Cooper was parked. She had come tearing in from Oldminster not more than ten minutes ago. He could hear her now, her bright, fierce young voice in conversation with her mother.

'But, darling, you owe it to your father to dress more like . . . well, more like a daughter of the aristocracy, to put it bluntly. Why pretend that you're something that you're not? Those wretched torn jeans are so *obvious*. And the same old sweater, day after day . . .'

Frank Renfield knew that Carole would be standing halfway up the great staircase, impeccably dressed, manicured and made-up. Jessica would be standing in the hall, defiantly casual, using slovenliness as a calculated weapon against her parents. That had been all very well when she was sixteen, but she was twenty-five now, and the time had come when she would have to toe the line. There had been plenty of boyfriends, some tolerably civilized, others horrendous, but she had been too free a spirit to commit herself to any of them. Well, the days of parental indulgence were now over.

'Daddy's living in a world of his own, Mother. He may be the twentieth baron, but he's on his uppers, isn't he? He should sell this place, and move into something modern and manageable. Nobody bothers about titles these days.'

He couldn't hear Carole's reply. Evidently mother and daughter had gone up to the drawing room to continue their pointless conversation — pointless because neither of them would give an inch.

There was another man in the room, a man of military bearing, who had kept silent until Lady Renfield and her daughter were out of earshot. Colonel Laxton had known Frank Renfield since they were both in the army. They had not been particularly close, but both had always been keen supporters of SSAFA, the armed forces charity. Laxton was there that day because he had come to collect Frank's annual donation. It had been a cheque for £50.

'It's all I can run to this year, Laxton. Things have been pretty tight of late,' Frank had said. He'd not heard Laxton's reply, because his whole attention had been given to his daughter's crude criticism of his way of life.

'Did you hear all that, Laxton?' he said, flushing with anger. 'Renfield Hall and its estate — such as it is, now — are both sacrosanct. They're part of an orderly universe that's not going to be changed. That silly girl doesn't know what she's talking about.'

Colonel Laxton could sympathize with his former fellow soldier. He suspected that Frank Renfield was heavily in debt, sacrificing his peace of mind to a theory of social station. Well, society was held together by hierarchies, and he could understand Frank's attitude.

'There have been Renfields at Abbot's Grayling for four hundred years, haven't there?' he ventured.

'Yes — yes, indeed. The house was Tudor originally, but it was largely remodelled in 1708. We've old Renfield portraits hanging here, Laxton, portraits by Reynolds and Gainsborough among others. Priceless. And you'll see the

Renfield achievements of arms blazoned in the windows in this room, and carved into the panelling in the gallery.'

'I wouldn't pay too much attention to your daughter, Renfield,' said the colonel. 'Girls can be very silly at times. My two were, but they ditched all their nonsense once we'd married them off.'

Colonel Laxton thanked Renfield for his cheque, and took his departure. Frank sat down and felt for his pipe and matches in the pocket of his tweed jacket.

Yes, Jessica was very tiresome at the moment, but when she'd said that he was 'on his uppers' — had Laxton heard that? — well, within the family, the truth of her assertion was an open secret. He had long ago sold off the farms for cash, losing valuable income in the process. There had been pressing debts that needed to be paid. They still had an investment folio, managed by his long-suffering solicitor, but everything now was held together by taking out long-term loans, with little prospect of them ever being redeemed.

But all this would change when Jessica married Karl Langer.

The simple act of recalling that name brought Lord Renfield out of his reverie. Leaving the oak parlour, as the great room was called, he crossed the entrance passage and went into the library. It was early September, and Lewis had lit a fire in the grate.

Framed to the left of the fireplace was a photograph of Renfield Hall in 1886, taken on the occasion of a visit from the Duke and Duchess of Fife. The royal couple stood in the centre, flanked by Lord and Lady Renfield. Arrayed on either side was the household of servants: butler, housekeeper, footmen in their smart liveries and the six maids in cap and apron. Today, the Renfields were served by Fred and Jean Lewis, known as a 'live-in' couple, and two young cleaning women who came in once a week from Abbot's Grayling to help Jean with what she called 'the heavy stuff'.

None of these people ever addressed him as 'my lord'. Fred managed 'sir' on most occasions, because he was a respectful man by nature. Jean never gave him any kind of title. 'There you are,' she'd say, putting down a tray. 'If there's anything else you want, give us a shout.'

But they were good staff in their way, and would dress up formally to serve dinner in the old fashion, standing against the wainscot until it was time to change the plates. Fred seemed to enjoy serving from the silver dishes, so that on those evenings when the family dined formally, there was a very faint echo of *Downton Abbey* in the proceedings . . .

And now the time had come to make Jessica marry Karl Langer. He was coming for dinner that night, and Carole would ensure that the girl dressed properly and behaved herself while he was in the house. He would arrive in his Mercedes C200, a splendid car that he had bought for cash on arriving in England from New York a couple of weeks earlier. He had three homes: something called a 'condominium' in Silicon Valley, an exclusive apartment in Manhattan, and a country estate in the Hamptons.

It was time for Jessica to grow up. Karl Langer was only twenty-eight, three years older than Jess, but he was already a multimillionaire. He had developed or devised various algorithms — whatever they were — that had delighted the manufacturers of computer games and made him a fortune by the time he was twenty-five. He had not been content to rest on his laurels, and had soon developed computer programs that were designed to be of interest to government departments concerned with national security. His fortune had doubled virtually overnight.

Karl Langer was fascinated by the aristocracy of the old country, and had hunted and shot with some of the foremost families in *Debrett's*. Frank Renfield had started to ensnare the young man just a year ago, showing him the sights of London, and wining and dining him in his club in Pall Mall. (He really must pay his dues there; the secretary was becoming rather strident about his arrears.) Now Langer was coming to dine, and if things went well, he could be persuaded to stay for a while at Renfield Hall. If the bait was sufficiently enticing, the quarry would irrevocably fall into the trap. It was an old story about to be repeated: a marriage of money and blood which would rescue Frank from the clutches of his creditors.

Lord Renfield glanced round the library rather like a producer surveying a stage set. The dark panelling and shaded lamps would create the right atmosphere when the two of them retired to sample some Napoleon brandy after dinner. They would occupy the two comfortable armchairs on either side of the fireplace.

In the centre drawer of his desk reposed the folder of documents that had arrived from the Lord Chancellor's Department a few days previously. They were there to show to Karl Langer, the innocent little fly who was about to blunder into his web.

* * *

Lady Renfield looked with distaste at her daughter, who was sitting, or rather slouching, on one of the antique brocade sofas that were a feature of the drawing room. It was a well-proportioned room, with a lofty plaster ceiling writhing with cherubs and acanthus leaves. Four fanciful Gothic windows looked out onto the rear gardens of the mansion.

Jessica was a very pretty girl with long, untamed blond hair and piercing blue eyes. She had behaved herself and done well at St Mary's, Ascot, but had left at sixteen to pursue an aimless sort of life on the fringes of the arts scene in Oldminster. She had begun, but never completed, a secretarial course.

She had toyed with the idea of studying for a diploma in cordon bleu cooking at Oldminster Polytechnic, but nothing had come of that.

Nowadays she hung around an antiquarian bookshop run by an appalling man named Guy Lavender. She had become far too friendly with the bookseller's nephew, Alan, who was supposed to be an artist. Well, all that would have to stop, now.

'Jessica,' said her mother, 'you will go now, wash, do your hair and change into something decent. Mr Karl Langer will arrive in an hour's time, and once he's here, you will entertain him, do you hear? You will be *nice* to him. You've met him on a number of occasions, so you should be at ease in his presence. He is a young American, rich as Croesus, who wants to ally himself with an English aristocratic family—'

The girl jumped up from the sofa, her face flushed with anger. It was at such moments that her mother saw her daughter's resemblance to Frank. The same bright red flush, the same clenched fists. Although Jessica did not realize it, she was very much her father's daughter.

'You want me to *marry* him?' Jessica cried. 'A boring computer programmer from Silicon Valley? Dream on, Mother. Yes, I've met him several times, each time manoeu-vred into the meeting by Daddy, who doesn't bother to con-ceal the fact that he wants to get his hands on his money. Well, I won't let him use me as bait. I shan't marry him, and that's that. We're not living in Victorian times.'

'Sit down, Jessica.'

There was such an imperious command in Lady Renfield's voice that her daughter did as she was bid. Her mother towered over her, suddenly threatening and intim-idating. Carole Renfield was fifty-three, but looked years younger. Jessica secretly envied her mother's confident beauty and poise. She was also afraid of her. She had been a wilful child, reducing her nanny to tears with her behaviour. When her mother had heard the nanny's anguished cries she had come into the nursery, told the nanny to go down to the kitchen, and had then proceeded to beat Jessica until she cried for mercy. Now she was standing over her, panting with anger. Her teeth were bared in something approaching a snarl.

'It was you, Jessica, who mentioned marriage, not me. But yes, what a good idea! We'll take it as a done deal, shall we? But if you won't marry him, you will break Daddy's heart. And, of course, he will stop your allowance. As for me

. . . well, I will devise ways of making you regret that you were ever born. I mean it, Jessica. Your father and I have our disagreements, but we are as one on this. The Renfields belong to Renfield Hall. We have been here for four hundred years. We are part of the fabric, part of its beating heart. And tonight, Daddy will tell Karl Langer a secret that will bind him to us as your husband and our son-in-law—'

'A secret? What secret?'

'You will be told later. Meanwhile, you will do as Daddy and I tell you.' Lady Renfield moved to the door.

'And you will stop seeing Alan Lavender and his degenerate uncle the bookseller. We have better things in store for you than an aimless existence with people of that sort. Go now, wash, change and go downstairs to welcome Karl Langer when he arrives. Waylay him before dinner, and talk to him nicely.'

* * *

Karl Langer leaned against his Mercedes and looked up at the front elevation of Renfield Hall. It was getting dark, so that the glimmer of shaded lights in the tall window embrasure of the oak parlour turned the coats of arms in the windows to dark roundels.

He had grown to love this old mansion in a way that only an American could. The house came with a history, and more important even than that, it was the home of a baronial family who had dwelt on that spot for centuries. In a few moments he would ring the bell, but first he would smoke a Marlboro in the little knot garden, which he knew lay beyond an archway to his right. It was still light, and the evening was warm, so he was quite happy to linger for a while until he'd soothed his nerves. He had been hobnobbing with English aristocrats for a couple of years now, but Lord Renfield still had the power to make him feel nervous.

He heard a door open, and turning, saw his host's daughter, Jessica, step out from a French window onto the path. Blonde like her mother, with her hair in a ponytail, she was wearing a floral dress and a string of pearls. The computing part of his brain duly registered her: *The Honourable Jessica Renfield, only child of Lord and Lady Renfield.* She was very pretty, but never had much to say for herself. But he liked her well enough. No, that was wrong. He liked her a good deal more than that. But then, he had to admit that he liked everyone and everything in Renfield Hall.

The girl stood rather awkwardly in front of him, holding out her hand, which he took. She treated him to what seemed to be an uncomfortably mocking smile.

'Good evening, Mr Langer,' she said. 'My mother has told me to be nice to you, so here I am. What are you doing in the knot garden? Why not try the front door?'

'I'm calming my nerves before I meet your father,' he said. 'In most houses I've visited in England, you're sent out into the garden to smoke. England is a very obedient country. Your parliament tells you not to smoke, so you stop smoking. They tell you to eat five a day, so you eat five a day. It's different in the States.'

Jessica laughed and made her way back to the window. 'Better finish that up, and ring to be admitted,' she said. 'And by the way, Daddy smokes like a chimney. So you needn't have risked getting a cold by loitering here among the flower beds.'

Karl Langer returned to the coffered porch and pulled the old-fashioned bell. Once again, he was to dine with Lord and Lady Renfield and their intriguing daughter. Each encounter drew him closer into their family circle.

The stout oak door was opened, and he was greeted by the family's butler. He could never remember the man's name, but he could recall his expression of hurt surprise on the first occasion they had met, when he had tried to give the man a tip. The man ushered him into the oak parlour and asked him to wait.

'The family will be down in a minute, Mr Langer,' he said. He made a gesture that was half nod, half bow and left the room.

Karl stood before the fireplace and took stock of his surroundings. By any standards, this was a splendid room of state. The fireplace was of old Italian marble, the mantelpiece supported by sculpted Tritons. The high ceiling of painted plaster depicted, he had been told, an English victory over the French in a battle forming part of the War of the Spanish Succession in the early years of the eighteenth century. 'If you look to the far end,' Lord Renfield had said on Langer's last visit, 'you'll see my ancestor, the twelfth Lord Renfield, who distinguished himself on that field. He was a very gallant soldier, so we've been told.'

A huge antique chandelier, converted to electricity, hung from the ceiling. There was a mirror on the far wall, and Karl Langer examined his own reflection in it. He saw a tall young man, with close-cropped fair hair. In his own estimation he was nothing much to look at, but he smiled when he considered that his great wealth gave him entrée to anywhere, with the possible exception of Buckingham Palace. He was wearing an evening dress suit which he had purchased in Savile Row earlier in the week. The tailor had demurred at the idea of 'off the peg', but Karl had prevailed.

The door opened and Lord and Lady Renfield entered. Evidently, Jessica would join them later. They greeted him with an unassuming welcome that always charmed him. These were aristocrats, part of the ancient fabric of England, and that added to their charm.

Lord Renfield never seemed to change. During the day, he liked to wear rather baggy slacks and what used to be called a 'sports coat', a comfortable tweed jacket with roomy pockets to hold his pipe and tobacco. That night, he was wearing evening dress, with an old-fashioned wing collar, but again, it seemed to Karl that his host contrived to make all his clothes look 'lived in'.

His face looked lived in, too. He was a handsome man in his mid-fifties, but his face was lined and ravaged, as though he had endured much suffering in his earlier years. Or maybe those lines were the bequest of dissipation, like Karl's uncle

Wilbur, who lived on a restricted diet of biscuits and mineral water in his mansion on Long Island. But old Wilbur didn't have Lord Renfield's piercing blue eyes, nor the sudden dangerous smiles that made him look like a satyr. And Lord Renfield could flush with anger at any imagined slight. A genuine, hundred-per-cent aristocrat, but a dangerous man to trifle with.

Lady Renfield, whose Christian name, he knew, was Carole, was a beautiful and charming woman. Tonight she was wearing a shimmering evening gown of some dark green material, set off with a diamond necklace and matching earrings.

The door opened, and the butler, now dressed in what looked like a hand-me-down penguin suit with its origin in some seaside café, entered the room.

'Dinner is served, Lady Renfield,' he announced.

'Thank you, Lewis,' she said, and Karl Langer followed his hostess to the dining room. Lewis, yes, that was his name. The decrepit butler who could refuse a tip from a multi-millionaire. A bizarre, wonderful country!

* * *

Dinner was uneventful. Lord Renfield talked expansively about the origins of his family and their titles, while his womenfolk remained more or less silent. When dinner was over, as though on cue, the ladies excused themselves and left the two men alone.

'Come into the library, Langer,' said Lord Renfield. 'I want to talk to you about family matters.' They were soon ensconced in Renfield's favourite room, with its dark panelling, old portraits and soft lighting. They occupied the chairs on either side of the fireplace, as Renfield had planned, and for a while sat in silent appreciation of their Napoleon brandy. Then Renfield spoke.

'I want to tell you something very interesting about my daughter Jessica,' he said. 'You like her, I think? Well, she's a fine girl, with many endearing qualities. But from the tenth of next month, she'll be something else. Just open that drawer in the desk, will you, and hand me the packet of documents tied with blue tape.' It was always a good idea to engage your dupe in some kind of activity. It helped to keep him off his guard.

'As you know,' said Lord Renfield, 'Jessica is my only child, and I have no brother or nephews. Carole and I hoped for a son, but it was not to be. So a few weeks ago I applied to the Lord Chancellor's Department and the College of Arms to have my daughter confirmed as my heir to the barony of Renfield by special remainder. Do have another glass of brandy, Langer. No more for me, thank you.'

He watched the young man as he busied himself with the decanter. He'd say nothing until Langer asked the inevitable question. Always leave the ball in your opponent's court.

'Special remainder? I'm not sure that I—'

'These peerages of ours are granted by letters patent from the Crown, and there are some situations in which the normal laws of succession through the heirs male can be modified to take notice of other claimants where no male heir exists. In such cases, known as special remainder, a peerage can be inherited by a daughter.'

Lord Renfield saw the light of excitement kindle in the young millionaire's eyes. Despite the complexities and obscurities of this particular branch of English jurisprudence, one point, he knew, had seized Karl Langer's imagination. The daughter — Jessica — could succeed to her father's title.

'I'm delighted to tell you, Karl,' said Lord Renfield, 'that my petition has been granted. After my death, Jessica will succeed to the barony as Baroness Renfield in her own right, and the twenty-first of that name. I can't tell you how relieved I am. There have been Renfields here at Abbot's Grayling for four hundred years.'

'So Jessica would be a baroness?'

'She would. If she is married at the time of my death, the title will pass to her, but her husband, of course, will remain plain "mister", unless she has married a man who already has a title. But the barony of Renfield will be inherited by the eldest of her male children.'

Got him! 'Thou shalt get kings, though thou be none.' So all hail, Karl Langer!

'It's just like what happened in the case of the late Lord Mountbatten of Burma,' Lord Renfield continued. 'After his murder, his earldom passed to his daughter by special remainder, and she became Countess Mountbatten of Burma in her own right. So there you have it. Now, before we join the ladies, let me show you some of the family portraits. I know how interested you are in the hall and its fascinating contents.'

They left the study, and Langer followed his host up the great staircase to a gallery on the first floor. Here hung a number of likenesses of members of the family, painted in previous centuries. Renfield stopped in front of a striking portrait of a gentleman in the sober dress of the late eighteenth century.

'I'm rather fond of this one, Karl,' he said, 'because he's my namesake. Frank. Not Francis, you know, but simple Frank. He was the fifteenth Lord Renfield, and by all accounts he was a bit of a rake, though he is said to have reformed in his final years. He died in 1812. That portrait is one of the last things done by Sir Joshua Reynolds.'

'It's a marvellous picture,' said Karl Langer. 'He's rather like you, Lord Renfield — in features, I mean. Is that a scroll he's holding? It looks like there's writing painted on it.' He bent down and peered at the scroll.

'It's a share certificate in one of the canal companies,' said Renfield. 'He made a goodly profit from that particular investment. And you can see Renfield Hall painted in the far distance. It looks very much the same as it does now, except that in those days the lawns came right up to the front door.'

'And who's this impressive old lady, sitting beside a dressing table? She's the only woman in this long line of men.'

'That's a Romney,' Lord Renfield replied. 'And the subject is Clarissa, Lady Renfield, the wife of the fourteenth baron. She was painted in 1776, and we still call that bedroom Clarissa's Chamber. It's said to be haunted by her restless spirit.'

Yes! This was the right moment to bring in the added fascination of a family ghost.

'Why is she restless? She looks rather nice to me. What did she do?'

'She didn't do anything. She was murdered in her bed on the twenty-fourth of June 1784. The culprit was taken up at the scene, found to be insane and died in a madhouse.'

The host led his guest further along the gallery, showing him more portraits.

'My father never had his portrait painted, and neither did I. But there's my grandfather, John, the eighteenth baron, who made quite a name for himself in the House of Lords. He was a friend of Asquith's. And that's Charles, painted by G. F. Watts. That's the finest painting of them all, I think. Charles was famous for doing nothing. He just lived here, and drew the income from the farms to live on. His wife was one of the Masefields of Compton Chase. Sound people, you know, but not much money there.'

He could see that Karl Langer was thrilled to have become the confidant of a noble family, sharing its family history. All was going well. Everything now depended on whether Carole could make their wilful daughter come to heel.

* * *

'So we've hooked him,' said Lady Renfield, putting down her copy of *Vogue* on the coverlet. She looked at her husband as he lay back with a sigh on his pillows. He looked flushed with success rather than brandy. She had heard him humming a little tune to himself as he prepared for bed in his dressing room, and knew that all was going to be well.

'Yes, my dear. Master Karl is well and truly hooked. But we must tread lightly. If we push too hard, she'll probably elope with the window cleaner out of spite. Silly girl!'

'Don't worry about Jessica, Frank,' said Lady Renfield. 'I will take her firmly in hand, starting tomorrow. She *will* marry Karl Langer, if not for love then out of fear of me. I've already warned her that I'll stand for no nonsense, and she knows that I'll keep my word.'

* * *

That night, Frank Renfield had a dream. It was a recurring dream that had come sporadically to disturb him for many years. He was standing on a river bank on a day of driving rain, looking down at the churning water, which was in full spate. It was dusk on a day in February, and he could just discern the thrashing limbs of a drowning man being carried away to his death downstream.

Then there was a tingling sensation in his back, and he knew that Victor Porteous was standing behind him. He could hear the quiet, cultured tones of his tormentor saying, 'I know it was you, Renfield, and I know why you did it. One day, when I judge the time to be right, I will expose your guilt to the world.' It was useless to protest his innocence. He just stood, trembling with fear, looking down at the churning waters, and the drowning man, and listening to Porteous's terrible threat.

He jerked himself awake and realized that he had broken out into a cold sweat. Had he awakened Carole? She knew nothing of these night terrors or what they portended, and she never would. One day, perhaps, he'd summon up sufficient courage to rid himself of this ghastly incubus, the obsessive investigator who was convinced that he was a murderer. There were always people to be found who would rid you of vermin for a suitable fee.

* * *

Next morning, Lady Renfield wrote a letter. It was something that her husband was absolutely not to see. All was going well, and it was time for her to indulge in a little private recreation — though it was more than that. She would post the letter herself in Abbot's Grayling, as she had done with the others. It wouldn't do to entrust that letter to Fred Lewis's hands.

2. THE ANGRY BOOKSELLER

The picturesque village of Abbot's Grayling, where Carole Renfield went to post her letter, stood half a mile east of Renfield Hall. It boasted a main street of eighteenth-century houses fronted by neat gardens. Its unspoilt appearance had resulted in it being used as a setting for a number of TV dramas, including a version of Jane Austen's *Emma* and two Miss Marple mysteries.

At the top of the village street stood the ancient parish church, opposite which was a huddle of old cottages and Victorian villas, known as Church Glebe. In one of these cottages lived a jobbing gardener called Matthew Grace, an elderly man stooped from years of working in people's gardens, but content with his lot in life. He was dependable, and unlike many men who called themselves gardeners, he knew all about flowers, and where shrubs should be planted so that they'd come up properly. There was only him and the missus living there now, as the girls were all married and away from home.

He sat at the kitchen table while Sheila, his wife, served him a cooked breakfast of bacon, eggs, hash browns and mushrooms. He'd already downed a mug of tea.

'Where are you off to today, Matthew? It's fine weather for September. You could do Lord Renfield's lawns. It's not going to rain, that's for certain.'

'I'll do Lord Renfield's lawns when he's paid me for the last two jobs I did for him. No, I'm going out to Forbes's Garage to give John and Flo a hand with their smallholding. It's only a mile out, so I'll be back about three.'

Matthew Grace left the cottage, climbed into his battered old Ford truck and set off on his journey.

Forbes's Garage was a petrol station housed in a centuries-old barn situated on one side of the Oldminster road. John and Flo Forbes were nice folk to deal with, proper Oldshire people, like Matthew himself. There weren't many incomers in this part of the county, thank goodness. John and Flo kept a little shop at the garage as a sideline, selling newspapers, a useful line of groceries and — something that Sheila loved — fresh vegetables from their own smallholding behind the garage. That's where Matthew was headed for now, to lend a hand with the heavy digging.

After a few more minutes he arrived at the garage and brought his van to a halt on the forecourt just as Flo Forbes came out to greet him. She was a pleasant, cheerful woman, just like his Sheila. She was wiping her hands on a teacloth.

'Hello, Matthew,' she said. 'You're nice and early! It's a lovely day, isn't it? Come inside. John's got something he wants to show you.'

John Forbes was sitting behind the counter of the little shop, where he had evidently been sorting out the day's newspapers. Behind him on a range of wooden shelves were displayed the bags of sugar, packets of tea, boxes of cornflakes and many other things that people suddenly found that they'd run out of. There was no longer a grocer's in Abbot's Grayling, and it was a long drag out to Robinson's supermarket at Binford, or the big Sainsbury's in Oldminster.

Matthew liked John Forbes. They were of much the same age, but John was going bald and had taken to wearing

17

glasses, which he kept perched on the end of his nose. He was falling into flesh, too, which was why he welcomed some help with the digging.

'Hello, Matthew,' said John, 'how are you? I've got something to show you here. It's an old book that I found in a box in the rafters when I was clearing out the attic last week. It might be worth a few bob. What do you think?'

Matthew took the book from his friend and examined it. It was obviously very old, and bound in cracked and stained leather. Its spine had snapped, and it was in danger of falling to bits. The best place for it, thought Matthew, was the bin.

'I'm not much of a reader, John,' he said, 'though I like John Grisham stories. They've a whole shelf of them in the library at Oldminster. But this old book . . . what's it about?' He handed it back to John. It was near nine o'clock. It was time to get on.

'Here, let me read what it says on the title page. I've got a reason for showing you this old book, Matthew. It says, "*The Farmer's Remembrancer*, wherein is contained all that is needed to conduct the skills of arable and dairy farming, together with a practical account of such an undertaking on the estate of a landed gentleman in Oldshire." Then it goes on to say that it was printed in London, by someone called Thomas Merton in Paternoster Row. Then there's a date: 1794.'

'Well, that's very interesting, John. But it's time we went out back—'

'Yes, but the odd thing is, Matthew, that we're mentioned in this book! You and me. Look!' He turned over some of the pages, and came to a list of names, which he began to read aloud. In spite of himself, Matthew began to take an interest.

'"These be the labourers working in the shippen or cow house, the sties, and other sheds on Lord Renfield's' estate: Matthew Grace, swine-master, John Forbes, cow-keeper" — that's you and me, Matthew! This old book's describing Lord Renfield's estate in the olden days. Perhaps Lord Renfield would be interested in buying it?'

Matthew Grace laughed. 'Oh, he'll be interested all right, and he'll give you a little promissory note in payment, but you'll never see your money. No, I tell you what: I'm working in Oldminster on Friday, all day. Now, there's a bookshop there, full of tatty old books like that one. Lavender's, it's called, on account of it being owned by a man called Guy Lavender. I'll take it with me, if you like, and ask him what he'd give you for it.'

'Well, that's a good idea, Matthew. Take whatever he offers. Let's get out in the field now. We'll work till twelve, and then Flo'll give us some lunch. I've got some John Brown's ale in.'

The two men went out into the field behind the garage and began the morning's steady digging. They were both thinking about the old book and the fact that their own names were recorded in it. Those men would have been their ancestors, thought Matthew, for he and John were both Oldshire born and bred. This was their land, their native home. If they wanted to, they could trace their own families back through the centuries.

* * *

Guy Lavender liked living in the ancient cathedral city of Oldminster. It was large enough to be a real urban hub, a vibrant working town, its streets lined with small shops, especially in the old quarter to the west of Cathedral Green. The high street still offered Marks & Spencer, with its enticing food hall, together with branches of Next, and other popular retail outlets. To the south, in what had been a fallow area of ruined meadows, a branch of Sainsbury's had recently opened.

Guy lived in a modern block of flats called Wyvern Court, built on the west bank of the River Ashe, at a point where the town petered out into picturesque countryside. Every weekday morning he would catch the red 26c bus in Vicar's Street, which took him as far as the Cross, when it turned sharp left into Folly Lane, and then into Abbey Flags, where it deposited him almost at his shop door.

From the front window of his bookshop he had a virtually uninterrupted view across the market square and Cathedral Green, and so to the majestic Cathedral Church of St Peter, rising on its mound. No other building in Oldminster had been allowed to surpass it in height. What you saw now was largely fourteenth century, though the top of the tower had been enriched with graceful pinnacles designed by Hawksmoor in the 1700s.

Guy was proud both of his shop and his reputation as an antiquarian bookseller. His many customers knew that they wouldn't find any bestsellers here, or remaindered memoirs of forgotten politicians, or the collected works of J. K. Rowling. They would have to go to Waterstones in the high street if they wanted things like that. His bulging shelves held countless volumes bound in antique leather or vellum, together with exceptionally valuable sets of Victorian classics. He could get you first editions of Dickens novels, early Brontes — all manner of marvellous things.

His nephew Alan helped him out three afternoons a week, and he paid him sometimes with money, sometimes with stock. Alan was a budding artist who sold some of his watercolours from a stall on market days. He was spending time with Lord Renfield's daughter Jessica, who hung around the shop, distracting him. She'd no interest in books — she only came so that she could flirt with Alan. Silly girl! Nothing would ever come of their little romance.

Love could be a damned nuisance. Guy had adored Roderick, who, like Oscar Wilde's 'special friend', had possessed a slim, gilt soul — among other things. Well, Roderick had left him for someone younger, his own tears and tantrums being to no avail. After Roderick, Guy hadn't wanted another serious relationship, and now he had to acknowledge that he was running to seed. Never mind. He took refuge from his difficulties in claret of various and varying vintages, with a goodly store of bottles from

Laithwaite's kept in the broom cupboard of his flat in Wyvern Court.

He had fallen into a reverie, and jumped with fright when the bell above the door jangled as a customer entered.

'Yes, sir, how can I help you?' he said. 'Why don't you sit down on that chair and take the weight off your feet?'

'Thank you very much,' said Matthew Grace. 'It's a warm day for September. I've brought an old book to show you that a mate of mine found in his attic. It's all about farming in the old days, and the funny thing is that there's an account of a working farm that's got our names printed in it — Matthew Grace and John Forbes. He doesn't want it, and wondered whether you'd give him something for it.'

Guy Lavender took the battered book and laid it on the counter. Matthew watched him in silence as he examined it.

The Farmer's Remembrancer, *wherein is contained all that is needed to conduct the skills of arable and dairy farming, together with a practical account of such an undertaking on the estate of a landed gentleman in Oldshire.*

Hmm . . . one of Thomas Merton's books from his shop in Paternoster Row, dated 1794. No author's name, which suggested that he was probably a farmer of noble rank, like the Earl of Leicester. Guy had had some of Merton's volumes on his shelves at one time, but not this one. He turned over the pages, noting some names and dates. And here was a letter, surely contemporary with the book, folded thrice over, and almost adhering to the surrounding pages. Very interesting. It would merit a thorough exploration, and after that he'd send it to a man he knew in Chichester, who'd repair and re-back it. He'd offer it for sale for £50.

'Well, Mr . . . er . . .'

'Grace. Matthew Grace.'

'Well, Mr Grace, as you can see, it's falling to pieces, and I can't see a sale for it. But I'll give your friend eight pounds for it.' He quickly opened the cash drawer, and displayed a crisp five-pound note and three shiny pound coins on the counter.

'That's very generous, sir,' said Matthew. 'Very kind. John will be very happy with that.'

When Matthew had gone Guy Lavender examined the book in greater detail. Yes, here was an account of the working farm practices on an earlier Lord Renfield's estate, with a list not just of the farmers and their men, but also one of the indoor servants, who were seen as a contribution to the efficiency of the whole working estate. Very interesting.

And this old letter . . . Very carefully, Guy opened the sheet of paper and spread it out on the counter. As he read, his face broke into a delighted smile.

Dear me! he thought. *How delicious! I should have given that chap a tenner! I'll lock this letter and the book in the safe before I close. And then I'll set to work verifying the assertions that its writer made two centuries ago. I can find a few things out myself, but it might be an idea to make use of Noel Greenspan . . . If all goes well, I'll be drawing a nice little income from this business. Well, well, who would have thought it possible? Maybe Alan will get his wish after all, and I will attend Oldminster's biggest society wedding of the year!*

* * *

Jessica Renfield had arranged to meet Alan Lavender in Oldminster's branch of Costa in Vicar's Street, on the far side of the Cross. She sat at a table in the window, her cappuccino surrounded by piles of uncollected used plates and cups. It was a noisy, hot place to be, but Alan liked it.

While she was dressing that morning, she had been thinking of Karl Langer, the man whom her parents were determined that she should marry. Imagine being tied to a man whose whole life revolved around computer programming! Okay, he had a flashy apartment in Manhattan, so he said, but how often would he occupy it? Men like him spent most of their time jetting from one business meeting to another. There was nothing very romantic about that.

Her mother had no patience with romance.

'If you don't marry him, my dear,' she'd said, 'your father will cut you off without a penny. And so will I. He's a very presentable young man, and you could always divorce him after a decent interval of marriage. They're used to that kind of thing in America, and you'd come away with massive alimony.' Well, Jessica wasn't going to marry him, and that was that. She'd move in with Alan, who had a gloriously untidy studio flat in Sable Court, behind the high street, where some Victorian warehouses had been converted into apartments.

That morning she had decided to wear her new denim jacket from Tommy Hilfiger, and her white cold-shoulder top. Her mother thought it was vulgar, but could hardly forbid her to wear it. Her skinny-fit jeans, also by Hilfiger, completed her outfit. Whenever she was allowed to dress in a way suitable to a girl of twenty-five, she had the knack of making casual look like smart.

Where was Alan? He'd said he'd be there at eleven, and it was nearly twenty past. A barista appeared at the table, and removed the used plates and cups. Jessica sipped her cold coffee and made a face. If he didn't come soon, she'd go.

At that moment Alan Lavender came into the café, dragging a framed picture through the entrance. It was crudely wrapped in brown paper, held together with little strips of Sellotape.

'Hello, Jess, I'm so sorry I'm late. I had to collect this painting from Michael Floss. He wants me to try and sell it for him at the arts fair next month. I'll just put this down, and then I'll get us some fresh coffee. Do you want anything to eat?'

'No, thank you.'

God, what a morning. They were supposed to be lovers, but he hadn't even kissed her. Him and his paintings. And why was he bothering to tout Michael Floss's pictures around? Couldn't he do that himself? Floss was supposedly the up-and-coming man of modern art. Every work of his consisted of different arrangements of black and red lines.

Why was she so grumpy? Maybe because he hadn't said how nice she looked. He hadn't even noticed her. She looked at him as he stood in the queue at the counter. What a mess! Nothing matched. He was wearing a skimpy zip-up windbreaker over a white T-shirt, and slim-fit chinos of sickly beige. His sneakers, once pristine white, had seen better days. And he was wearing that awful, *awful* blue bucket hat.

And Alan was starting to take her for granted. She was becoming an appendage, something that he dragged around with him, like he'd dragged that painting through the doorway. She thought of the quietly elegant Karl Langer, enjoying his cigarette in the knot garden, and bit her lip. Karl had never made a secret of his admiration for her, even when she went seriously out of her way to snub him.

'Here we are!' Alan plonked the tray down on the table and dropped into the plastic chair opposite Jessica. He *was* handsome, with a fair complexion, soulful brown eyes, and a shock of fair hair. When they were married, she'd take his wardrobe in hand. She'd take him to Hugo Boss in Winchester Street and tell them to kit him out.

'You're looking great this morning, Jess!' he said. 'Is that a new jacket?' He paused. 'What are you blushing for?'

She was blushing for having doubted his love for her. Karl was all very well, but there was something languidly superior about him that made him seem older than his years. Alan was vibrant with life and vigour. It was exciting to be with him. If her parents persisted in hating him then they'd elope. But there were things to tell him first.

'Alan, Daddy told me last night that when he dies, I will inherit his title. I will become Baroness Renfield, and if I have a son, he will inherit the title after me.'

Alan Lavender paused with his cup halfway to his lips. He looked startled, and an expression crossed his face that Jessica could not interpret.

'A baroness? Wow! So if I married you, would I become a baron?'

'No, of course you wouldn't. You'd still be plain mister. And why "if"? I thought there was no doubt that we were getting married.'

'Yes . . . I mean, no, there isn't.' Alan looked distinctly uncomfortable. 'Look, I must get this picture to the gallery. We can talk about this later at my place. And then I've got to call on Uncle Guy.' He gave her a peck on the cheek, retrieved the painting, and all but ran from the shop. He had not drunk his coffee.

Jessica Renfield burst into tears and fumbled in her pocket for a tissue. An elderly woman came across from another table and sat down beside her.

'Do forgive me, my dear,' she said gently, 'but I couldn't help overhearing what you two were saying. Don't cry, he'll be back — that is, if you still want him. Do you know what made him rush out like that?'

'No.'

'It was because you were talking too much about marriage. That kind of thing puts a young man off, you know. I know we're living in the days of gender equality and all that, but young men can't be rushed. So try to be patient with him. I hope you don't mind me speaking to you like this, but I have three grown daughters of my own.'

'No,' said Jessica, 'I don't mind at all. It's very kind of you. My name is Renfield, by the way, Jessica Renfield.'

'Yes, my dear,' said the woman, 'I know who you are. My name's Sheila Grace. My husband sometimes cuts Lord Renfield's lawns.'

When Mrs Grace had gone, Jessica sat in thought for some time. Her second cup of coffee had also gone cold, so she gathered together the little round biscuits that came with it and ate them.

That woman, Sheila Grace. How lucky Jessica would have been to have had *her* as a mother! She'd brought up three daughters. Had she ever threatened them with unimaginable torments, as Jessica's mother had done to her?

She left the café and made her way to the town hall car park to collect her Mini Cooper.

Her parents were right about one thing. The time had come for her to settle down and find some purpose in life. She loved Alan Lavender, but would he ever settle down? He'd had a string of girlfriends before he'd met her at Duke's nightclub, where she had gone with that sad loser Neville Jobling. Alan had swept her off her feet quite literally, and she had danced with him for most of the night in a fog of strobe lights and smoke, and the drumming of the club's band.

They'd now been seeing each other for close on a year. It had been an on-off relationship, but they had always come back together again. Alan had no parents, his only relative being his Uncle Guy, and he protested that Jess was the only person of significance in his life. But she was determined he would not take her for granted. It was time for him to stop rushing round, doing errands for the likes of Michael Floss, and settle down to a purposeful future.

3. A QUESTION OF TITLE

The Renfields had decided a few years earlier to abandon the fantasy of breakfast in the dining room, with hot dishes on the sideboard presided over by Fred in his old waiter's suit. Jessica had flatly refused to connive in this fiction that they were wealthy aristocrats and would help herself to what her father described as 'noisomely healthy' foods from the fridge. Lord Renfield had seen her eating a bowl of muesli and cold milk, standing up with her back resting against the sink. So now, they breakfasted in the kitchen, a vast room with long-disused ranges and enormous cast-iron ovens lining one wall.

'I was listening to *The Archers* last night,' said Lord Renfield, 'and was suddenly struck by the fact that they all drink coffee. What's happened to tea, for God's sake?' He poured himself another cup of tea and buttered a piece of toast.

Carole put down the paper that she was reading and looked at her husband. Why on earth did he listen to *The Archers*? He could no longer sustain the fiction that he was a gentleman farmer, as nearly all their land had gone. And he wasn't a life peer — he was a thoroughbred aristocrat.

'I see Fred's brought us some letters,' she said. 'Anything for me?'

'Let's see . . . Here's one from British Gas: "We've revised your monthly payment schedule." In other words, they've put the price up. Well, they'll have to wait. Here's one for you, a catalogue from one of those Scottish tailors who'll sell you a waxed jacket. It's addressed to Lady *Carole* Renfield. Can't these people ever get a title right? Why must they always include your first name? Oh, here's another one for you. Chichester postmark. Looks like your friend Margaret's writing. And here's . . . Hello! Whoever do I know who uses purple envelopes?'

'Maybe it's from a lady admirer,' said Lady Renfield. 'Is it perfumed?'

'I'm not sure. Let's see who's sent it — oh! It's from that fellow Lavender. What the devil can he want?'

'That wretched boy who's spending time with Jess?'

'No, the uncle. Guy Lavender, the bookseller in Oldminster. If you don't mind, I'll go out into the garden and smoke a pipe while I read this.'

'As you wish, Frank. Tell me if it's anything interesting.'

She opened the letter that she'd received, and her husband went out into the kitchen garden. He sat on a bench near the cold-frames, and read Guy Lavender's letter.

My dear Lord Renfield,

I have come into possession of a letter, written in the early years of the nineteenth century, that could perhaps throw an interesting light on the legality or otherwise of your family's right of succession to the barony of Renfield. If you would care to call upon me at my shop in Abbey Flags, Oldminster, perhaps we could discuss its contents.

Yours sincerely,
Guy Lavender.

Frank Renfield's face flushed a dangerous red. The nerve of the fellow! What was he talking about? They may be impoverished, but there had never been any question about the legitimacy of the family's succession. Had the Reids put him up to this? They were distantly related, and were entitled to bear the Renfield arms — with a crescent to make the distinction. No, the Reids were a decent couple, and probably made more from running their hotel at Church Eaton than he could amass in a year. He'd see this Lavender without letting Carole know. If the scoundrel wanted to embark on some kind of blackmailing spree, he'd chosen the wrong victim!

'Frank,' said Lady Renfield as her husband came back into the kitchen, 'this letter was indeed from Margaret Cowles. It was to tell me that the Steynforths have gone bust. They're putting Stanton Old Place up for sale. There'll be an advertisement in next week's *Country Life*.'

'Damn!' said Frank Renfield. 'Another of our sort on the blink! I spent some happy times in my boyhood on holiday at Stanton. The Steynforths were related to my mother's family, and I often stayed there with their son Robin in the holidays.'

'Didn't we visit once, not long after we were married? I seem to recall it was a beautiful black-and-white-timbered Tudor grange, with old-fashioned gardens in the Elizabethan style.'

'Yes, it was a marvellous place. I wonder what John and Marjorie will do?'

'She thinks they'll emigrate to Canada and buy a house near Robin and his wife in Toronto . . . You see, don't you, Frank, why we must do whatever it takes to stay here? God forbid that you and I end up like the Steynforths! I'll do anything — *anything!* — to ensure that there will always be Renfields at Renfield Hall.'

* * *

It was raining on the day that Frank Renfield chose to visit Guy Lavender's shop, and he was glad that the 18a bus from Abbot's Grayling deposited him almost at the bookseller's door. It had been hot and stuffy in the bus, and he'd developed a headache.

Frank Renfield was not much of a reader, and the dusty overflowing shelves held no appeal for him. The old-fashioned wooden counter was piled up with more volumes, and behind them sat Mr Lavender, wearing a green tweed suit, an orange open-necked shirt and a flowing silk scarf. God, what rotten taste!

'You sent me a letter,' said Lord Renfield, brushing aside the bookseller's attempt at a greeting. 'Whatever this thing is, you'd better show it to me.'

'Very well, my lord,' said Guy Lavender. 'I know you don't like me, but I hope we can be civil? Here is a copy of the document that I mentioned. Sit down on that chair and read it.' He added, inconsequentially, 'You won't catch anything, you know.'

The copy had been scanned and printed on the shop's photocopier. It was from a man called Jethro Evans, and the recipient was someone called Charles Blazey. It was dated 7 June 1818.

> *To my friend Charles Blazey, advocate, at Gray's Inn,*
> *I have now proof positive that the Renfield family of Abbot's Grayling, in the county of Oldshire, gained their lands and title through an act of murder, and that the slaughter of Lady Renfield in 1784 was brought about not by Timothy Reid, as determined by the magistrates, but by a member of the family. It would be imprudent for me to write the name of that murderer here, but I have it closed up fast in my bureau, and if you are willing to undertake the matter, you will advise me of what the due procedure would be.*

'I have done some research, my lord,' said Guy Lavender, 'and have established that this man Jethro Evans was librarian to the fifteenth baron. He had been dismissed for dishonesty and obviously bore a grudge against his former employer. Charles Blazey was a lawyer practising at the chancery bar in the eighteenth and early nineteenth centuries.'

Lavender suddenly stood up and leaned over the counter. His expression of twisted venom would have frightened a lesser man than Frank Renfield.

'Interesting, isn't it, my lord? A noble title obtained by murder! English law allows for no such thing. What would happen if somebody delved deeper into the matter? Perhaps the lands and title would pass to that nice young couple Tim and Linda Reid—'

'How much do you want?' Renfield could hear the panic in his voice, and saw the smile of triumph on his tormentor's face.

'My dear Lord Renfield, not so fast! The original letter's not for sale at present. It's in that safe over there, together with the old book in which it had been hidden. It's quite safe there. Safe in the safe, you know!' His gloating voice rose to a kind of bellow, ending in a dry, wracking cough. 'No, my lord, what I am hoping for is that you will look more kindly on my family, particularly on my dear nephew Alan. He's *the* upcoming artist, you know, and would welcome your patronage. So would I, for that matter. A little something every month . . . I'd also like you to look kindly on my nephew's courtship of your lovely daughter, the Honourable Jessica Renfield—'

'That's enough! You're wasting your time with all this. Give me the letter. I'll make it worth your while.'

'Oh, no you won't, Renfield. I can start a deep investigation of that letter, and the more I unearth, the nearer you are to being plain old Frank Renfield, landless, and reduced to "Mr" like the rest of us. That copy of the letter I've given you is worthless compared to the original. I'll give you a week to come to your senses.'

As Frank Renfield tore out of the shop, nearly knocking over a passer-by as he did so, he heard his tormentor's high snickering laugh of triumph.

* * *

31

Lord Renfield was known as 'the Major' at the British Legion Club in Station Street.

Housed in what had once been a pub, and acquired by the Legion in the 1950s, it had all the attractive qualities of a spit-and-sawdust establishment, serving proper draught beer, real butcher's meat pies and packets of crisps, but no fancy meals. There were dartboards and pool tables, and a fruit machine in an alcove leading off the bar.

'Nice to see you again, Major,' said a shifty-looking man in his forties, a man whose acne-ravaged face was half hidden by his grey hoodie. 'You've not been in for ages.' The man gulped down the remains of his pint, and the Major offered him another. Both men were hunched up on stools at the club bar. It was an hour after Renfield's visit to Guy Lavender's shop.

Frank Renfield had joined the Oldshire Light Infantry, the county regiment, soon after his father had died in 1973. Most of the Renfield barons had served in this regiment, and he'd enjoyed his five-year stint, attaining the rank of captain. He had retired with the courtesy rank of major, and that was how he was known in the British Legion Club.

'The fact is, Gorman,' said the Major, glancing round the room, 'I'm in rather a tight spot, and I need a bit of help.' He half slid his hand out of his pocket, and Gorman saw what was at least a hundred pounds in ten-pound notes.

'You was always good to me, Major, in the old days,' he said. 'Come out into the garden and we'll talk about it.'

The 'garden' was the back yard of the club, where the big commercial bins were stored. There was a sickly, neglected plant in a tub and a supermarket trolley full of empty beer cans. They sat on a couple of barrels while Renfield told Gorman what he wanted.

'Now, Major,' said Gorman, 'do you want everything out of the safe? It's often the best way, you know. What you don't want you can always throw away.'

'That sounds like a good idea. Will you do that?'

'Yes. Now, think carefully. Did you happen to see the name of the maker on the safe door? It's usually on a brass plate. It don't matter, but it would save a lot of time.'

'As a matter of fact, Gorman, I did, because the man who owns the shop told me he put the letter I'm talking about in the safe. It was called "The Regent Lockfast".'

Gorman chuckled.

'No problem there, Major,' he said. 'Useless things. I'll be able to pick that lock in no time. So it'll be a case of in and out.'

'What about the shop door? It may be alarmed.'

'Don't you worry about the shop door. I've served my time to this trade.'

'Yes, I know you have. You've served time on more than one occasion in the county gaol.' Both men laughed. Renfield took the wad of notes from his pocket and pressed them into Gorman's hand.

'That's something in advance,' he said, 'non-returnable if you can't do the job. I'll give you another couple of hundred if you bring me the contents of that safe.'

Even in his army days Pat Gorman had been a thief. After he was demobbed, he'd made thievery his profession and had twice been brought up before Renfield in his capacity as a magistrate. His sentences had been extremely lenient.

Lavender would know that Renfield had engineered the robbery but would never be able to prove it.

Suddenly, the phantom of Renfield's vile dream came unbidden into his mind. Once again he imagined Victor Porteous standing behind him, watching. *I know you did it . . .* He felt the blood pounding in his ears as he turned to Patrick Gorman. 'Gorman, if ever I had need of someone who would . . . If ever it came to pass . . .' His voice trailed away into appalled silence. Gorman said nothing for a moment. When he did speak, he was careful to avoid the Major's eye.

'If it ever does come to that, sir,' he said, 'I know a man who'd oblige. But it would cost you a good deal of money. We'll say no more for the time being, Major.'

On his way back into the town centre, Frank thought he saw Lady Renfield hurrying down an alley leading to the back of the town hall. But he must have been mistaken, because Carole could have had no conceivable business there.

* * *

The Victoria Arms was to be found at the end of an alley in the huddle of half-derelict streets lying behind Oldminster train station. The whole area was scheduled for demolition, to make way for a development of affordable housing. To those in the know, the Victoria Arms was Oldminster's gay bar, but it welcomed customers of any orientation.

Alan Lavender had assured Jessica that it would be 'cool' to go there one evening. It was crowded with people, all chattering loudly in an attempt to make themselves heard above the din of the very loud, high-pitched techno music. They sat at a rickety wooden table near the door, where Alan, still in his infuriating mishmash of garments, told her all about the pub and its origins. A young man in a black tank top asked them what they'd like to drink. He had a shock of hair dyed an iridescent emerald-green. Jessica had decided to stick to her mother's favourite, gin and tonic, but Alan ordered drinks for both of them.

Jessica couldn't hear much of what he was saying because of the pounding music, so she busied herself by examining the clientele. There was a very strong, muscular man behind the bar, wearing a short-sleeved shirt open to the navel. Every inch of his body seemed to be covered in tattoos. There was a gaggle of young men in tight black jeans talking together at the bar and laughing uproariously at what were evidently their repertoire of jokes. Some of the men had girls with them, but most of the good-natured assembly of males were clearly interested only in each other.

Why had Alan brought her here? She'd nothing against gay people, of course, but it was nice to see other guys' heads turn when she was out with Alan. That wasn't going to happen here.

The drinks arrived, and she was rather pleased to see that Alan had got her a tall, refreshing glass of red Sangria. Still, he should have asked her what she wanted. He'd been brought a bottle of some kind of ale. She asked him what it was, and he told her that it was a Fierce Peanut Porter. She smiled to herself. What would her father say if he could see her here, now?

There were long banquettes along one wall, where various couples were deep in conversation. One young man, though, sat alone, shoulders slumped, his eyes gazing into space. He wasn't drunk; no, he was ill. Poor lad! She beckoned to the waiter and asked him who the young man was.

'He looks really ill. Isn't there anyone with him?'

'It's very kind of you to ask, love,' said the young man. 'That's Leslie Blackmore, and he *is* ill. In fact, he's dying. No one can say exactly what's wrong with him . . . he's kept that part to himself. But he sits there for most of the day, full of anger and despair. But he's surrounded by friends here, and when he dies, he'll not be alone.'

Tears sprang unbidden to Jessica's eyes. To see someone terminally ill was truly a terrible thing, but when they were so young, with what should have been so many years ahead of them? Life really could deal the cruellest of blows.

She looked up at Alan, but he seemed to have dozed off. He sat with his head thrown back, his eyes closed and his porter only half drunk. She poked him roughly in the ribs, and he awoke with a start.

'Wh-what?' he said. 'Sorry — that's what comes of having a late night.'

'A late night? Out boozing with your artist friends?'

'Something like that.'

'Let's drink up and get out of here,' said Jessica. 'Thanks for the drink, but I want to go home.'

'Won't the Dragon be lying in wait for you?'

'It's nearly midnight, and the Dragon will have gone to bed. But I still want to go home.'

Alan shrugged his shoulders and drank up, and together they left the Victoria Arms. Before setting out on foot for his flat in Sable Court, he saw Jessica into a taxi which would take her the three miles to Abbot's Grayling.

Why had he taken her to that place? Suddenly, and quite unbidden, she saw in her mind's eye Karl Langer in his elegant tuxedo. She saw him not as the wealthy multi-millionaire, but as the young man who always sought her out whenever he came to visit them at Renfield Hall. Did she like him? Yes. But she was not going to marry him to repair her father's fortunes. Alan just needed a bit of management and he'd be all right. He wasn't after anything except her.

* * *

The frontage of Guy Lavender's shop had been cordoned off with fluttering blue-and-white crime scene tape to prevent nosy parkers from trying to get in. Inside, Detective Sergeant Glyn Edwards was trying to issue the bookseller with a crime number. It was proving to be an uphill task.

'Why haven't you dusted for fingerprints? All you've done so far is look around the shop. They've cleared out the safe and riffled the till—'

Edwards sighed internally and caught sight of himself in a dusty mirror over the counter. Did he really look that old? Gaunt, hatchet-faced, tired. He was only thirty-eight.

'And they picked the lock on the front door!' Lavender carried on. 'Why aren't there any officers on the beat these days? When I was a boy you could leave the door open all day.'

Inspector French had warned him about Lavender. 'He's one of those sensitive plants, Sergeant, so he'll probably throw a wobbler. Try to calm him down and give him a crime number. We'll round up the usual suspects, but I don't suppose anything will come of it.'

'Have you got a piece of paper, Mr Lavender?' asked DS Edwards. 'Write down this number and keep it safe.' He explained to Guy Lavender what a crime number was. 'And you're quite sure that there was no money in the safe? Only documents and papers?'

'Quite sure. Just letters and papers, an old book worth a couple of pounds, and some old ledgers.' The bookseller suddenly seemed to lose interest in the burglary. He gave a sigh of resignation and shook his head.

'Well, Sergeant,' he said, 'I suppose there's nothing more to be done. When can I reopen for business?'

'You can open straight away, Mr Lavender,' said DS Edwards genially. He was relieved there wasn't going to be any more fuss and tantrums. 'We'll move our paraphernalia off the pavement now.'

When the police had gone, Guy Lavender sat behind the counter and thought about the robbery. Rifling the till had been a blind. Renfield knew that he would place the old letter in the safe and had got someone to retrieve it. It had to be Renfield. God knows what thugs and killers he consorted with. Why hadn't he taken the letter home with him to Wyvern Court?

Well, Frank Renfield had won the first skirmish, but not the battle. It was time to delve into the past to find the proof that Renfield and his tribe were holding their title, and what land they had left, illegally.

He conjured up an image of Lord and Lady Renfield trying to fit themselves into one of the properties of the Oldminster Housing Association out at the Redwing Farm Estate . . .

What time was it? Eleven thirty. He'd walk down now to Canal Street and see if Noel Greenspan was in his office. Greenspan was an Oxford graduate, a redundant journalist who had turned private detective. He was a very smart, well-organized fellow. Give him something of interest to pursue and he'd worry at it for weeks, if necessary, until his digging and delving was done. He was good at raking up scandal and bringing buried secrets into the light of day. Greenspan would start the ball rolling in the process of putting Frank Renfield firmly in his place.

4. AMONG VELLEITIES AND CAREFULLY CAUGHT REGRETS

Noel Greenspan, knowing that his secretary Chloe was in the other room, felt no self-consciousness as he spoke aloud to the various pieces of furniture in his airless office.

"'We are the hollow men, we are the stuffed men, leaning together, headpiece filled with straw.'"

That was how he felt most mornings in the run-up to autumn, with its inevitable promise of winter to come. Hollow and stuffed with straw.

He had absorbed a great deal of poetry at school, because he had a retentive memory, but it was at Oxford that he had discovered poetry as the language of deep meaning, as an endless series of conversations about shared realities. That was why the poems of T.S. Eliot had found a resting place in his bruised and doubting psyche.

There are no eyes here
In this valley of dying stars

Chloe came in carrying a sheaf of letters. She had only to enter the room to banish his gloomy meditations on Eliot's stoic losers. A slim, handsome woman in her forties, she wore her short fair hair in a style which swept over her brow and accented her bright grey eyes.

She favoured wrap necklines and knee-length tailored dresses. He knew that she had a number of treasured jackets and skirts from Jaeger. He was quietly pleased that she liked clothes to have clear simple lines, without a lot of fussy adornment.

'It's twenty past nine, Mr Greenspan,' said Chloe. 'You're seeing Mr Guy Lavender at half past.'

'Why am I seeing Guy Lavender? Did he make an appointment?'

'Yes. He came in yesterday morning when you were out. I booked him in for today. He sat down at the desk and wrote you a letter, which I've read and noted. Shall I make some coffee?'

Chloe always called him 'Mr Greenspan' in the office, though occasionally she would forget her self-imposed propriety and call him 'Noel'.

'Yes, please. But first, sit down, Chloe, and give me your take on Mr Lavender. I've never met him, though I recall that he was an innocent bystander in that Speaking Clock fraud that we cleared up last year.'

Chloe had been with Noel for six years, during which time he had deliberately trained her to be something more than a secretary in a thriving detective agency. She was his eyes and ears, skilled in the art of eliciting information from people who were only too willing to talk to a stylish and sympathetic woman.

They both pretended that their relationship was entirely professional, but they knew, deep down, that it was more than that. She was a widow. He was divorced.

There was something very dignified about being a widow, but being divorced was a kind of failure. People wondered who had been the 'guilty party', as though the anguish of that kind of final separation was the culmination of a battle between good and evil. Life was more subtle than that.

'As an antiquarian bookseller, Guy Lavender is second to none, apparently,' said Chloe. 'He's highly regarded in the trade, and also by serious collectors. But he's not a very endearing man: he's too self-absorbed, too convinced that everybody should like him, and he's hurt when they don't. He can fly into passions over any imagined slight.'

'How did you find all that out?'

'I've a neighbour on my side of Wellington Square who buys books regularly from him. If he ever dares to question the provenance of some book or other, Mr Lavender can get very shirty. My neighbour says that he's a prickly personality, but first class at his job, which is why he doesn't mind being insulted or scolded by Guy Lavender from time to time.'

She picked up a cardboard file from Noel's desk and flicked it open.

'In this letter that he wrote to you he stated that he had something of "the highest import" to reveal to you. Maybe he has. That's the kind of expression that Sherlock Holmes's clients would use. "Mr Holmes, I have come to consult you on a matter of the highest import." He may be a fantasist. He . . . I should watch him carefully, if I were you.'

She handed him the letter, which he glanced at and then returned to the file.

Noel Greenspan's office, situated above a stationer's shop, was a sterile kind of place, neat and tidy, its floors covered in beige carpet. An Apple iMac glowed and gleamed on its own desk, but there were also two classic filing cabinets. Chloe was his computer wizard. Noel himself preferred to file information away on paper in cabinets.

Noel Greenspan thought: *There's something else that she knows about Lavender. I can tell by the way she stiffens a little and won't meet my eyes that she's holding something back. She was about to tell me and then cried off. But she will have had her reasons. When the right time comes, I'll make her tell me what that 'something' is.*

A rasping buzzer above the glazed door told them that their client had arrived.

'Good morning, Mr Lavender,' said Noel Greenspan, 'please take a seat. This is my secretary, Mrs McArthur. You sound a little out of breath. Those stairs can be tiresome, I know. Would you like some coffee?'

Guy Lavender nodded and murmured his thanks, as Chloe brought out a pot of coffee and two cups. Really, he and Lavender were very much alike in appearance: rather bulky but not fat, and dressed in slightly crumpled business suits. Lavender contrived to look bohemian, whereas Greenspan looked merely unkempt.

Both men were developing double chins, but Lavender's was meticulously smooth. Greenspan regarded him ruefully. His own chin was covered in unsightly stubble, not displayed as a fashion statement, but because shaving was difficult owing to his suffering from an outbreak of psoriasis. It would clear up in a week or two, but it made him self-conscious professionally. On this occasion, his client had the advantage. They both, he noted, had dark brown eyes, but whereas his were said to be essentially kindly, Lavender's eyes were unfathomable.

The walls of the office, which were painted in magnolia, held a range of framed photographs, some very faded. They were images of decidedly foreign-looking men with beards, some wearing skullcaps and others sporting turbans. Greenspan watched his client looking at them with curious interest and knew what he was thinking.

'Have you ever heard of the Grand Turk?' he asked.

'What? Why, yes,' Lavender stammered. It was another name for the Sultan of Turkey. 'You saw that I was looking at your collection of old photographs. Your ancestors, perhaps? Was one of them a Grand Turk?'

'No, he was not. But I saw that you were quite ready to believe that he was! But come on, Mr Lavender, spill it all out, whatever it is. What do you want me to do? What is this matter "of the highest import"? Don't be embarrassed. You can treat this room as though it were the confessional.'

He listened while Guy Lavender quite unconsciously revealed himself as a potential blackmailer. He told Greenspan how he had acquired an old book which contained a letter concealed within its pages, a letter which called into doubt the right of the Renfield family to their title and possessions. He described how he had summoned Lord Renfield to the shop, their altercation and the subsequent burglary. He left no detail out. Chloe McArthur took down a verbatim account in shorthand.

When he had finished, he sat back in his chair and treated them both to a self-satisfied smile. Noel Greenspan looked at him. Here was another hollow man, this one stuffed with resentment and jealousy, eager for revenge against various slights, real or imagined.

'And what do you want me to do?'

'I meant to take that book and the letter home with me that very night,' said Lavender, 'but foolishly left them in the safe. I'd made two photocopies of the letter, one of which I gave to Renfield. I told him that it was the only copy that I'd made, but in fact I made another. Here it is.'

He produced a folded-up sheet of A4 paper from his pocket and remained silent until Greenspan had read it.

'Neither copy will mean much in law, of course,' said Guy Lavender. 'They could be copies of a forged document written on modern paper. But I can assure you that the original was a genuine nineteenth-century document. What I want you to do is to unearth evidence that will prove that the Renfield family have no right to their titles and lands—'

'You want to tarnish *my* reputation with your vindictiveness?'

'I want you to search for the truth. I know that you're more than adept at this kind of work. People have told me about things that you've done — wills overturned, old documents bringing ancient wrongs to light . . . It's rather a speciality of yours, isn't it?

'I'm quite content to yield the moral high ground to you, Mr Greenspan. I've no illusions about my own motives. I detest that man, and want to see him brought low. He thinks his daughter is too good for my nephew, Alan, and that rankles, I can tell you. But there is an issue of justice here! There's a very decent young couple, Tim and Linda Reid, who I believe to be the true inheritors of the Renfield estate. You will not tarnish your reputation by seeking justice for *them*.'

Noel Greenspan started to laugh.

'What a moving speech! I'd no idea you were so virtuous, Mr Lavender! "An issue of justice", you say? Let's have none of that, shall we? You want me to collude with you in a plot to destroy another man's security and peace of mind because you feel inferior to him. Let's call a spade a spade, shall we? Justice be damned. You're out for blood.'

Guy Lavender looked suitably subdued. He watched while the detective produced a notepad from a drawer and made some notes with a pencil, licking the point as he did so.

'This book that was stolen from your safe — can you remember its exact title?'

'Oh yes, I took care to write its title down in this little jotter that I carry everywhere with me.' He handed the notebook to Greenspan, who copied the title out laboriously by hand.

'And the man who sold the book to you? You said a man came into your shop and asked you to buy the book. Can you recall his name?'

'I'm afraid I can't, really. Matthew something. Oh, hang on. Grace. Matthew Grace. And he mentioned a friend of his, somebody Forbes. He showed me how both their names had been printed in the book. He was a local man to judge by his accent, so it's quite possible that the men mentioned in the book were ancestors of theirs.'

The detective made a note of the names. *Matthew Grace and somebody Forbes.*

It was evident that Guy Lavender had nothing more to offer. He was becoming restless, thinking, no doubt, of his secure little world in the bookshop, and anxious to return. He had set something in train that he was already half regretting. Men like him shied away from developing action, creative or destructive.

The heavy burden of the growing soul
Perplexes and offends more, day by day.

'So, Mr Lavender,' said Greenspan. 'How badly do you want Lord Renfield punished for his transgressions? Do you want to see him ruined?'

'Yes.'

'Do you want to see him robbed of his title?'

'Yes.'

'Would you like to see him sentenced to life for murder?'

'*What!* What on earth do you mean?'

'If your answer to my question is yes — and I can see that it is — then you and I will go to see a man in London who will work with us to see Renfield locked away for life.'

'Well, this is very unexpected. I mean, surely Renfield can't be personally culpable for a murder that took place all that time ago?'

'I have reason to believe Lord Renfield may be responsible for a great many things, Mr Lavender.'

'Oh. Well if that is indeed the case then my answer is definitely yes.'

'Very well. I'll undertake this quest for you, Mr Lavender, but be advised — which means be warned — that I will pursue the truth of this inheritance business, and when I've found it, I'll convey my results not just to you but to the relevant authorities. I'm not a man who's prepared to cook the books over a matter like this. Mrs McArthur and I will undertake a special search in various archives, both here in Oldminster and in London, seeking out old documents, wills and suchlike. And when we have finished our research, you and I will go up to London to see the man I told you about. Oh, and I'll keep your personal confession to attempted blackmail a close secret.'

'And your fees?' said Guy Lavender nervously.

'I'll be charging you £1,500, plus any unforeseen extras. I'm quite certain that you can afford such a modest sum. Let's shake hands to conclude our bargain.'

As they moved towards the door, Guy Lavender put an arresting hand on Greenspan's sleeve. 'You're one of us, aren't you?' he said.

Noel Greenspan jumped in alarm.

'Why, whatever do you mean? I'm a married man! At least, I *was*—'

In spite of himself, Guy Lavender laughed.

'Good heavens, I don't mean that! I mean, you're Jewish, aren't you?'

Noel Greenspan glanced at the faded photographs on the wall.

'Ah! You're thinking about my photographs again. Those were taken in happier times. The people in those pictures came from Iraq — or Mesopotamia, as it used to be called. They were there for three hundred years. They're not there now.'

'I suppose your family were Sephardim?'

'And I surmise that yours are Ashkenazim?'

'What else? We can't all be aristocrats.' His face flushed with sudden ill-concealed anger.

'There you go again, Mr Lavender. You're still angry about other people's rank and position. Try to calm down and see things in proportion.'

'I've never seen you at Pitt Street Synagogue—' Lavender's lips snapped shut, and he clenched his fists.

'No. Anyway, never mind all that. Let's not get bogged down in theology. Good day, Mr Lavender. I hope to have news for you very soon.'

When the bookseller had gone, the detective and his secretary sat in silence for what seemed like an age. Chloe spoke first.

'Noel, you could feel that man's anger like a blow to the body. I don't like him. He's a dangerous man to have as a client.'

'Dangerous?'

'Yes. He's one of those clever men who feel contempt for life as it's lived by the vast majority of us. He thinks we're intrinsically inferior. But I'd say that emotionally he's still a petulant child. Be careful, Noel.'

'Yes, I'd agree with all that. He's imprisoned by his intellect. He's a very knowledgeable man, drowning in facts. But in one sense, the emotional sense, he's dead. All that animates him is anger and a lust for vengeance. Men like him no longer look up at the stars.'

Because these wings are no longer wings to fly
But merely vans to beat the air.

'But you know something else about Guy Lavender that you've not told me,' he said. 'Now is the time to do so.'

Chloe looked vexed. Noel could always read her like a book.

'I have a friend who's a nurse at the Princess Diana Hospital. She told me once that Guy Lavender had done something quite frightful — something to do with one of their patients. I asked her what it was, and I think she realized that she was about to break some medical confidence that would get her into trouble, so I didn't pursue the matter. Cora's a level-headed woman, so when she used the word "frightful" I know that she meant it.'

'Well, frightful or not, I've accepted him as a client, and you and I will do the very best we can to give him value for his £1,500. Of course, nothing may come of all this, in which case he'll be sadly out of pocket. So he's locked in combat with a member of the aristocracy. Lord Renfield's family have lived at Abbot's Grayling for four hundred years. I've met him on several occasions, and he seems to be quite a decent sort of man. He has a beautiful, very elegant wife, and an equally attractive daughter. Served in the army. Sat as a magistrate. That sort of thing. So yes, I rather hope nothing comes of this investigation.'

'Noel, why on earth did you let Mr Lavender think you're Jewish? You're nothing of the sort. You're an old-fashioned Prayer Book Anglican.'

Noel Greenspan laughed. 'It's what he wanted to hear. Maybe he felt that hiring a co-religionist would earn him a discount. You will have noticed that at no time did I actually say that I *was* Jewish. I wanted to see how perceptive he was to the nuances of language. No reason really, just curious. He failed the test miserably.'

'What made him think you were Jewish in the first place?' asked Chloe.

'Well, he saw all those old photographs that Professor Temperley gave me after I'd run that bogus antique dealer to earth, and obviously assumed that they were my ancestors.'

Chloe sat down at the desk. She looked uneasy.

'There's nothing funny about this case, Noel,' she said. 'You plan to involve Victor Porteous in this business, don't you? I know that you worked with him years ago in London, but it's an open secret that he's become unhinged.'

'Admittedly, it's fifteen years or more since I worked with him on bringing the truth of the Maybury House scandal to the light of day. His undercover work on that case was quite brilliant, and it helped to seal an already first-class reputation as an investigator. I know that he's had mental troubles since then, and that he's had lengthy sessions with a psychiatrist, but they must have done him the world of good because he's still in practice, and I think you'll agree that he's the ideal man for us to consult on anything concerning Lord Renfield.'

'I agree that Guy Lavender and Victor Porteous were made for each other, Noel,' said Chloe. 'They both hate the same man, but Lavender's hatred is only recent, and we know where it originates. But Porteous's has been festering for years, and nobody knows the full story. What connection could he have possibly had with a peer of the realm? Oh, he's the obvious man to meet Guy Lavender, but the two of them together could lift the whole matter out of your hands if you're not careful.'

'I realize the danger of that, Chloe, but I'm prepared to take the risk. Nothing ventured, nothing gained. Forget Victor Porteous for the moment. It's time to embark on our research. See what you can find in the library here in Oldminster, and I'll stay in London for a few days in order to visit the British Library and the Public Record Office at Kew. And after we've done our research, I'll take Lavender up to London with me to consult with Victor Porteous. I don't know what Porteous has got against Lord Renfield, but now's the time to find out.'

* * *

Guy Lavender didn't much care for Canal Street. It was in an area of the town that the Americans would have described as being 'on the wrong side of the tracks'. Most of the street was occupied by small factories and warehouses, where lorries and vans stood on concrete forecourts behind tall iron fences. Some of the warehouses were empty and were used by drug dealers as safe places to peddle their wares.

Why couldn't Greenspan have his office in the high street or one of the thriving little shopping streets to the west of Cathedral Green? Still, a ten-minute walk would bring him back to civilization. He'd go to Troxler's Café and think over his consultation with Greenspan over a cup of coffee.

Halfway along Canal Street he saw a young man camping out on the pavement, accompanied by the inevitable dog and begging bowl. How he despised these parasites! Somebody had told him that they could make more in a week of begging than a decent man could earn by his honest labour. He skirted round the impediment on the pavement and continued on his way.

Here was another beggar, lurching out of an alley to his left. This one wore a balaclava with a hoodie pulled over it. It was half past ten. Any decent man would be at work at this hour — himself excepted, of course.

Suddenly the man punched him in the stomach, and he fell down in agony on the pavement. Oh, God! He was being mugged! The man rummaged through his pockets and found a few coins. Guy Lavender began to struggle to his feet, but the man pushed him back onto the pavement with his foot. The bookseller found that his view was now confined to a dirty trainer crushing the air out of his lungs. Why had no one rushed to save him? Was he going to die? Suddenly, the man stood back for a moment and then began to kick him viciously as he lay helpless on the ground. To add to the horror, the man started to sob, as though he were the sufferer. Kick and sob, kick and sob. Guy Lavender knew that in a few moments he would faint with shock.

His attacker walked away from him, and he saw him drop the stolen coins into the begging bowl of the pavement-dweller twenty yards back. He braced himself for another bout of kicking, but instead, he saw the man run away into the maze of alleys leading out of Canal Street.

Was this Renfield's doing? A warning to back off? He heard a voice shouting, 'Hey! There's a guy there, he's just been beaten up! Call 999.'

* * *

'It was a cowardly, brutal attack, Mr Lavender,' said the doctor in A&E, 'but there are no bones broken and no significant contusions. You'll be stiff and sore for a few days. I'll give you a prescription for an analgesic cream and some co-codamol. You might want to see your own doctor when you get home.'

'It was a mugging,' said Guy Lavender. 'I suppose it's one of the facts of life these days. There's no need to trouble the police about it.' *If Frank Renfield's behind this, there'll be more of the same if I make a fuss.* 'Thanks very much, Doctor. When you say I can go, I'll get a taxi out to Riverside.'

'Believe me, Mr Lavender, these assaults are on the up and up. The police do what they can, but they don't get the funding they deserve. However, this assault must be logged and reported to the police. You've given us your address, so an officer will call upon you later today or maybe tomorrow morning.'

In fact, the police called upon him at Wyvern Court just an hour after he had got home. DS Edwards greeted him like an old friend.

'Why, Mr Lavender,' he said, 'fancy meeting you again! I'm very sorry to hear that you've been assaulted. I can assure you that we'll work very hard to find the culprit. Now, I'm going to issue you with a crime number—'

Guy Lavender tried to laugh, but the pain turned it into a groan.

'I want you to believe me, sir,' said DS Edwards, 'when I say that we'll pursue the perpetrator of this assault until we find him. Don't be put off by this business of being given a crime number. Can you give me any idea of what your assailant looked like? Height, build, what he was wearing . . . Any little point will be of value.'

'He was a young man, in his twenties, I suppose. Thin and wiry. He was wearing tight blue jeans and a balaclava that covered most of his face. He had his hoodie up. Dark grey, I think. He said nothing, but he did sob from time to time, which was odd. I can't imagine why he picked on me.'

But of course I can, he thought. *He was sent to give me a warning not to mess with Lord Renfield.* Well, he'd take more care in future, and when he next came to Canal Street, he'd come by taxi. But he was not giving up. His high-and-mighty lordship had to be cut down to size.

5. ARMY GAMES

Lord Renfield sat down at the desk in the writing room at Renfield Hall and took a sheet of crested notepaper from the drawer. It was time to write to Karl Langer, inviting him to Carole's birthday bash on 10 October. It would be a lavish affair, with professional caterers and florists, and the Lyceum String Quartet were to provide some agreeable musical background to the chatter. The Lord Lieutenant and Lady Broome were coming, together with a few other titled folk from the county. Carole would love it, but it was being staged for Karl Langer's benefit.

Last Saturday he had sat up late, waiting for his daughter to come home. She had gone with that fellow Alan to some dive in town, and he had caught her sneaking in by way of the kitchen passage. She had looked rather despondent, but he had accosted her for a purpose and was in no mood for conciliation.

'Jessica,' he'd said, 'you're to come to your mother's birthday party on the tenth. Karl Langer will be there. Do you hear me?'

He had braced himself for a row, but none had been forthcoming.

'Oh, Daddy,' Jessica had pleaded, 'must I? It'll be so boring. And there'll be no proper band. And those horrible old men you always invite will be coming on to me—'

'Don't be silly. And you will wear something fitting for the occasion. Buy a new frock, have your hair done at Mummy's hairdresser — good God, girl, you're twenty-five. Do I have to tell you how to do these things?'

He had seen that she was on the verge of tears and had let her go upstairs without answering. But she would be there all right. She'd never be able to stand up to the two of them.

The new edition of *Country Life* had contained the advertisement offering Stanton Old Place for sale. 'This exceptional historic property', etc. The Steynforths wanted five million for it. Their debts must be even greater than his. Five million? They'd be lucky to get three.

The noise of the vacuum cleaner in the hall was very loud, and when it stopped and the door opened, he expected to see Jean in her wraparound floral overall, but it was her husband Fred.

'There's a gentleman to see you, sir,' he said. 'I asked for his card, but he said he hadn't got one with him.'

'A gentleman?'

'Well, I say that out of courtesy, sir,' said Fred drily. 'He's dressed like a gentleman. Says his name's Hollingworth.'

'Ah! Hollingworth! I'd forgotten he was coming. Well, he's come at just the right time. I really need a secretary to take charge of my engagement book . . . Show him into the oak parlour, Fred. Then Jean can come and hoover in here.'

Mr Hollingworth was a smooth young man with a high-bridged nose and a supercilious smile. He wore his hair combed back from his forehead, and Renfield saw that it was slicked down with some sort of goo. Lord Renfield shook hands. He was about to sell this man something that would pay for Carole's party, with a goodly bit of cash left over.

'Pleased to see you, Hollingworth,' he said. 'As you know, there are many priceless paintings here at Renfield Hall, and I have a few small works that I'm willing to part with to the more eminent London galleries. If you'll come over here, I'll show you one of the smaller gems in my collection. It's a Van Dyck.'

'Indeed, Lord Renfield? Well, we'd be more than interested in that.'

Frank Renfield led the art dealer to a dim corner of the parlour, and showed him a portrait in an oval gilt frame. It depicted a young man with flowing golden hair and a beautifully painted lace collar. He was looking rather haughtily at the artist.

'This is a seventeenth-century ancestor of mine,' said Frank. 'The Honourable Fulke Renfield, a young confidant of Charles the First. I'm prepared to let it go for whatever sum you think is fair.'

Hollingworth peered closely at the painting. 'The frame is certainly of the period,' he said. 'Do you mind if I take this down and examine it more closely on that table?'

Renfield nodded, and watched him as he took it down from the wall and began to peer at the portrait through a lens.

'I need to look at this portrait out of its frame,' said Hollingworth. 'You can be assured that I will not harm it in any way.'

'Of course. What . . . er . . . what do you think a painting like that would fetch?'

The young man made no immediate reply but began to remove the canvas from the frame. He had produced a little tool-kit in a leather case from his pocket and had already removed a back panel of stiff cardboard.

'What do I think it would fetch?' he said, without looking up. 'Well, last month a Rembrandt much like this one went at auction for one and a half million pounds.' Time itself seemed to hold its breath. *One and a half million?*

Finally, Hollingworth carefully lifted the canvas out of the frame. He crossed the room and laid it carefully on another table in the great window embrasure, where he used his lens to examine not the painting itself, but the rough edges of the canvas that had been hidden from sight in the frame. After what seemed like an age, he spoke.

'I'm sorry, Lord Renfield. It's a copy. Very well done, but worth no more than fifty pounds. You'd get a couple of hundred for the frame.'

'A copy? How can it be a copy? It's been in my family for hundreds of years!'

He must stop his voice shaking. This fellow mustn't know how much he'd staked on this picture.

'The copyist has left his initials on this blank piece of the canvas: J. P. John Podmore was a noted copyist who flourished in the 1860s. He did a lot of work for noble families who were running short of cash, and because his initials would be hidden within the frame, they could pass them off to visitors as the originals. He'd then sell the original work on to private collectors and take five per cent of the proceeds. That's what's happened here.'

God! Was he never to have an even break? It must have been Charles, the seventeenth baron, the man who was famous for doing nothing. Carole's party was in a couple of weeks' time. What was he going to do?

'I tell you what, Lord Renfield,' said Mr Hollingworth. 'I'll give you two hundred and fifty pounds for the lot, frame and all.'

'Done. I don't suppose you could make that cash?'

The young man produced an enormous wad of twenty-pound notes from an inner pocket and counted out the agreed sum on the table. Renfield saw the art dealer's respect for him dissipate because he had asked for 'money on the table'. One day, soon, after Jessica had married Karl Langer, he would be free of all this.

His heart pounding, he had just regained his comfortable chair in the library when Fred came in. Renfield had heard him seeing the visitor off at the front door and wondered what it was Fred wanted. Renfield was suffering from profound shock and was in no state to see anyone else.

'There's another visitor to see you, sir,' said Fred. 'A Detective Sergeant Edwards. Shall I show him in here?'

'A police officer? What on earth can he want with me?' Although, of course, Renfield knew very well why he was here. Lavender was bound to have given up Renfield's name as soon as he'd discovered his safe had been burgled. 'Yes, please do show him in, Fred. And could we have a fire lit in here after he's gone? There's a touch of autumn in the air today.'

The sergeant looked a decent enough fellow, but his face was showing strain, and he had a hangdog, defeated attitude, unusual in a police officer. No doubt he had personal trials of his own. Who didn't?

'This is a beautiful room, sir,' said DS Edwards. 'Grand and cosy at the same time. Now, I've come to clear up some details of a break-in at Mr Guy Lavender's bookshop. I understand you two know each other?'

'Yes . . .' said Renfield warily.

'Now, I know that Mr Lavender wasn't a friend of yours. It appears you had a falling out with him in his shop on Monday, the eleventh. What one might call "an angry exchange". What was all that about?'

'How did you know that I'd been to visit Lavender?'

'Well, sir, you rushed out of the place in a right state, and barged into a man who recognized you. This witness called in at the police station and reported the incident.'

'Oh, "incident" is too strong a word, Sergeant. Lavender had sent me a letter, claiming that he had evidence that the Renfield family had no legal right to the barony and the estate that goes with the title. I considered this the height of impertinence and decided to tell him so to his face. Naturally there was "an angry exchange", as you put it. I knew he was going to blackmail me, or attempt to do so. I told him to go to the devil and left the shop. I think he got the message.'

The sergeant seemed to have mastered the art of sitting perfectly still, like a heron waiting patiently to seize its prey. It was unnerving, to say the least.

'And then, in the early hours of Wednesday morning — yesterday, the thirteenth — Mr Lavender's shop was burgled, and certain items were removed from his safe.'

'Really? How very unfortunate. But I can assure you that it wasn't me, Sergeant. I have neither the agility nor the necessary tools to carry out a successful break-in!' No, he'd left that in the capable hands of Pat Gorman.

'So, can you tell me where you were last night, then, sir?'

'Why, I was here, of course! I retired to my bed shortly after ten. My wife will vouch for that, although frankly I find it rather absurd that you should even ask me such a thing.'

'Just a routine question, sir, I assure you. Have you heard anything more from Mr Lavender about this evidence he's allegedly found, calling in question your right to your title?'

'I have not. I rather think he's had second thoughts about the legality of his intentions! It would be prudent of him to forget the whole business. If he does so, I shall certainly follow suit.'

'That would be very handsome of you, sir,' said DS Edwards. 'Let's leave the matter there for the moment. Meanwhile, the file on the burglary will remain open.'

When Edwards had gone, Frank Renfield poured himself some brandy and tossed it down in one gulp. He had begun to tremble with fear. Was he to lose all of this? Would his creditors force him to bankruptcy? It was not the police sergeant's visit that had so unnerved him but the knowledge that the Van Dyck was a mere copy. Carole's party alone would cost a few thousand pounds. What was he to do?

He thought of Charles, the seventeenth baron, and a chill hand seemed to clutch at his heart. What if all those priceless paintings in the gallery — the Reynolds, the G. F. Watts and the others — had fallen victim to Charles Renfield, the man famous for doing nothing? What if they were now all fakes?

When Gorman had brought him the book and the deadly letter, his first instinct had been to burn them. But as he handed his accomplice the £200 that he'd promised him, he had balked at the idea. It was, after all, irreplaceable. And the instinct to squirrel it away was more than he could resist. He had secured that cash by engineering yet another loan, this time from a bookmaker who operated a discreet little moneylending business in town. So he had locked away the book and the letter in his bureau.

What was he to do? Edwards clearly suspected him of engineering the robbery. The police could turn up any time with a search warrant and find that damning evidence, the fruits of burglary.

Ah! An idea. He'd tried to fob off DS Edwards by hinting that Lavender was harmless, but he knew better than that. Rather than let sleeping dogs lie, he would carry the battle into the enemy's lines.

He would pretend that he'd received the book and letter in an anonymous parcel, and he would take them not to the police, but to a man who had the ability to dig and delve into old archives and libraries in a search for the truth, a private detective called Noel Greenspan. With those items out of his house and off his hands, he would ask Greenspan to conduct a piece of research to see whether there was any truth in Lavender's claims. He had always taken risks, and he would deal with Greenspan's results when the detective presented them to him. If he hadn't the cash to pay him, he'd give him a note of hand charged to the estate.

The fit of trembling had subsided, and Renfield felt very much better. He'd arrange to see Greenspan within the next few days. Meanwhile, he must find new ways of raising money. Last year Coutts Bank had closed his account, and he'd transferred his meagre deposits to the TSB. At all costs he must keep the house and estate until he had lured Karl Langer into the family. What should he do? Take a leaf out of Baron Charles's book and replace Carole's inherited jewellery with paste?

He went into the library and dialled Noel Greenspan's number. The woman who answered told him that Mr Greenspan was in London with a client for a couple of days.

Would he care to book an appointment? He arranged to call at their offices on the following Thursday, 28 September.

* * *

Noel Greenspan drove his battered Ford Mondeo into a little square off Islington High Street and turned off the engine. Guy Lavender had evidently been relieved to find that he was a skilled driver, very much used to motorway traffic, and totally unfazed by the intricacies of the London traffic system. He had boasted that he could find somewhere to park anywhere in London and had proved his point by locating an obscure little square, where he was able to park with ease beside one other car and a bicycle chained to some railings.

'I made enquiries about Victor Porteous, the man we're going to see,' said Greenspan, 'and it seems that he's moved his office from Oxford Street out here to Islington, to a place called Lubeck Street, which is the second road on the right, down there.' He waved vaguely at the windscreen. 'He knows we're coming today, so let's hope he shows up.'

'Why shouldn't he?' said Lavender. 'That's what you do when you make an appointment.'

'Well, you see, Porteous hasn't been very well for the last couple of years. He's . . . Well, you'll form your own judgement when you see him. If, that is, he turns up. He claims to know something about your Lord Renfield that would put him away for life.'

'Claims?'

'Yes, I don't know whether he has documentary proof, but we'll find out more when we meet him. His offices are situated over a greengrocer's.'

'Are all detectives' offices over shops? Is it a custom?'

'It's a question of cheap rents in my case, and probably in Porteous's. But some agencies have big swanky offices. It depends on what you want to achieve.'

They saw the greengrocer's as soon as they turned into Lubeck Street. They went inside, and Greenspan told the woman behind the counter that they had an appointment with Mr Victor Porteous.

'Well, dear, there's a door just to the right of the shop,' said the woman. 'Just push it open and go up the stairs. There are different little businesses with offices there. I do hope Mr Porteous is alright. We don't see much of him these days.'

'Oh really?' asked Greenspan.

There was a beaded curtain behind the counter, and the woman, a cheerful person in a wraparound overall, pulled it aside and shouted, 'Alf, come here a minute, would you?' A little bald-headed man appeared.

'That Mr Porteous, we don't see much of him these days, do we, Alf? These gentlemen here are looking for him.'

'No, not so much now. He was never the same after he got knocked on the head. He was in and out of all sorts of places after that. Mr Porteous, I mean.'

'Knocked on the head?'

'Yes. Some case he was on, and this man turned nasty and belted him with a hammer. After that, he only came to his office off and on. They say he had to go into one of them mental homes for a spell. When he does appear, he'll pop into the shop for a little chat. He's a very nice, quiet-spoken man, isn't he, Maggie?'

'Oh yes, very nice,' she agreed.

Greenspan thanked them both, and they left the shop.

'I don't much like the look of this place, Greenspan,' said Lavender. 'Let's give it a miss and get back to Oldminster.'

'Nonsense. You're too . . . What's the word I'm searching for?'

'Pusillanimous?'

'Yes. You've got a grudge against Lord Renfield. Do you want to do something about it or just touch your forelock and creep away? Come on, man. Nothing ventured, nothing gained.'

The door next to the shop was in dire need of a coat of paint, but it opened easily enough, and they found themselves looking at a steep flight of uncarpeted stairs which took them up to a wide landing. A long passage contained a number of doors to individual businesses, and they could hear the sound of voices and the clatter of coffee mugs. They walked along the passage, reading the names of the businesses painted on the doors. Roland Thorn, Importers. Thompson & Walsh, Wholesale Merchants. Charles Mason, Hairdressers' Sundries. Bobbie & Mary, Office Cleaners. But no Victor Porteous.

Greenspan could sense that Lavender's uneasiness had increased. The passage was narrow and covered with time-worn lino. A couple of electric lights hung from the ceiling on the end of old-fashioned flex. Dim and dusty places like this probably unsettled him. No doubt he was already regretting having started his silly vendetta against Lord Renfield.

The downstairs door opened, and they heard heavy, dragging footsteps climbing the stairs. Suddenly, an elderly man wearing an overcoat over his suit and carrying an old-fashioned suitcase appeared on the landing. He stopped in front of the door of Roland Thorn, Importers, and peered at them through thick glasses.

'Can I help you, gents?' he said. 'You seem to be lost.'

'We're looking for the office of a Mr Victor Porteous,' said Greenspan. 'He's a private detective.'

The man put his case down on the floor.

'Victor Porteous?' he said. 'We don't see much of him these days. He might be there, I don't know. Go to the end of this corridor and turn right. You'll see another flight of stairs going up to the attic storey. That's where his office is.'

They walked further along the passage and found the narrow stairs leading to the attics. They could be closed off by a door that was held back on a brass hook.

Porteous's premises was the only office in the attic storey. The landing was lit by a grimy skylight, and the floor was covered in dust. The door of the office announced its owner in neat black lettering painted on a pane of obscure glass.

Victor Porteous, Private Investigator
Member of the Association of British Investigators,
established 1913
Please walk in

Cautiously Greenspan pushed the door open and stepped into the room. Lavender followed him.

Porteous's office was festooned with cobwebs, and the furnishings lay under a thick pall of dust. There was a pervading smell of organic decay. On the desk they saw a plate of sandwiches which had turned green with mould. A mug which had once held tea or coffee now contained the skeleton of a mouse. A pile of unopened letters lay behind the door.

'Gas and electricity bills,' said Greenspan. He pressed down the switch by the door, but the lights didn't come on. He picked up the phone, but that, too, was dead.

Another door led to a small wash room, which had a barred window looking out onto the roof. It contained a dirty sink, with brass taps turned green with neglect. Greenspan turned on one of the taps, but no water came out, only a hissing sound. The water had been turned off.

Victor Porteous hadn't been there for years.

They heard the door that was held open by a hook suddenly slam shut. Somebody had released it. More heavy, dragging footsteps on the narrow stairs, and then Victor Porteous came into the room. He greeted Noel Greenspan — 'Hello, Greenspan, how are you?' — and treated him to a broken-toothed smile. His voice was courteous and low, with the remains of a refined accent that suggested a public school education, long ago, in another world.

Noel could see how Lavender looked at the London detective with fear and revulsion.

He was a little man, not much more than five feet tall, but he had an uncanny power to intimidate. And that polite smile . . . It was a conspiratorial smile, implying that he knew your secret, whatever that secret might be, and was amused by your unwillingness to tell him all.

He had a round, fleshy face, a stubbly chin and watery grey eyes. He wore an old-fashioned belted mac, buttoned up to the neck. Greenspan met the man's eyes and saw there the unsettled spasms of a man on the verge of insanity. He'd seen that kind of unhinged expression before. He began to regret renewing Porteous's acquaintance for the sake of his rather dodgy client.

'I must apologize for the state of this room,' said Victor Porteous. 'I am not often here these days. But your letter interested me greatly, Mr Greenspan, and I thought that this would be the best place to meet. Let us sit down, and I'll tell you a very nasty secret about Frank Renfield. Perhaps you'll introduce me to your client?'

They wiped the thick dust from a couple of Windsor chairs and sat down at the desk. Porteous seemed not to notice the disgusting decayed sandwiches or the skeleton of the mouse entombed in the mug.

'This gentleman is Mr Guy Lavender,' said Greenspan. 'He's a most distinguished resident of Oldminster who has been wronged and slighted by Lord Renfield. But more than that, he and I have uncovered documents that prove the illegitimacy of Renfield's claim to the lands and titles that he currently holds. He had no right in law to either, and we intend to see that he is deprived of both.'

'Documents?'

'Yes. My colleague and I have located certain damning documents in various libraries, and when we return to London, I'll show photocopies of these items to Mr Lavender here and outline my proposal as to what action we should take. But first things first. Let us hear your story, Mr Porteous.'

'It's providence,' said Porteous in a quiet, courteous tone. 'Providence has brought us together, Mr Lavender, to see justice done on that man. You say he's a thief and usurper. I can tell you that he is also a murderer.'

'Your fee—'

'I don't want a fee. All I want is to see that man brought to justice. Let me tell you the whole story.

'In 1976 my twin brother Alexander and I decided to join the army, in order to receive a regular wage and solve the problems of hunger and homelessness. That's another story, which I shan't burden you with. We signed on for three years. We were both Londoners born and bred, but as fate would have it, we were posted to the Oldshire Light Infantry Regiment, far away from our home. We did our basic training there, and as neither of us was very athletic, we made a hash of many of the outdoor tasks, like crossing rope bridges or getting across streams. As a result, we were often put on fatigues and sessions of "spud-bashing".'

Victor Porteous appeared to shrink as he told his story, and the unsettled expression in his eyes seemed to intensify. Greenspan wondered whether he had lost sight of them completely.

'It wasn't long before we fell foul of the drill corporal, a mean, vindictive and stupid young man called Patrick Gorman. He was a favourite with the company commander, Captain the Lord Renfield, one of the blue-eyed boys favoured by the brigadier, who had been a friend of his father. He was only twenty-three but had just been promoted from lieutenant. Renfield and Gorman were birds of a feather, each as corrupt as the other.

'One wet day in January our platoon was taken out for an exercise at Potter's Wood, a restricted area not far from Chichester, over the county border in Sussex. We swung from tree to tree like monkeys — some of us, me included, falling from the wet ropes and landing in the mud. The army wished to break our spirit, and it nearly succeeded.

'Finally, we came to a river, in which a pontoon bridge had been moored. It was teeming with rain, and visibility was poor. On the opposite bank, beautifully dressed in his captain's khaki uniform and his officer's Crombie overcoat, stood Captain the Lord Renfield, observing the exercise. He had field glasses slung round his neck. Beside him, wearing a beret and gas cape, stood Corporal Gorman. You could tell that they were savouring their power of life and death over us, their humble slaves, half dazed, soaked to the skin and blinded by the rain.'

Greenspan could see that Lavender had forgotten his revulsion for the man and was listening, fascinated, to his story.

'Then somebody behind us gave an order, and we ran down through the trees to the river, which was dangerously in spate. I think Alexander was quite desperate by this time. I saw him wade through the water and clamber onto the pontoon, which was the object of the exercise. I made to follow him, but the bridge suddenly ripped from its moorings and began to rush away downstream. I stood in the muddy water on the edge of that cursed river and watched my brother being swept away to his death.'

'Terrible, terrible,' said Guy Lavender. 'And what did Captain Renfield do?'

'Corporal Gorman, who was a strong swimmer, threw off his cape, and prepared to dive into the river. But I saw Captain the Lord Renfield put a hand on his arm to restrain him. I saw him shake his head, and although the rain still blurred my vision, I could swear I saw him smile. I never forgot Gorman's attempt at a rescue. He was one of nature's thugs, and in later life I found out a number of unsavoury things about him, but I have always stayed my hand because of it.'

Suddenly, the quite measured tones gave way to a shriek of agony that made both men jump in alarm.

'Something gave me superhuman strength, and I half waded, half swum across that river. I scrambled up the bank and hurled myself at Renfield, fastening my hands around his throat. Had Gorman not interfered, I swear I would have killed him!'

Porteous resumed his quiet tones, and they both saw his shoulders sag as though admitting some ultimate defeat.

'I was court-martialled, found guilty of a murderous assault on an officer and was sentenced to five years in a military prison, later reduced to two. The latter was none of Renfield's doing. It was the work of a very decent senior officer, a Major Laxton, who secured my early release on compassionate grounds.

'Renfield and Gorman enjoyed a fruitful career in the army before returning a couple of years later to civilian life. Things were different in those days, but now this story of mine would be viewed very differently. If it would be somehow added to Mr Lavender's discoveries about that blackguard, I think he would be obliged to serve a term of imprisonment for dereliction of duty.'

'I have a lawyer friend who could look into that, Mr Porteous,' said Greenspan. 'Here's my card. If you'll send me a written statement, endorsed by a Commissioner for Oaths, I'll set the whole business in train. I can see him facing financial and social ruin, but there's also a strong possibility of securing some kind of financial compensation.'

The three men stood up, and Greenspan produced a wallet from his inside pocket. He removed a couple of twenty-pound notes and handed them to Porteous. 'I hope you'll accept this for expenses today, Mr Porteous,' he said.

Porteous took the money without comment.

'I'll bid you good day, gentlemen,' he said. 'I'll stay here a while and tidy things up a bit. I'll get that affidavit to you within the week.'

Greenspan and Lavender made their way to the little square where Greenspan had parked the car.

'That poor man's near the end of his tether,' said the detective. 'He looks as though he's living on handouts, and I think his mind's turning. But that story of his will be more ammunition for our campaign. There's a garage near here where I can top up the petrol, and then we'll make our way back to Oldminster.'

6. THE PAIN OF LIVING AND
THE DRUG OF DREAMS

Chloe McArthur was no stranger to the Oldminster Record Office, which occupied a rather strident Victorian Gothic building in Walpole Square. She had been a frequent visitor when researching the lives of three prominent citizens of Oldminster who had brought wealth and prosperity to the ancient cathedral city in the early years of the nineteenth century. Chloe was a member of the Oldminster Historical Society.

Noel had gone up to London to pursue his own lines of research. It was Thursday now, and he had texted her to say that he would be home on Saturday afternoon. That morning she was peering at a number of pale microfiche copies of the *Oldminster Clarion*, a newspaper that had retailed news, gossip and scandal of interest to the good people of Oldshire from 1748 to 1832. It was vexing to think that the record office had still not got round to scanning these old journals and making them available on the internet. Peering at microfiches strained her eyes.

In the issue of the *Oldminster Clarion* for 7 August 1791, she found a reference to Jethro Evans, the man who had written the letter to his friend Charles Blazey, casting doubts on the Renfields' right to their barony.

> *We hear today that one Jethro Evans, librarian to Lord Renfield at Renfield Hall, near Abbot's Grayling, has been dismissed from his post as librarian to His Lordship. Enquiries have elicited the fact that Evans had taken and sold two pieces of silver belonging to his master, in order to pay off a threatening creditor. Evans was a highly educated man, a Bachelor of Arts and sometime exhibitioner of Jesus College, Oxford. Later. We have heard that Lord Renfield is unwilling to prosecute the delinquent, but has summarily dismissed him without a reference.*

Unwilling to prosecute . . . Perhaps Jethro Evans had found out things that Lord Renfield didn't want to see emerge into the light of day. In his letter to Charles Blazey he had spoken of 'proof positive' that a murder had been committed by 'a member of the family'. This disgruntled, socially ruined man could only have been talking of his employer. Only fear of prosecution and imprisonment had kept him from writing that name.

Chloe had already consulted *Debrett's Peerage* and found out that the Lord Renfield concerned was the fifteenth baron, another Frank, who had been born in 1750 and had died in 1812 at the age of sixty-two. It was only when his old master was safely dead that Jethro Evans had transferred his vendetta to the next generation in the person of George Renfield, the sixteenth baron.

Sitting in the quiet side room where the microfiche machines were housed, savouring the silence and the slight perfume of lavender polish, Chloe McArthur began to wonder whether the whole business was simply a dead letter. All these people had long since fallen to dust, and lived on only in the printed word.

What had happened to the wretched Jethro Evans? His letter had given no address, but it was unlikely that in those days he would have strayed far from his native town. Leaving the microfiche room, Chloe went downstairs to the long gallery housing the historical registers of births, marriages and deaths. She spent over an hour thumbing through three volumes of bills of mortality, and in the volume for 1826, she found him.

April 8th. Evans, Jethro. Aged 84. In the Poor House at Oldminster. Dropsical.

Thumbing through the earlier pages of the old volume, Chloe's eye hit upon the name Forbes. There he was, 'John Forbes, cow-keeper', whose name Guy Lavender had seen in the old book before it was stolen from his safe.

February 13th 1826. John Forbes. Gentleman Farmer. Aged 72. Funeral paid for by Lord Renfield of Abbot's Grayling. £7 8s 6d. Buried in churchyard.

The churchyard in question was that attached to the parish church at Paul's Acre, a village some twelve miles out from Oldminster.

* * *

Noel Greenspan and Chloe McArthur lived in flats on opposite sides of Wellington Square, a now rather battered Regency gem in the area east of Cathedral Green. There was a railed garden in the centre of the square, and at one time the residents had had their own keys to open the gates. However, since all the properties in Wellington Square had long ago been converted to flats and offices, the garden was more or less public property.

Noel returned from London on the afternoon of Saturday, 23 September, and made his way across the garden to the opposite side, where Chloe McArthur occupied a ground-floor flat. She was waiting for him in the kitchen-diner, where she had brewed some Blue Mountain coffee, which was simmering in an electric percolator. They sat down at the kitchen table and prepared to compare notes.

'You first, Chloe,' said Noel. 'What did you find out at the Oldminster Record Office?'

'Well, for starters, I tracked down that man Jethro Evans. I found an entry in the *Oldminster Clarion* for the seventh of August 1791. It reported that he had been dismissed from his position as librarian to Lord Renfield for stealing silver in order to pay a pressing debt. That was the fifteenth baron — another Frank, like the present one—'

'Yes, I've got him here in my notes too. The fifteenth baron. Born 1750, died 1812.'

'Yes, that's the one. The article said that Lord Renfield was unwilling to prosecute, which suggests that Evans had indeed known something the baron would rather he hadn't. We know Evans had written to someone called Charles Blazey to enlist his help, but nothing seems to have come of it. I found Evans in a volume of bills of mortality. He died on the eighth of April 1826. Described as a pauper. He died in the poor house.'

'While I was in London, Chloe, I called at Gray's Inn and was able to run this Charles Blazey to earth. He was a very successful lawyer, practising in the Chancery Division in the late eighteenth and early nineteenth centuries. He had been a student of Jesus College, Oxford—'

'So was Jethro! So they were old college friends.'

'He seems to have been a very worthy man, very successful. I somehow can't see him wanting to get involved with someone who wanted to overthrow the rights of a titled gentleman. Not in those days. Blazey died in 1832, and there was an obituary of him in the *Law Gazette*.'

'I think the saga of Jethro Evans and Charles Blazey can be left to lie on the file. It's a dead end, Noel. The only useful thing that we can deduce is that there was something odd about the Renfield succession.'

'I agree. It's clear that nothing ever came of it. But my visit to London proved very fruitful. I found most of what I wanted in the British Library, but I also visited those marvellous collections in the Guildhall and the London Library, and spent a fruitful morning at the National Archives in Kew. It was there that I unearthed the last will and testament of the fifteenth Lord Renfield. I have a photocopy of it here. It was proved on the fifteenth of August 1812 and consisted largely of bequests to individuals, as both the house and the estate were entailed to his heir, George Renfield, who was only eighteen, below the age of majority in those days. His affairs were overseen by his mother's brother until he reached the age of twenty-one.'

'And these bequests to individuals . . .'

'I shan't keep you in suspense, Chloe. Lord Renfield left £500 each to "Matthew Grace, formerly my swine-master, and John Forbes, quondam cow-keeper, in recognition of their singular and devoted faithful service." He left each of them a fortune. At the start of all this they were mere servants. At the time of Renfield's death they were important managers of his farmland.'

'Fourteen years later,' said Chloe, 'John Forbes had become a "gentleman farmer", and I suppose something similar had happened to Matthew Grace. They both knew something, or connived at something, and somebody bought their silence.'

Noel Greenspan rummaged through the papers in his folder and produced another photocopy.

'I found this at the British Newspaper Archive. It's a page from the *Bow Street Intelligencer* for Friday the twenty-fifth of June 1784. It seems to have been a popular broadsheet recounting the week's most sensational crimes. It tells us just about all we need to know.' He handed the photocopy to Chloe and sat back in his chair, watching her. Would she draw the same conclusions he had?

CRUEL AND BLOODY DEATH OF
CLARISSA, LADY RENFIELD
We hear that this day gone, being a Thursday, in
the County of Oldshire, at Renfield Hall there,
one Timothy Reid, Gentleman, ran frantick, and

discharged a pistol at his relative Clarissa, Lady Renfield, a lady aged 52, and wife of James, Lord Renfield. It appears that Lord Renfield and his son Ralph, heir to the barony, are absent from England at this time, in their plantation in the West Indies. The following account of the atrocity was given to our correspondent by John Forbes, a footman in Lord Renfield's employ.

Myself and my fellow-servant Matthew Grace were sitting in the servants' hall here at Renfield when a gentleman known to us, Mr Timothy Reid, burst into the room and demanded that we convey him to Lady Renfield, who was lying abed, much troubled with the toothache. It was late in the day and drawing on to dusk. Mr Reid knew his way about the house, and without waiting for us to conduct him, he ran up the great staircase. He seemed out of his senses, his eyes rolling wildly, and I feared for our safety. We were the only servants resident, as the house was partly closed up because our master was abroad. Lady Renfield's maid was nearby, visiting her sister in the village of Abbot's Grayling. I felt great fear, and told Matthew Grace to run for the thirdborough, or any man of the watch to hand, and followed Mr Reid up the stairs. I heard a violent altercation, followed by a shot and a scream of anguish. I rushed into the room, and there saw my lady lying back dead in her bed. Her bosom was covered in blood, and her face still held the look of terror which it had assumed at the moment when she had feared for her life. Mr Reid was standing in the centre of the room, the smoking pistol still in his hand. I made to detain him, but he felled me with a blow and ran from the room. He had killed my mistress, and I shall be present, God willing, to see her avenged, when he is hanged from the gallows.

Timothy Reid was seized by the thirdborough and his constables, and conveyed to the Bridewell. He will be examined by a competent surgeon, who will declare whether or not he is fit to plead.

'So what do you think, Chloe?'

'It's a stitch-up. Those two footmen connived with somebody to frame this man Timothy Reid for a crime that someone else committed. They both grew fat on their treachery, and so did the man who corrupted them.'

'I've some other extracts here, from different papers of the time. James Renfield, the fourteenth baron, died together with his son in Jamaica, a week after the tragedy, apparently from malaria. The sole surviving heir was Frank, who became the fifteenth baron. He was thirty-four years old. That's where the trail ends. I haven't yet found out what happened to Timothy Reid, the man who supposedly "ran frantick". He's next on the list. I think Frank did the deed, or somebody employed by him. That's what Guy Lavender suspected. That's why he thought that the present Frank Renfield had no right to the title and estate.'

'It certainly makes sense. Now, I've been waiting to tell you about a rather interesting development in your absence, Noel. On Thursday, while I was still in the office, I received a call from Lord Renfield asking to consult you on what he called "a very private matter", and could we be trusted to keep a secret?'

'Well, well, Chloe. I think we both know what that "very private matter" is going to be. Did you give him an appointment?'

'Yes, for next Thursday, the twenty-eighth. I told him that detective–client confidentiality was sacrosanct.'

'I suppose it is, up to a point. But Guy Lavender got here first, and we owe our prime duty to him. Let's see what happens. Meanwhile, I think we should celebrate our success among the archives by dining out tonight at the Escoffier. I'll come across for you at eight.'

* * *

The Escoffier restaurant in the high street was a spin-off from an expanding hotel chain. It had proved to be a first-rate venue for young and not-so-young. There was a fitness club in the basement and a Michelin-standard restaurant, where Noel and Chloe had been given a table in an alcove.

For one night, Noel forgot all about pizzas and takeaways. He ordered lamb chops with balsamic sauce. Chloe chose one of the house specialities, herb-crusted halibut. Their white wine came properly chilled.

'This is going to cost a fortune,' said Chloe.

'Mr Lavender is going to give us £1,500. Eat up. These chops are superb. And they're not presented on a disgusting mound of crushed spuds. Bully for the new chef. He's a very young man, I gather.'

'Noel, do you see that young couple sitting at the table near the door? That pretty, slim girl is Lord Renfield's daughter, Jessica. And that untidy blond lad with her is Guy Lavender's nephew. I don't like him. He's deliberately come in that bomber jacket and no tie in order to create a stir — which he would have done, forty years ago. That self-absorbed type always manages to be embarrassingly passé.'

'She looks very taken with him, Chloe,' said Noel. 'I can't think why.'

'Well, he *is* very handsome, you know. Quite a stunner, in fact. But he's not my type.'

'What *is* your type?' asked Noel, and for some reason Chloe blushed.

'If you don't know that,' said Chloe, 'then you've not been very observant over the past few years. I like decent, trustworthy men who can quote reams of poetry and who are not above telling a few outrageous lies in the line of duty.'

'Men like me, do you mean?'

'Your lies are not just outrageous,' said Chloe, 'they're preposterous. Like letting Guy Lavender think you're Jewish. Now he thinks that your ancestors came from Iraq.'

'Well, as I told you, that's what he evidently wanted to believe. It won't do him any harm.'

Coffee arrived, accompanied by a plate of petits-fours.

'The loving couple left a couple of minutes ago,' said Chloe. 'I noticed that . . . No, that's mean. Never mind.'

'Let me guess,' said Noel. 'Their meal was paid for by the young lady's credit card.'

They walked home from the restaurant, skirting Cathedral Green and making their way through some little side streets until they reached Wellington Square. It was warm for September, and neither of them felt the need to hurry. The square was still illuminated by gas lamps, which gave the place a certain magical feel. Noel conducted his secretary to her front door, where she thanked him for a lovely evening. When she had closed her door, he walked thoughtfully to his own house on the opposite side of the square.

* * *

Ecstasy was Oldminster's latest nightclub, the place to go for the young and liberated. It consisted of two large rooms, one of them a basement and the other the entire ground floor of what had been a wholesale warehouse.

Jessica Renfield sat in one of the booths in the basement room with Alan Lavender. She'd enjoyed the dinner at the Escoffier and readily agreed to Alan's suggestion that they should go on to see what Ecstasy had to offer. A girl dressed as Charlie Chaplin, complete with a little pencilled-on moustache, brought them their drinks from the long mirrored bar. Apparently it was a Hollywood-themed night, but only the waitresses had risen to the occasion. Jessica and Alan would grab some more food later, but it was only eleven thirty.

She had not seen him all that week. Jean, their housekeeper, who knew all about her love for Alan, thought she'd seen him at the train station on Tuesday but couldn't be certain. 'It certainly looked like him,' she'd said. 'He was wearing that funny hat like a bucket. But maybe it was someone else.'

Jean was Jessica's cuddly, protective honorary 'auntie'. She could tell Jean things that she dared not tell her mother.

Jessica knew that Alan was talking to her, because she could see his lips move. A battery of speakers was belting out bass-heavy rock music, which made conversation impossible. The room was evidently designed for the old folk, people over twenty. A few couples were dancing, but not with much conviction.

The real attraction of Ecstasy was in the room upstairs on the ground floor, where a live band was performing head-shredding hard rock. Tossing down his drink, and not waiting to see whether Jessica had finished hers, Alan grabbed her wrist and led the way upstairs to the centre of attraction.

The air was thick with smoke, which was caught by the frantic strobe lights. The hot room was thronged with ecstatic teenagers, screaming and singing, arms waving in the air. She and Alan began to dance, and in spite of herself Jessica was caught up in the general euphoria.

There was a vocalist, a rangy, tattooed man with a flowered bandana, whose singing style alternated between screaming and choking. He was accompanied by two frantic guitarists and a demented drummer. Alan shouted to her that it was Vince Voodoo, from Birmingham. There was a sudden lull in the pandemonium, and a little man, incongruously wearing a tuxedo, seized the microphone. He told them all that next Friday was glitch-hop night, and that they would be welcoming the Desperadoes, with Britain's own Shula Savage. The little man disappeared, and the music resumed. Everybody began screaming and singing along to Vince Voodoo.

> *I wanna see ya, I wanna see ya at my place, baby,*
> *No one's nice, no one's nice no more.*

Alan was wearing a white shirt open almost to the waist, a silver neck chain and the inevitable black trousers. It all made him look rather seventies. A beam of strobe light crossed his face, and she almost gasped in awe at his raw beauty. Okay, he wasn't exactly polished, but he was a real man.

Neither of them let up in the frantic dancing. Their skimpy clothes were soaked in sweat. Jessica was disappointed not to be pressed against Alan. Her mother's generation always touched each other when they danced, just as she and the other girls at St Mary's Ascot had done when they attended ballroom dancing classes. She could dance like that too, at a pinch.

They found themselves at the bar, and Alan bought them drinks. She wasn't quite sure what it was that he gave her, and it would be pointless to try to ask him above the din, but it was very nice, very strong and very cooling. She pulled herself up on to a bar stool, cradled her head on her arms and went to sleep.

Karl Langer was being presented to the Queen at Buckingham Palace. He looked so elegant and suave, and seemed quite at ease in Her Majesty's presence. 'It's nice to see you again, Karl,' said the Queen. 'I hear you're marrying Lord Renfield's daughter?'

She woke with a start to see Alan smiling at her. 'Are you up for this, Jess?' he asked, and she joined him again on the dance floor, where the teens were still screaming and cavorting as though the night had just begun.

Jessica suddenly recognized one of two young men who were dancing together. It was the young waiter with emerald-green hair who worked in the Victoria Arms. She smiled at him, but he didn't seem to recognize her. There were black shadows under his eyes, and he was as pale as a ghost. She recalled how he had told her the name of the dying boy. Leslie Blackmore. Alan saw the young man too and frowned. From that moment he seemed preoccupied. Taciturn by nature, he hardly spoke another word.

Some hours later, when their energy was finally spent, Jessica and Alan stepped out of Ecstasy and gratefully gulped in the fresh night air. Jessica felt that she was getting too old for nightclubs, but she had enjoyed dancing away at least some of her cares.

They walked in silence through the deserted streets towards the all-night taxi rank in Town Hall Square.

Although it was getting chilly, she had very sensibly brought a double-breasted jacket with her to cover her light clothing when they left the hot club.

'Alan,' she said, as they reached the square, 'are we good?'

'Yes,' he muttered, 'of course we're good. I wouldn't have asked you out tonight if we weren't good, would I? See you tomorrow in town. Maybe at Costa.'

He saw her into a taxi and strode rapidly away in the direction of the high street. 'Where to, love?' asked the driver.

'Renfield Hall. It's just outside Abbot's Grayling. Will you wake me when we get there?'

She settled back in the seat and closed her eyes. Karl, she felt sure, would have given the driver a twenty-pound note to cover the cost of the journey plus a handsome tip. But Karl wasn't there. He was at Buckingham Palace with the Queen . . .

* * *

Jerry Carter, working on what he was convinced would be his masterpiece, *Christ Visits the Gorbals*, found that he'd run out of paint. He tried squeezing the tube as he did with his toothpaste, but it was useless. It was Monday, 25 September, and Heller's, Purveyor of Artists' Requisites, closed on Mondays. He needed this particular shade because Christ was to be depicted as being of African origin, the oppressed visiting the oppressed. A friend had told him that the Gorbals had long gone, but that didn't matter, did it? In this case, the medium was the message.

Jerry left his attic studio and clattered downstairs to the next landing, where Alan Lavender had his pad. Alan never seemed to run out of anything, and if he wasn't in, he'd nick a tube and repay him later.

As usual, Alan's door was open, and Jerry went in. Alan's flat had all the untidiness of a student squat. The living area was dominated by a threadbare green and orange carpet, which had belonged to a previous tenant. There was a battered sofa, a rickety Formica-topped kitchen table with a set of chairs, and an electric fire. Various items of clothing were strewn around the room. A professional artist's easel stood in the window, displaying one of Alan's unfinished paintings. His palette and paints — or 'colours', as he persisted in calling them — lay where they'd been carelessly thrown on the Formica table.

Great! There was an almost full tube of paint, which he quickly pocketed. It was as he was leaving the room that he heard from the bedroom the unmistakeable sounds of two people enjoying sex. Alan had got someone in there with him. The noises rose to a crescendo, and then all fell silent. Alan had probably got Jessica Renfield with him, lucky lad. Jerry tiptoed out with the paint, went back upstairs and returned to his work by the window. He heard the door downstairs slam shut a few minutes later and peered out. This would be Jess Renfield coming out now. She—

Oh no! It couldn't be! Surely, not even Alan would do a thing like that? But he had. Jerry gave an involuntary shudder and went back to his attic. He tried to forget what he'd seen by throwing himself wholly into the details of the divine visit to the long-vanished Gorbals.

7. DEATH IN THE AFTERNOON

Guy Lavender's apartment in Wyvern Court was on the first floor, with a large picture window in the sitting room, looking east across the River Ashe. Though some may have questioned his sense of style in the way he dressed, his taste in fabric and furnishing was unerring. Antique pieces, including a Regency dresser and bureau, sat comfortably beside an avant-garde dining table and chairs from the latest in aristocratic furniture makers. Silver and crystal gleamed in appropriate settings.

Guy sat in a reclining armchair and looked out across the river to the fields beyond. He felt reassured by his visit to Noel Greenspan, and their interesting though rather frightening excursion to London. Greenspan had a reputation for delving into all manner of secrets and revealing them, if not exactly to the world, then to those who were willing to pay for them.

He had almost recovered from the vicious mugging he'd suffered in Canal Street and had become something of a celebrity in Wyvern Court, where a number of residents had brought him presents of chocolate, bottles of wine and other goodies. He'd invited them in and repeated his account of what had happened to him, adapting the details to suit each particular listener. He'd received a phone call from DS Edwards, assuring him that his case was still actively under investigation.

His nephew Alan had set his heart on that girl Jessica, and he would have her. Take Renfield's title away and what would be left? A red-faced, coarse bully living on his wits. Once reduced to plain 'mister', he'd have the sense to leave Jessica to her own devices.

Renfield still had that book and the all-important letter, but he'd probably destroyed them by now. But Greenspan would dig up enough dirt from other sources to cook Renfield's goose.

Guy heard footsteps in the corridor, and a moment later somebody rang his bell. Who could it be at this hour? He didn't usually get callers mid-afternoon. Rising from his chair, he crossed the room and opened the door. When he saw his visitor, he gave a start of resentful surprise.

'Oh, it's you, is it? I'm surprised you have the gall to come here. You'd better come in.' He stepped back to let his visitor cross the threshold.

* * *

The following morning, Dr Raymond Dunwoody, the medical examiner, was still kneeling beside the body when DS Edwards, accompanied by his immediate superior, DI French, came into Guy Lavender's sitting room. Dunwoody, clad in his white space suit, looked as though he was offering a prayer for the repose of the bookseller's soul. They both knew that he was mentally arranging the facts of his examination into some kind of coherent pattern. Unlike the hard-bitten men and women in TV dramas, Dunwoody was always emotionally affected by the bodies he had to examine and cut open.

The SOCO team had finished their preliminary work, and two uniformed officers were busy packing away various items into plastic boxes.

DI French was a man in his late forties, quietly dressed in a dark suit of clerical grey, white shirt and Police Federation tie. He wore old-fashioned rimless glasses. French had chosen to remain in the background, knowing that his sergeant had interviewed Guy Lavender previously.

'What have you got for us, Ray?' asked DS Edwards. Dr Dunwoody rose to his feet. He was a man nearing sixty, with thinning grey hair and long, delicate fingers.

'Well, as you can see, this is a particularly brutal murder. The victim has suffered a blunt force trauma, his skull crushed by a series of rapid blows from that brass table lamp lying by the bookcase, where it was thrown by the perpetrator.'

'Can you give us any idea of the time of death?' asked Edwards.

'As you can see, he's lying in a pool of his own blood, which has now congealed. Rigor mortis has passed away, and there are indications of putrefaction commencing. Taking into account the temperature in this room and the state of the body, I'd say he's been dead for about seventeen hours. He'd have been killed at about three to three thirty yesterday afternoon.'

Dr Dunwoody sighed, and began to peel off his boiler suit.

'Poor Mr Lavender! I bought several historical medical textbooks from him over the last year — he had a genius for finding the unfindable when it came to books. Whoever killed him did so with almost insane savagery. The skull really is a tough nut to crack, but as you can see, there's little left of poor Lavender's cranium. If you'll send him along to the morgue later this morning, I'll do the autopsy straight away.'

When Dr Dunwoody and the SOCO team had left the room, French and Edwards surveyed the murder scene.

'Well, Glyn,' said DI French, 'what do you think? Premeditated or spur of the moment?'

'The body's not been moved, sir, and is lying where it fell, so we know that the decedent was not killed elsewhere and then dumped here. There's no sign of forced entry, suggesting that Mr Lavender opened the door to his murderer and was probably acquainted with them. It *could* be premeditated. Or it could have been the result of a heated argument of some sort. A sudden flare-up of anger. You can see that the cable is still attached to the plug, which didn't leave the socket when the assailant seized the lamp as a weapon, but the plug is half out of the socket.'

'That could suggest a spur-of-the-moment crime,' said DI French. 'Somebody coming here yesterday bent on murdering Lavender would have brought a weapon with him.'

DS Edwards looked down at Guy Lavender's body. Despite the destruction of his skull, the corpse still looked like the bookseller, and Edwards had the sudden unnerving idea that he would suddenly spring up from the floor to ask what was going on. But no; this was now simply so many pounds of human flesh and bone waiting to be opened by Dr Dunwoody's scalpel and afterwards consigned to the grave or the cremator.

'SOCO will have bagged any diaries or letters,' said DI French. 'We'll be able to look at those when we get back to Jubilee House. Do you think Lord Renfield could have done this?'

The question was so unexpected that DS Edwards did not reply for a moment.

'Lord Renfield?' he said at last. 'Well, of course, the two men had quarrelled openly about the question of the Renfield inheritance, but would that have necessarily resulted in Lord Renfield murdering Lavender? I don't much care for the idea, sir.'

'Neither do I, but it's a possibility. Renfield has been known to fly into rages when he can't get his way. And there are things I know about the noble lord that don't redound to his credit. Frank Renfield has some very shady friends and associates. Interview him, will you, Glyn? Do it this morning. Find out where he is and put the frighteners on him. But for the moment we'd better find the constable who was brought to the scene and then interview the woman who found the body.'

The constable had been on his routine patrol in the Riverside area of the town. At 8.45 a.m. he had been accosted by a near-hysterical woman who had run from the gardens surrounding Wyvern Court. She told him that she had discovered the body of one of the residents murdered in his sitting room. He had ascertained the truth of what she had told him and radioed the information through to Jubilee House. The woman was Guy Lavender's cleaner, and she had very little else to tell them. She had taken one look at the dead man and rushed out of the house to tell somebody. Had any of the other residents appeared? No, they had all stayed in their flats. Well, they would, wouldn't they? Everyone here minds their own business.

'Constable,' said DI French, 'radio for another constable to come out here, and then the two of you get written statements from all these shrinking violets who won't even open a door when one of their neighbours is murdered. If any of them have left already, come back this evening and take their statements. I'm sure you know the type of people we're dealing with here — they don't want to be dragged into anything "unpleasant".'

As the two detectives left Wyvern Court, they were approached by a smart, well-made-up woman who had evidently been waiting for them. She seemed nervous, and was evidently plucking up the courage to speak to them.

'Excuse me,' she said, 'are you the two policemen who've come to find out who murdered poor Mr Lavender?' They confirmed they were. 'I'm Brenda Parle. How do you do? I don't live here, you know. I have a very nice house further up the river from here at Abbot's Weir, but I like to take a stroll whenever I'm able.'

'And what can we do for you, Ms . . . ?'

'Mrs. Mrs Brenda Parle. I'm a widow.'

'I'm Detective Inspector French, and this is Detective Sergeant Edwards.'

'Pleased to meet you, I'm sure. These are very expensive apartments, and this is a very select neighbourhood. We don't expect this kind of thing here. Murder, you know. I was returning yesterday afternoon from a meeting of the Friends of Oldminster Cathedral and walked this way on my way back. About four o'clock it would have been. Mr Lavender was a very quiet gentleman who lived alone, though he used to have the occasional party — nothing scandalous, you understand, mainly booksellers and people of that sort. I used to live here, you see, until about five years ago. So I was surprised to see him sort of skulking through the gardens as I was coming in from Riverside Road.'

'You saw Mr Lavender skulking through the gardens?'

'Well, no, Officer, not Mr Lavender. It was Lord Renfield. I'm sure it was him. He's very well known, as he's often sitting on committees and things like that. Lady Renfield is patron of the Oldminster Flower Show.'

'You're absolutely certain that it was Lord Renfield?'

'I can't utterly swear to it, but I'm as sure as I can be. If it wasn't, then he's got a double walking about. I thought you should know. I've never been involved with the police, but I hope I know my duty.'

'Go *now*, Glyn,' said DI French when Mrs Parle had left them. 'Find Renfield and ask him where he was yesterday afternoon. Put the wind up him. You've come across him before. He won't be able to hide behind his title if he's added murder to burglary.'

* * *

DS Edwards found Lord Renfield at home. Fred the butler ushered him into the library, where Frank was sitting at a table poring over an account book.

'Come in, Sergeant Edwards,' he said, 'come and sit down. Have you further news of the burglary? Poor Lavender. I'm very sorry for him, though he was unforgivably impertinent when I confronted him in his shop.'

DS Edwards saw the twitching of a nerve in Renfield's temple, saw the faint trembling behind his hearty tones, saw the naked fear in his eyes.

'It's not the burglary I'm here about, sir,' he said. 'I'm very sorry to tell you that Guy Lavender was murdered yesterday afternoon in his home, at about three thirty. After that, there was no possibility of him being impertinent to Your Lordship a second time.'

Edwards hoped that the form of address would goad Renfield into some kind of admission. He saw the wary look that displaced the fear in the nobleman's eyes.

'Good grief! Well, I very much hope you're not suggesting I killed him?'

'Can you account for your movements at the time Mr Lavender was killed?'

'I expect so. Let me see . . . Yesterday afternoon? Yes, I was in the bar at the British Legion Club, chatting to a few old comrades. Anyone there will tell you.'

'Because you see, sir, a witness claims that she saw a man matching your description hurrying away from Wyvern Court not long after the murder.'

'Well, your witness is wrong. Did she identify me by name? Oh, she *thought* it was me. A lot of people look like me. I'm nothing very special in that respect. You're very thorough and meticulous, Sergeant Edwards, but I fear you're wasting your time pursuing me as a murderer. People of our sort don't commit murder.'

'Very well, sir,' said Sergeant Edwards. 'Thank you for agreeing to see me. I'll be on my way.' He turned at the door. 'Don't forget Lord Lucan, sir. *He* was one of your sort.'

When Edwards had gone, Lord Renfield sat as though mesmerized in his chair. A witness! Of all the cursed luck. But all he had to do was bluff it out. It was true, he looked very like hundreds of other men of his age and class. He remembered looking down at Guy Lavender's dead body, lying like a stranded whale on a beach, and thinking, *Well, my enemy, that's well and truly done for you. You delved too deeply into the past. Now your delving days are done.*

* * *

Later that day, Jean Lewis caught the bus into Oldminster to visit the NatWest branch in the high street. There'd been a small branch in Abbot's Grayling until last year, when it had been closed. Lord Renfield said that the Oldminster branch wouldn't be there much longer either. Maybe he was right.

The bank was crowded, as most of its floor space was taken up by little island offices where people were supposed to talk about investments with nicely made-up young ladies. There were also two cash dispensers, both rising from a floor littered with discarded receipts. A lengthy queue had formed at the single little counter, and Jean had time to look out of the window into the thronging high street while she waited to pay in a cheque. It was then that she saw Lady Renfield going into the post office. She'd have come out this far because the post office in Abbot's Grayling closed on Wednesday afternoons.

Lady Renfield was carrying a parcel wrapped in brown paper, a parcel that Jean was sure she recognized. It had come in the post earlier in the week, addressed to Lady Renfield, from Spearman's, the gentlemen's outfitters in Chichester. The parcel she was carrying now looked exactly the same size and shape, with the same brown paper and distinctive claret label in the corner. Lady Renfield must be posting it on to somebody else — but why? What was she up to? Why hadn't she told Fred to post it? After a few minutes Lady Renfield emerged from the post office and went into Eliot's card shop next door.

Ah! At last! The counter was clear. Jean Lewis paid in her cheque, but her mind was elsewhere for the rest of that day.

* * *

Alan sat beside Jessica on the bed, holding her hand. She had called to offer her condolences on his uncle's death and wanted to be there to support him.

'He was all I had, Jess,' said Alan. He sighed. 'I just don't understand it. He never did any harm to anyone. He didn't deserve to be murdered.'

'Of course he didn't,' Jessica soothed, stroking his hand tenderly.

'I had to identify his body in the mortuary. You can't even imagine how terrible he looked. Battered to death with a brass table lamp — I mean, who on earth could do such a thing? I tell you, Jess, if I find out who did it before the police do, I'll kill him.'

Jessica hugged him as he continued to stare into space. Poor, untidy, loveable Alan! She would never leave him, especially now that he was alone in the world. She had some money of her own, inherited from her grandfather. They could go away together, away from all this. They could go to London, where Rachel, a friend from her days at St Mary's Ascot, had run away with the lead guitar player from a pop group. Alan would prosper in London, away from the cloying atmosphere of this provincial town. And Jessica would be out of her mother's clutches at long last.

Alan sighed and got up. He brought a letter from a bedside table for Jessica to see. She was about to take it from its envelope when he suddenly snatched it away. She saw that he had gone white.

'Sorry, wrong letter,' he said. 'Here's the one I wanted you to see. It was delivered by hand. It's from Uncle Guy's solicitor, Mr Cantor. He wants me to see him to read Uncle's will to me. It says he'd appointed Rabbi Hertzberg as his executor. I don't suppose poor Uncle Guy had much to leave. The shop in Abbey Flags was rented.'

'Do you want me to come with you?'

'No. Better not. But when I see you again I'll tell you all about it.'

The words sounded like a dismissal, so she left. Alan remained standing in the middle of the chaotic room, looking at the letter. Jessica very much wondered what was in the letter that he had snatched away from her. For a brief moment she thought she'd recognized the handwriting on the envelope, but the letter had gone before she could focus properly. He had not even given her a perfunctory kiss. She recalled what that woman had said to her in the café. *Too much talk of marriage puts them off.*

* * *

'It's best not to tell me your name, dear,' said Mrs Gladys Osbourne. 'All I need is for you to give me a handkerchief or one of your gloves to hold. Once I'm attuned to your vibrations, I'll be able to seek guidance from Spirit.'

Lady Renfield sat gingerly on the edge of a chair in Mrs Osbourne's cramped sitting room, which looked as though it hadn't been altered since her grandmother's time. The room smelt of camphor, mingled with a lingering odour of boiled cabbage. She peeled off one of her elegant leather gloves and gave it to the medium. Mrs Osbourne was a stout, comfortable woman wearing a flowered dress and a string of false pearls. There was nothing particularly creepy about her. The sitting-room curtains had been drawn, but there was still plenty of light in the room.

'Ah, yes. You're evidently a lady of quality, as we used to say. Greatly troubled. You feel afraid every day. C. Is it Caroline?'

Carole Renfield made no reply. She had no intention of helping this woman out. Her friend Margaret had told her about Mrs Osbourne, a widow who lived in one of a line of attractive terraced houses in a quiet road behind the cathedral. 'She's marvellous, Carole,' she'd said. 'She has this spirit guide who acts as a kind of compere for all the spirits that come flocking around her. It's only twenty-five pounds for a sitting.'

Mrs Osbourne sighed and closed her eyes. Carole looked at her watch. Why had she fooled herself into coming to this ghastly place? What would Frank say?

Suddenly, the medium began to speak, but it was a man's voice that Carole heard — a hearty, sophisticated kind of voice. It surprised her. She wasn't sure exactly what she'd been expecting, but it wasn't this.

'Good evening, my sisters,' said the voice. 'It's Dr Brosius speaking. The medium sleeps. You are greatly troubled, my sister. Afraid of a picture that hangs in your house. C. It is a picture of a fine lady from a previous century. Why will you not tell me her name? I sense only the letter. Your name, too, begins with C. Do you share a name?'

'We share the same initial letter—'

'Wait! She is *here*!'

This time a woman's voice took over from Dr Brosius. 'Carole, you have summoned your husband's ancestor to reveal herself here through the medium of this witch. It is I, Clarissa, Lady Renfield. Why have you come here? Why should you fear my portrait in the gallery?'

'It's not just your portrait,' Carole faltered, 'it's *you*. I fancy that I can see and hear you in darkened rooms and on the back stairs at night. What do you want? Why are you haunting me?'

'I'm not haunting you. I'm haunting the house. I was murdered there, and my spirit is trapped until the High Powers see fit to release me. I can do you no harm. I wish you no harm. If you see me about the house, you may ignore me if you wish, but if you speak to me, I may answer back.'

The voice of Dr Brosius came back from the ether. 'Clarissa Renfield has gone. Heed what she says — she means you no harm. Do not be afraid of her portrait, it is nothing but a picture. Goodbye. I am called to service elsewhere.'

Mrs Osbourne's eyes opened, and she blinked for a few moments.

'Did anything come through, dear?' she asked.

'Yes. Thank you very much. I feel so much better for having heard her speaking directly to me. Let me tell you more about her—'

'No, no,' said Mrs Osbourne. 'Don't tell me. I'm just the medium between folk in this world and folk in the next. That'll be a donation of twenty-five pounds.'

Lady Renfield put the cash on the table.

'There's no spiritualist church in Oldminster,' Carole said.

'No, but there are a number of house circles, quite private and exclusive. If you are interested—'

'I am. It's no good talking to the vicar. He'd say it was all wicked nonsense.'

'There are many pathways to the truth,' said Mrs Osbourne. 'This leaflet gives all the details of the house groups. All the sitters are anonymous, though of course you're bound to recognize someone you know at times. Goodbye, my dear.'

When Lady Renfield had gone, an elderly man came into the sitting room and sat down beside Mrs Osbourne.

'Well? What did you think of her?' said her husband.

'I knew who she was, of course — it's difficult not to recognize Lady Renfield in a small town like this! I was able to deduce a lot from her face, and from the way she sat, and as you know in that letter she sent me under an assumed name she mentioned that she was being haunted by a picture. Well, the story of the celebrated murder at Renfield Hall is set out in that guide book to the Renfield family and their house that you can get in Smith's. And it's got a section on all the pictures in their gallery.'

'So what did you do?'

'I brought Lady Clarissa to talk directly to her and to assure her that she meant no harm. When I say I brought Lady Clarissa—'

'I know exactly what you mean, Gladys. You'd have made a fine ventriloquist!'

Mrs Osbourne laughed. 'It's harmless enough, God knows,' she said. 'But I'm worried about that poor woman. You see, there's nothing psychic about her. She's not a "sensitive". So when she says she sees things . . .'

She leaned close to her husband and whispered in his ear.

'What? Poor woman. Let's hope you're wrong, Gladys. I wouldn't wish that fate on anyone.'

* * *

David Cantor, who had been Guy Lavender's solicitor, occupied a set of chambers in the old guildhall building opposite the Cross. The solicitor was a red-faced, comfortable man in his fifties, with unspectacular but profitable clientele. He wore a dark pinstriped suit, spotless white shirt and a Wellington College tie.

He looked at Alan Lavender and thought, *He could do with a good scrub, a comb through his hair and a friend, preferably female, who could knock some sartorial sense into him.* Aloud he said, 'Sit down, Mr Lavender. I'm so sorry for your loss. Now, I'll not keep you in suspense. You'll want to know your uncle's testamentary dispositions.' He loved these legal phrases. It didn't matter whether his clients knew what they meant.

'Did Uncle Guy leave me anything?'

How crude.

'You were his only living relative, Mr Lavender, which means that you are the sole beneficiary. Your uncle's shop in Abbey Flags was rented, of course, and there is one quarter's rent to run. I can obtain a rebate on that for you. Get an expert in to buy his stock of books, because they'll be worth a goodly sum.'

'What about his flat?'

'I was coming to that. His apartment in Wyvern Court was owned by him outright, with no outstanding mortgages. It will take me a week to transfer ownership to you. I expect you'll want to live there yourself—'

'How much is it worth?'

David Cantor gave up. This moron was incapable of playing the game.

'Two hundred and fifty thousand pounds.'

'Wow! God! Are you sure?'

'Yes, I'm quite sure.'

'Can you turn it into cash for me? I don't want to live there with all those old men and women staggering around on Zimmers.'

'Quite. Now let me tell you about your uncle's deposits in Barclays Bank. He invested well with Barclays, and after probate has been proved, you will receive the proceeds, just over three hundred thousand pounds. I will arrange all the necessary transfers. I assume you have a bank account?'

'What? Yes. I can't believe this. So I'm rich?'

'Comparatively rich, yes.' *Much good may it do you.* 'Are you prepared to leave all pending transactions in my hands?'

'Yes, transactions. Whatever.'

Alan Lavender pushed his chair back and blundered out of the room.

8. THE INVESTIGATORS

While Lady Renfield was consulting Mrs Osbourne, her husband had arrived at Noel Greenspan's office in Canal Street. He brought with him a small parcel clumsily wrapped in brown paper and tied with coarse string. He placed it on Noel's desk without comment and burst into speech.

'You will appreciate, Mr Greenspan,' said Lord Renfield, 'that I was acquainted with Guy Lavender, although he was no friend of mine. That said, I'm truly sorry to hear that he's been murdered. I'm also upset at the attitude of the police — they seem to regard me as a suspect. That's nonsense, of course, and if they take the trouble to check out my alibi, they will leave me alone. They came to see me yesterday. The police, I mean. It's very disturbing, to say the least. But I've come today to enlist your help in another matter. May I tell you my story?'

'Indeed you may, Lord Renfield,' said Noel Greenspan. 'Do please take a seat. This is Mrs McArthur, my colleague. You look rather put out, if I may say so, sir. Would you care for a glass of whisky?'

'Why, that's very decent of you. Thank you very much.'

Lord Renfield sat down, cradling his glass of whisky between his hands. He proceeded to repeat Guy Lavender's story of the old book and the mysterious letter, and the confrontation between the two men in Abbey Flags. He clearly had no idea that Guy Lavender had already consulted them. Noel had an uncanny feeling that poor Guy Lavender's spirit was present in the room, waiting to explode into contradiction if Lord Renfield strayed from the truth. But it was only a feeling.

'So you see how I'm placed, Mr Greenspan? I don't for one moment believe that I have no right to the title that I bear, but I would like you to do some delving into the matter, in order to disprove these assertions. Will you agree to help me?'

'I will, Lord Renfield,' said Greenspan. 'I have nothing very pressing to do at the moment, and your case presents an interesting challenge. This parcel that you've placed on my desk — does it have anything to do with this business?'

'It has. It's quite extraordinary. My butler found it on the kitchen doorstep yesterday morning. We opened it together and found that it contained the old book and the letter that had been stolen from Guy Lavender's safe. I think that the thief must have panicked and disposed of the items by giving them to me. But they'll provide you with an excellent starting point for your investigation.'

Extraordinary, my foot! thought Noel. *Poor Lavender was right. You arranged to have these things stolen, and now you're fobbing them off on me. Well, so be it.*

'I'll be in touch with you in about a week's time, Lord Renfield. Thank you for coming to see me. I'll start work immediately.'

When Lord Renfield left, Noel undid the parcel and removed its contents. The book had obviously been misused and undervalued. It had fallen into halves, held together by a few threads of twine, but the contents were fresh and unfoxed.

The Farmer's Remembrancer, *wherein is contained all that is needed to conduct the skills of arable and dairy*

farming, together with a practical account of such an under-
taking on the estate of a landed gentleman in Oldshire . . .

'We know all this, Chloe,' he said, 'but it's nice to see the actual volume. Are there any more letters concealed in it? Any enlightening pencilled notes in the margins? No . . . Ah! Here's the passage where those two men, Matthew Grace and John Forbes, found their own names mentioned. Very interesting. And here's the letter from Jethro Evans to his friend Charles Blazey. Renfield doesn't know that we've already done all the research while we were working for poor Guy Lavender.'

'What do you think we should do next?' asked Chloe.

'We need to turn over our findings to a legal eagle who will know where to look further. I'll see whether I can lure Lance Middleton down here with promises of gourmet food at the Escoffier.'

'Lance Middleton QC,' said Chloe. 'He was quite brilliant when he tackled that Weeping Statue business. He's a bit like Sherlock Holmes, in a way. He'll go to the ends of the earth to verify a single obscure point. And for a well-built man he's very light on his feet. I rather like his blue double-breasted suits.'

'He's not well-built, Chloe, he's *fat!*'

'You're not supposed to use that word anymore,' said Chloe. 'You have to say "obese". It's an epidemic, apparently. All our children's lives are in danger.'

'Be that as it may, Lance won't refuse an invitation to dine and investigate. He loves an audience, and will hold forth to you and me for hours if he feels like it. He's in Europe on business at the moment, but we should be able to contact him next week.'

* * *

There were times when Karl Langer liked to disengage himself from his English friends and hide away for a few days to clear his mind, and to conduct various matters of private business. To do this, he retired for a while to White's, the venerable gentlemen's club which occupied a fine Portland stone building in St James's Street, Piccadilly. Established towards the end of the seventeenth century, it was still an all-male enclave, and it was not exactly easy to secure membership. Karl had proposed himself and had been seconded by a minor member of the royal family.

He was feeling very much content with his own particular world that day. Daily reports from New York and Los Angeles showed that his many business ventures were flourishing. A renowned general physician in Harley Street had assured him that he was in excellent health. It was time now for him to conduct a little private business of his own.

He had just finished an excellent meal arranged around a game pie, a meal that he'd shared with Jayden Hopper, who was sitting opposite him in White's dining room, making little entries with a gold pen in a small leather-bound notebook.

'So, Jayden,' he said, 'can I trust you to do the thing discreetly? I don't want any British gumshoes in on this. Some of them are very good, but they don't go about things in the way our native products do. You get my meaning? Fly over someone from the States, someone savvy enough to keep out of the limelight, someone who's not going to get himself locked in a battle of wits and wills with English 'tecs.'

Jayden Hopper was a very heavy, double-chinned man who looked as though he was in his fifties, but he might have been thirty or anywhere in between. A few strands of hair were carefully arranged across his shiny scalp. He poured himself a glass of wine and shifted in his chair.

'They don't like toothpicks in the UK, do they?' he asked.

'Some places provide them, but it's not really kosher to use them. Whoever you get can work on commission. You'll get your usual bonus.'

'I can get you Homer Piatkus,' said Hopper. 'I could have him here by tomorrow evening. He'll do a good job

— after all, it's not much that you're asking for, is it? Just routine stuff.'

'Get him here tomorrow, and set him to work straight away.'

'Are you going after this guy because he's a rival for this swell girl you're after?'

Karl Langer laughed. He'd known Jayden Hopper too long to take offence. Hopper was his 'Mr Fixit', his enabler. There was nothing that he couldn't make happen.

'Maybe you're right about that — damn it, Jayden, of course you're right! But there's more to it than that. I keep my ears open, you know, and I hear things. Things that Lord Renfield's staff say. Of course I hate Jess hanging out with this Alan Lavender. From what I hear, he's a dumb no-hoper, a talentless parasite who's got his claws into Jess in order to get his hands on some of her father's loot.'

'Kinda reverse situation to yours, Mr Langer. This Lavender's skint, whereas you're the guy with the dough. Is Lavender his real name?'

'Yes, it is.' Karl checked his watch. 'Right, we're finished here, Jayden. I'll stop here overnight, and then head back to Oldminster tomorrow morning. Tell Piatkus to deal only with you. I don't want to appear in the matter. When he's got enough low-down on Alan Lavender, you can come here to lunch again and tell me all.'

* * *

Homer Piatkus glanced in the mirror and nodded his approval. It was one of his greatest assets that he looked just like anyone else. He was of average height, average weight, average everything. He would never stand out in a crowd. The Avon Guest House, situated in a quiet suburb of Oldminster, was just the right kind of place for him to set up his stall. Jetlag had set in, and he was dog-tired, but no amount of fatigue would make him any less alert. When you worked for Hopper, you did the job properly.

He had booked in to the Avon Guest House on Saturday morning, travelling on the same train from London as Karl but in a different compartment. He had spent Sunday exploring the town centre, in order to get a feel for the place. Early on Monday morning, 2 October, he had positioned himself in a dim corner of Sable Court and waited for Alan Lavender to emerge from his flat. He would follow him for the day, logging everything that he did, and, with the aid of acute hearing and the ability to lip-read, everything that he said. Everyone had their own underworld, and this Alan would be no exception.

When Homer Piatkus arrived in Abbey Flags he saw a couple of white vans parked half on the kerb in front of Guy Lavender's shop, tail lights flashing. Men in brown overalls were busy dragging crates of books out on to the pavement. A poster in the window read: 'Closing down. Books at bargain prices.' The door of the shop had been wedged open by a chair under the handle, and he walked in.

He recognized Alan Lavender from a couple of photographs that Jayden Hopper had sent to his phone. There he was, behind the counter, wearing a zip-up windcheater over jeans and T-shirt. He had a peculiar blue hat on his head. No fashion model, then. But gee! He was one of the most handsome guys that he'd ever seen. No wonder this high-class girl was after him!

'It says you've some bargain books for sale.'

'Over there, on those shelves. We're closing down, and that's all stuff we can't sell to dealers.'

The shelves on one side of the shop were crammed with sets of old encyclopaedias, and the complete works of Sir Walter Scott, Charles Dickens and other classic writers. They all looked faded and tatty, and were being offered for a few pounds per volume. All the really valuable stock was even at that moment being loaded into the two white vans.

Alan Lavender's phone rang, and with a little grunt of vexation he answered it. 'Yes? Oh, hi. I'm in the shop, getting rid of Uncle Guy's stuff. What, now? All right, in Costa. I'll be there in ten minutes.'

'Can I buy this copy of *David Copperfield*?'

'Two pounds. If you want a bag, it's another 2p.'

'I'll take it as it is, thanks.'

'Are you American?'

'No, Canadian. I'm here to visit my sister. Thanks for the book.'

A quarter of an hour later, Alan Lavender emerged from the shop. Piatkus followed him to Vicar's Street, where he entered the city branch of Costa. He disappeared into the crowd at the counter but emerged in a couple of minutes carrying a tray with two cups of coffee and some little packets of sugar on it. He sat down at a table near to where Homer Piatkus was sitting, reading that morning's *Oldminster Gazette*. He hadn't ordered anything, but he knew that the frantically overworked baristas wouldn't bother him.

Alan could do with a haircut, thought Homer, and someone to teach him some elementary dress sense. You could dress very informally and still look smart. His fancy girlfriend must be dead keen to put up with him. Alan turned to look at the door, and his profile looked like that of one of the gods of Olympus. A guy had no right to be as beautiful as that.

A young man came into the café and sat down at Alan's table. A nice, open-faced lad, thought Homer. The way he looked at Alan, with a kind of awed respect — fear? — showed that the scruffy rival to Karl Langer had managed to establish some kind of ascendancy over him.

'Well, Tommy,' said Alan, 'did you get it? Have a cup of coffee. It's on me.'

'Thanks,' said Tommy. 'There it is. Why did you get me to buy it for you? It's not as though it's the really hard stuff.'

'I don't want Jessica to know that me and my friends are using at all. It wouldn't go down well up at the big house. Anyway, I'm keeping out of her way at the moment, because if she knew I was going up to London, she'd want to come with me — and that would never do. I think she's started to follow me round, which is a bit creepy. Here's your money. Thanks again.'

Tommy stood up.

'So I won't see you tomorrow?' he asked.

'No, I'll be away all day on business. I'll be back at eleven, on the last train out from Victoria to Oldminster. See you later!'

* * *

The following day, Homer was content to be crushed and jostled as he followed Alan Lavender on the Victoria Line to Oxford Circus, and then on the Bakerloo Line to Maida Vale. He relished the anonymity of crowds, knowing that he would merge into the background of any throng of people. Alan may have seen him in Costa the day before, but he would not have registered as a viable individual in his mind.

Homer followed Alan through a maze of prosperous-looking streets until they were bordering the Regent's Canal, where the young man made his way to a less affluent area of houses clustering around a red-brick Methodist church. He stopped at a house in a narrow street of Victorian terraces and knocked on the door. It was opened almost immediately by a pale, thin young woman who greeted him warmly and pulled him into the house.

Homer Piatkus looked around him. At the end of the terrace was a huddle of small shops, two of them boarded up. One of the remaining shops was a thriving convenience store. It was there that Homer would start his investigation.

He gave a cheerful greeting to the man behind the counter and proceeded to buy an array of items from the ample stock. Some sweets, a pound of apples, a copy of the *Daily Mirror*, two scratch cards, a box of cook's matches and a tin of Heinz soup. The shopkeeper, a middle-aged, balding man with glasses, positively warmed to Homer, and went as far as to give him a plastic bag for his purchases without charging him. Homer seemed in no hurry to depart.

'Do you know, mate,' he said, 'I was born in a house in this street, number nine, just over the road. We had some happy times there. But when I was twelve we emigrated to Canada, which accounts for my accent.' He pointed to a shelf behind the counter. 'I'd better have one of those big bags of crisps.'

'Did you now?' said the shopkeeper. 'Well, that's very interesting. Number nine, you say? There's a young lady living there now — well, I say young, perhaps twenty-five or so. I don't think she's very well, though. Pale, she is, and coughs a lot.'

'Yes, I heard something about her. A Mrs Kilpatrick, I was told.'

'Kilpatrick? No, she's a Mrs Lavender. Funny name, but there was that character in *Dad's Army* who was played by an actor called Lavender. She comes in here every day or so to buy a few things.'

'There was a young man calling on her just now. A handsome young chap, he was. Fair hair. She seemed very taken with him.'

'That's Mr Lavender. He doesn't live with her. He just calls when he feels like it. Mary!'

A pleasant-looking woman came out from a door behind the counter.

'This gentleman's been asking about Mrs Lavender,' said the shopkeeper. 'He was born in number nine. I need to go out for half an hour. Pleased to have met you, Mr . . . er . . .'

'Green. Tommy Green. I used to go to school round here, me and my sister.'

'That'd have been at Naylor Street Council School, yes? It's still there, I'm glad to say.' When the shopkeeper had gone, Homer bought a ballpoint pen to add to his hoard of shopping.

'Your husband — it was your husband, wasn't it? — said that Mrs Lavender didn't look well. Has she been ill?'

Mary's face hardened into a frown.

'Not ill in the usual sense, Mr Green. That husband of hers — did you see him? Handsome is as handsome does. He turns up from time to time to give her some money, though she works part time in a café somewhere. But he's a wastrel if ever there was one. He doesn't live with her. I don't think he lives in London, come to that. I'll tell you why she looks ill, and why she's pining away.'

Mary leaned forward, and like a little girl, cupped her hands round his ear to whisper the words that she could not bring herself to speak aloud.

* * *

It had been an unexpectedly easy investigation, Homer thought. After his visit to the shop, he had returned to town, where he had offloaded his purchases beside a surprised street dweller and made his way to Piccadilly. He had made enquiries at the local government offices in Maida Vale and elsewhere, and obtained copies of documents that Jayden Hopper would welcome with open arms. A visit to St Mary's Hospital, Paddington, had provided him with what he hoped would be the final nail in Alan Lavender's coffin.

9. TIMOTHY AND LINDA REID

On Friday morning Chloe McArthur hurried across the garden in Wellington Square and let herself in to the house where Noel Greenspan had his flat. She found him in his rather sombre workroom, as he insisted on calling his study. There were no photographs of his mythical 'ancestors' here: the walls were adorned with a fine collection of water colours by Samuel Palmer. The room was crammed with heavy Victorian bookcases, and over the fireplace were some replica death masks of notorious criminals.

'Noel,' said Chloe, 'what do you think? I've received an invitation to Lady Renfield's birthday party on Tuesday! It was on a printed card, with a family crest at the top. Did you get one?'

'Yes, I did. Evidently Lord Renfield wants to keep in his detectives' good books. I suppose it'll be a semi-private affair, but I suggest we keep our eyes peeled while we're dining off rubber chicken at Renfield Hall. That will be Treat Number One. And after I've lectured you on the Renfield family tree, I'll tell you about Treat Number Two.

'In the letter that the late Guy Lavender brought us,' Noel continued, 'Jethro Evans stated he had "proof positive" that the Renfield family gained their lands and title through an act of murder. He went on to say that the murder of Lady Renfield in 1784 had been committed — and I quote — "not by Timothy Reid, as determined by the magistrates, but by a member of the family." Now, Chloe, what was said about Mr Kurtz in Conrad's *Heart of Darkness*?'

'"Mistah Kurtz — he dead." I did *Heart of Darkness* for A level.'

'I know you did. Hence my question. It's very laconic, isn't it? And it turns up in T.S. Eliot's "The Hollow Men". To which I will add my own contribution: "Timothy Reid — who he?"'

'What's the matter with you this morning, Noel?' asked Chloe, laughing. 'What's all this about Conrad and Eliot?'

'It's just that we learned quite a lot about the Renfields during our research, and no doubt Lance Middleton will come up with more facts and theories. But so far, the man called Timothy Reid has been a mere shadow. So I've been trying to bring him out into the light.

'Look at this family tree, which I've drawn up from some of our own sources. Here is George Renfield, the thirteenth baron. He married a lady called Jane Carew. They had "issue", as they say: two children. Their son James became the fourteenth baron. He was the one who died in Jamaica with his son Ralph, in 1784.

'The second child of George Renfield and Jane Carew was a girl, Mary, who married into the Reid family. It was *her* son, Timothy Reid, who was found guilty of the murder of Lady Renfield.'

'Well, if what it said in that letter was true, then Timothy Reid — the present-day one — has been cheated of his legitimate inheritance. He and his ancestors since 1784.'

'Yes, Chloe, and there's the rub. We find ourselves in the odd position of working for both the late Guy Lavender and the present Lord Renfield. Two sides of the same question. What to do? No man can serve two masters.'

'How about serving the cause of justice?' said Chloe.

'Yes, it has to be that. "I was about to say the same thing myself," said he, without a blush. So the time has come for action.'

'What do you propose to do? Am I to be included in this action?'

'You are, which brings me to Treat Number Two. We know quite a lot about the Renfields, past and present, but the Reids are no more than a name. So, starting tomorrow, you and I are going to take a few days' break at the Church Eaton Hotel and Spa, which is owned and run by Timothy and Linda Reid.'

* * *

'Auntie Jean,' said Jerry Carter, 'there's something that I want to tell you.'

Once a week Jean Lewis visited her nephew, her brother's son, to bring him a parcel of groceries. She always included two sandwiches from Marks & Spencer, and they'd have a little lunch together. Her brother Stephen, Jerry's father, had been killed in an accident on the railway, and his mother had long since consoled herself first with gin, and then with anything alcoholic that came in a bottle or a can. Jerry was a good lad who fancied himself as an artist. He supplemented his meagre income by working on the market stalls for a large part of the week. He was well liked there, and was quite comfortable in his little flat in Sable Court.

The trouble was that Alan Lavender, who considered himself to be Jessica's boyfriend, lived in the flat below. He wasn't fit to lick Girlie's boots, but you could never talk sense to a girl once she'd fallen for someone.

'There's a BLT and a smoothie, Jerry,' said Jean. 'I've got a cheese and ham. Now, what is it you wanted to tell me?'

'It's something about Alan,' said Jerry Carter. 'Something I heard one day . . . It was wrong, and I can't get it out of my mind. That's why I've got to tell you. You're very fond of Jessica Renfield, aren't you?'

So that was it. Poor lad, did he really think that she didn't know? Jessica had confided in her that she'd been sleeping with Alan. Girlie could tell her things like that, things that she'd be too terrified to tell her mother.

'Oh, Jerry, there's no need to look so embarrassed. I know perfectly well that Alan and Jessica are an item. I wish it wasn't so, but that's the way things are.'

'No, no, Auntie, you don't understand. It wasn't that. I went down to Alan's flat one day to borrow a tube of paint, and I heard him having sex in his bedroom. I went back up to my room and when she came out of Alan's flat, I saw her through the window. It wasn't Jessica. *It was her mother!*'

* * *

Timothy Reid stood on the rear terrace of the Church Eaton Hotel and Spa, and surveyed his own particular kingdom. It was now five years since he and Linda had sunk all their savings, together with loans from their parents, into acquiring the empty manor house at Church Eaton and commenced the gruelling work of start-up hoteliers.

They had both been thirty in 2012, when he had been made redundant from his job as a civil engineer. When he had mooted the idea of going into the hotel business, Linda, a kindergarten teacher, had wholeheartedly agreed. Now, five years on, they were doing very well indeed.

The eighteenth-century manor house had been standing empty for over ten years, and it had been a herculean task to restore it to something like its former glory. But they'd done it. Each of the original twelve bedrooms had been themed around a Dickens character, because it was rumoured (but never proved) that Charles Dickens had stayed there as a guest of the original owners in 1854. An inventive barman had created a whole range of Dickensian drinks. Hoping that they would survive with just twelve bedrooms to start with, they had opened the spa side of the business immediately. It occupied a purpose-built wing, with state-of-the-art

106

treatment rooms, its own indoor swimming pool and jacuzzis, and a private terrace for sunbathing, when that was possible in the English climate.

Now there were sixty bedrooms, most of them housed in an attached wing built in the style of the old manor house and cunningly covered in fast-growing ivy. The hotel's unique ambiance had attracted visitors from America. There was one staying here now, a wealthy young businessman who gave an address in Manhattan.

It had been Linda's idea to lease the spa to a specialist company and take a cut of the profits. It was Linda, too, who had developed 'history trails' to stately homes and picturesque villages in the neighbouring countryside, including special entry to places not normally open to the public. They were only four miles from Oldminster, in a particularly beautiful part of the county. Earlier that year, Tim had started coach tours over the county border to Chichester.

'Mr Reid! Mr Langer wants to know if he can make a couple of photocopies from your office?'

'Of course he can, Mike,' Tim called to a young waiter in a white jacket who had appeared on the terrace. 'Whatever he wants, let him have it. And if we haven't got it, we'll get it, okay?'

Their debt with the bank was now under £1.5 million. They had good credit with their merchant bank and no difficulty meeting the agreed repayments.

Linda appeared on the terrace. As always, he felt a rush of thankfulness and incredulity that she had ever agreed to marry him. She was what was sometimes referred to as a 'willowy blonde', and that was true enough. She looked good in anything, like the trouser suit she was wearing now, or her favourite black satin evening frock that she'd wear for formal dinners and the like.

'Tim,' said Linda, 'will you stop standing there like a statue? Come inside and have a drink with Mr Greenspan. He's quite a well-known detective, you know, no doubt doing some hush-hush work for someone or other.'

Linda Reid had found herself attracted to Noel Greenspan and his secretary, Chloe. He looked rather untidy and uncared for, and his face was badly afflicted with some kind of skin rash, but he was a well-educated man and a good conversationalist. He was a complete contrast to Tim, who was a strong, heavily built man, handsome and with a mercifully clear complexion. Her mother called him 'the blond giant'. Chloe McArthur was an elegant and intelligent woman. They seemed totally at ease in each other's company. Linda wondered whether there was anything going on between them. What qualities were needed for a woman to become a detective's wife?

The four of them sat at a table in the window of the Mr Pickwick bar, the walls of which were hung with coloured prints showing scenes from *The Pickwick Papers*.

'We were due for a few days' break,' said Noel Greenspan, 'and heard about your hotel from the Rennisons, who stayed here in August. I gather that you're related to Lord Renfield, Mr Reid?'

'Yes, the Reids were connected with the Renfield family centuries ago. I've no idea in what way we're related, but there's a connection of some sort going back into the dim and distant past. Lord Renfield and I are on Christian name terms, but that's always been a convention in both families. Linda and I get invited to parties, which is very nice, and very decent of Frank to remember us.'

'You could use one of those online sites to trace your ancestry,' said Chloe.

'Quite frankly, Mrs McArthur,' said Tim, 'I'm not remotely interested in that kind of thing. Okay, Frank Renfield is a true aristocrat. But as far as I know, the Reids have always been ordinary people who earned their own living. We're more than content with what we've got, aren't we, Linda?'

'Yes, we are. But Tim, wouldn't Renfield Hall make a marvellous hotel? I can just see it in my mind's eye . . .'

Timothy Reid laughed. 'Thinking of branching out already? Still, you're right, Linda. If you could establish a

Michelin-standard restaurant, like the Escoffier in Oldminster . . .'

Half an hour later, Tim and Linda went about their business, and the detectives retired to the hotel lounge for a while. It was called the Uncommercial Traveller, and over the door was a silhouette of a grand lady being conveyed somewhere in a sedan chair.

'They're a very nice couple,' said Chloe. 'I believe Tim when he says that he's not interested in his family's history. The present is all he's concerned with. And the future of his business, of course.'

'Well, let's hope all goes well at dinner tonight,' said Noel. 'I believe their American guest, Karl Langer, has accepted our invitation to join us. Rumour has it that he's got his eye on Jessica Renfield. Maybe he has.'

* * *

In a world where every hotel claimed to have a restaurant, the Church Eaton Hotel and Spa preferred to have a dining room. Guests appreciated the old-world atmosphere of the large, pleasant room, with its tables covered with crisp damask cloths and full silver service. At night, each table was lit by its own shaded lamp. People came from far and wide to celebrate special occasions there. It was one of the very few provincial hotels that still offered flambé work.

Karl Langer had readily accepted Noel and Chloe's invitation to dine with them. Chloe found him immediately appealing. He was a handsome young man, tall and elegant, and with an invitingly relaxed manner that came from his consciousness of having enormous wealth. There was nothing, she thought, that he could not command — except, perhaps, love.

Chloe was content to listen while Noel talked about places that he had visited in his extensive travels as a young man. He told Karl about the treasures of Egypt and the best hotels to patronize in Cairo. Karl, for his part, enthused about Rome and Florence and the hill towns of Tuscany. His words were not those of a rich American 'doing Europe'. He spoke with taste and deep appreciation of all that he had seen.

Chloe turned her attention to the excellent dinner, served by a team of young waiters. She began to think about their hosts, Tim and Linda Reid. They were an attractive couple, enthused by what they were doing, and living, quite rightly, for the present and the future. Tim was a man of the present day.

She knew something about Linda that Noel didn't. Earlier in the day, the two women had met in the ladies' room to repair their make-up, and Linda had asked Chloe whether she had any children.

'No, Linda,' she'd said. 'I was unable to conceive. We tried everything, including IVF, but in the end we had to face up to the fact that we were destined to be a childless couple. My husband has been dead for seven years.' It was not something that she usually talked about to comparative strangers, but she readily accepted Linda as a confidante.

Linda, still looking in the mirror as she attended to her eyebrows, said, 'Tim and I had a little girl. Sonia. When she was six, she was killed by a hit-and-run driver. We couldn't face the thought of having another child after losing her.'

' . . . but the best place on earth for me,' Karl Langer was saying, 'is England. I have an estate in New York, but here in England I can stay as a guest in the house of a man whose family has lived there for five hundred years. I've been on shoots with men whose ancestors came here with William the Conqueror. Perhaps I'm a romantic, I don't know. But I'm a businessman too, and I take my time when I'm considering making a purchase.'

'Do you mean a property, Mr Langer?'

'I do. I'm talking about Renfield Hall. I'm proud to call Lord Renfield a friend. I've stayed with him and his lovely wife so often now that I'm considered almost one of the family.' The young man blushed. 'I'm hoping to bind myself closer to the Renfields by marrying their daughter Jessica. Did you know that when Lord Renfield dies, Jessica will inherit his title? She will be a baroness in her own right, and her first child, male or female, will inherit her title. It's something called a "special remainder".'

Well, well, thought Noel. So that's it. Renfield wants to lure this wealthy man into his family so that he can take care of his debts. Langer and Jessica would live as inheritors of Renfield Hall. If that ever happened, Lord Renfield would probably be quite happy to move to another, more manageable residence elsewhere.

'Will you walk into my parlour?' said the spider to the fly.

'I expect you've been invited to Lady Renfield's birthday party on Tuesday?' asked Chloe. 'Noel and I are doing some professional work for Lord Renfield, and he's very kindly invited us.'

'Yes, I'll be there. Lord Renfield tells me that it'll be a very spectacular do. So I'll look forward to seeing you folks again at Renfield Hall on Tuesday.'

* * *

In a little lane leading off East Pallant, in Chichester, was to be found the premises of Spearman's, the old-established gentlemen's outfitters. Jean Lewis, wearing her smart tailored suit, sat on a chair at the counter, talking to a handsome, white-haired man in his sixties, the type of genteel salesman who could always find time to chat with his customers. It was that kind of shop, where there were always a couple of chairs for the use of customers. *Their days are numbered*, she thought, *both the shop and the man*. There was little call these days for the high-quality merchandise that Spearman's were offering. In a year or so, this dim, hushed shrine to sartorial elegance would be replaced by a bright, brash branch of a corporate tailor, staffed by clueless youths.

'So you see, Mr Preston,' said Jean, 'Her Ladyship was so pleased with the things that you sent her that she told me to come into Chichester especially to thank you.' It was a lie, but one told in a good cause.

'How very kind,' said Mr Preston, smiling. 'I expect it was a present, but not, I think, for His Lordship. It would have been far too skimpy for him!'

He laughed, and Jean did likewise. It was time to venture a question in the form of a statement. It would be a shot in the dark, as of course she'd never seen the contents of the parcel that Spearman's had sent to Renfield Hall — the parcel that she'd seen Carole despatching to some unknown address from the Crown post office in Oldminster.

'His Lordship still favours the old-fashioned style of evening dress,' she said, 'the type he can wear with a wing collar — the proper ones, you know, fixed to the shirt with a stud.'

'Ah, yes,' said Mr Preston. 'I expect His Lordship would get his suits from a certain shop in Brooke Street, St James's. I happen to know that his father patronized that establishment.'

So it had been a suit of evening clothes.

'I rather think it was meant as a present for one of his nephews,' said Jean. What a liar she was! Poor Frank had no nephews or nieces. He only had Girlie, and Girlie's stuck-up cow of a mother.

'Those young men never have any real clothes or proper shirts,' she said. 'Just T-shirts and the like. Nothing formal, even in those exalted circles.' *Steady on, Jean. Don't overdo it! You're beginning to sound like nice Mr Preston.*

'Ah! I thought it would be something of that sort. Yes, Her Ladyship bought an off-the-peg evening suit, a shirt and a ready-made-up bow tie. It's no good giving those young fellows a proper tie. They've no patience with them these days.'

After a few more pleasantries, Jean left the shop. Mr Preston had not expected her to buy anything, and had certainly not pressed her to do so. It was that kind of shop. They'd be gone in a year or two.

That was as far as Jean's detective work could go. Only a policeman could go asking questions in the post office. But she knew all that she needed to know about that parcel. Jessica's mother had bought those clothes for her fancy-boy, Alan Lavender, so that he could come to her birthday party.

What kind of woman had sex with her daughter's boy-friend? Was that incest? Whatever it was, it was disgusting and evil. Poor Girlie! She could never tell her, of course. It would break her heart and wreck her family. All she could do was watch and wait.

10. THE BIRTHDAY PARTY

Renfield Hall was a blaze of light as Noel Greenspan drove his car through the entrance pillars that gave onto the twisting drive. White garden lights twinkled a welcome along the grass verges. The trees flanking the drive were festooned with coloured fairy lights. He came to a halt in the forecourt, and as he and Chloe left the car, they could hear the slamming of doors and the murmur of couples as they walked to the entrance. It was a mild, dry evening, and a clock somewhere was striking seven.

A grand, grey-haired butler, impeccably dressed in white tie and tailcoat, stood at the open door to welcome the guests.

'Somehow, I thought it would be more subdued than this,' said Noel. 'They're supposed to be living on a shoestring, but this sparkling welcome makes me think otherwise.'

Chloe motioned to a couple of vans parked discreetly on the far side of the forecourt. 'They're from Mayfair Cuisine, the caterers. Shoestring or not, it looks as though no expense has been spared.'

She glanced up briefly at the darkened windows above the ground floor.

'This is the house in which Lady Renfield was shot dead in 1784,' she whispered, and gave a slight shudder. Together they climbed the steps, to be greeted by the stately butler. A gaggle of girls in black dresses and non-functional pinafores stood behind him, holding highly polished silver trays. The butler glanced at their invitation cards.

'Mrs McArthur, Mr Greenspan, welcome to Renfield Hall,' he said. 'Cocktails and canapés are being served in the oak parlour, to your right. Presentations will be made in the library, to your left, at eight o'clock. Dinner will be served at nine.'

'Do you think he's been hired for the purpose?' asked Chloe. 'I assume that fronting an event of this type would have been too much for Lord Renfield's skeleton staff.'

'Very likely. This one's too much like Carson of *Downton Abbey* to be a real butler. I expect he belongs to Mayfair Cuisine.'

They found the oak parlour thronged with guests talking animatedly in little groups. A string quartet was playing gentle classical jazz. Another group of waitresses circulated, offering tall cocktail glasses to the guests. A number of earnest young men in white shirts and black ties presented a selection of enticing canapés.

'This is a beautiful room,' said Chloe. 'Just look at that magnificent window! And the furniture! Some of these pieces must be priceless. They filmed some indoor scenes here for an episode of *Midsomer Murders* a few years ago.'

'The carpet's a bit worn,' said Noel. 'But yes, you're right. Whatever doubts there might be to the succession, there seems to be plenty of money here. That butler, and all these waiters — this birthday dinner must have cost a bomb.'

'Several thousand at least,' Chloe agreed. She noted that most of the men were in evening dress, though some were wearing lounge suits. The ladies exhibited a dazzling range of evening frocks. Diamonds glittered at wrist and throat.

'No sign of Lord and Lady Renfield as yet,' said Chloe. 'I expect they'll make a grand entrance soon. I'd no idea it would be like this. It was very nice of them to invite us. This cocktail is very nice, too. I wonder what it is?'

'It's a Sink the Pink, gin-based, and very popular with A-listers this season.'

'How did you know that?'

'I don't know how I knew. I just know these things.'

They began to mingle, stopping occasionally to talk to someone they knew. They caught snatches of conversation as they moved around the room.

'I think she's fifty-three or fifty-four today, though nobody's saying . . . It's just her birthday. Best not to ask.'

'They say he'll go bust any day soon . . .'

'Langer, his name is. I believe he's an American industrialist, or Hollywood mogul, or something . . .'

'Oh, didn't you know? Jessica's madly in love with the nephew of that bookseller who was murdered the other day. Guy something.'

The butler appeared at the door to usher them all into the library.

The vast kitchen had been commandeered by Mayfair Cuisine, and as Lady Renfield walked cautiously along the adjoining passage, she could hear the near-bedlam of professional caterers doing a first-rate job. Would they see her? Well, what if they did? She reached the garden entrance, which she opened to admit a special guest of her own, a very handsome young man in evening dress. He treated her to a knowing smile but said nothing.

She led him back down the corridor, but as they reached the darkened open pantry opposite the kitchen door, she pulled him into the room and gave him a voluptuous kiss. 'There,' she whispered, 'that's a little something to be going on with. You'll need to mingle unobtrusively with other guests until dinner is served. Just don't go anywhere near my husband, or Jessica! When dinner's announced, go straight into the banqueting hall and find your place at the second table on the right. The place card will read "Derek Lloyd".'

'And will you really do as you said? About — you know what?'

'Yes, I will. It will happen later, in the cellar. That and a few other interesting things. Don't worry. Enjoy your dinner. It'll be one of the best that you've ever eaten.'

Lady Renfield looked at her watch. Seven forty-five. She ran lightly up the stairs to join her husband.

* * *

'*Where is she?*'

Frank Renfield stood in the upstairs drawing room with his wife, waiting for their daughter to appear. In ten minutes' time, the presentations would begin. He glanced at himself in the mirror. He looked every inch an aristocrat, but he could see how ravaged his still handsome face looked, worn with care and guilt.

'Where is she?' he repeated. 'If she's let us down tonight, skulking off with that fifth-rate so-called artist, I'll—'

'She won't let us down, Frank. She dare not. Don't upset yourself.'

Carole Renfield looked very much the grande dame that night. She was wearing a white sheath dress by Adeline André, one of the top Parisian designers, along with a diamond necklace, matching earrings and a heavy silver bracelet. Yesterday she had gone up to London to have her hair cut and coloured by Luke Hersheson in Berners Street. Nothing about her looked provincial or 'county'.

Karl Langer would soon be leaving his suite in the guest wing. He intended to stay for at least ten days. Frank had asked him what airline he favoured, and he had replied that he had come to England in his private jet. It was imperative that tonight's events should create the illusion of considerable wealth. If Jessica let them down . . .

'Goldstein had a chat with me at the club last week,' Frank stammered. 'He said he'd give us three million pounds for the house and the estate—'

'*No!*'

117

Carole's face flushed with anger, and her eyes blazed with a fury that subdued her husband.

'No, Frank. We belong here. Without this house and estate we're nothing. You remember how my mother ended up when Father's investments went smash? Living in a so-called "apartment" in Bournemouth, reduced to doing her own shopping. Aristocrats must hold on to their land or go under. It's something that I've tried to drum into that stupid girl's head.' She smiled, and it was such a dangerous smile that her husband flinched. 'Jessica *will* marry Karl Langer. She will marry no one else, that I can promise you. Here she is now.'

Jessica was clad in a knee-length dress of white silk, complemented by a single string of pearls and a matching clutch bag. Her fair hair shone in waves over her shoulders.

'Well, my dear,' said Jessica's father, 'you look very . . . er, very nice.' He felt an overwhelming sense of relief. She was going to play the game.

Her mother smiled her approval, but she remained tense and suspicious.

'Oh, Mummy,' said Jessica, 'that dress! You look absolutely fabulous!'

'Thank you, my dear. Ah! Here's our principal guest now.'

Karl Langer joined them on the landing. Like his host, he knew how to wear clothes. Tall, with close-cropped fair hair, he bore no resemblance to the popular conception of a 'nerd'.

'Hello, Jessica,' he said. 'Are you going to be nice to me again? I rather enjoyed it last time.' He had the quiet, amused tones of a cultured American gentleman. Her response was only a smile, but really, he *was* a refreshing change from Alan!

* * *

It was time to descend the great staircase.

By now, the guests were partly in the library, with an overflow still in the hall. As the family descended the stairs,

118

there were gasps of admiration as the assembled guests saw Carole Renfield in her full glory. The Parisian couturière had done her proud.

What the printed invitation had called 'The Presentations' took place in the library, which had been decked with lavish floral decorations. Lord Renfield, listened to with rapt attention by his adoring wife and daughter, told his audience how delighted he was to see so many distinguished people at his wife's birthday party. He was gratified, too, to see so many presents and cards displayed on the library table for all to see.

He took a long black jewel case from his pocket and presented it to his wife. She opened it and gasped in surprise. It contained a beautiful ruby necklace. Lady Renfield kissed her husband lightly on the cheek, and they saw her mouth the words, 'Thank you.' It had been carefully rehearsed and had gone off well. Carole was a good actress. The necklace, obtained on approval from Asprey of New Bond Street, would be returned first thing the next morning.

The presentations had lasted only half an hour, so the guests remained in the library, chatting and admiring some of the cards and presents. Lady Renfield excused herself and left the room. Frank Renfield stayed close to Karl and Jessica, silently willing them to become a couple.

At nine o'clock the stately butler rang the gong and announced that dinner was served.

It was served not in the family dining room but in the great salon, famed for its gilded and painted coffered ceiling and its Italian marble fireplace, brought from Florence by the sixteenth baron in 1830. Mayfair Cuisine had brought a vast collection of silver and glass, together with table ornaments and jardinières, so that the long tables glittered and glowed as though laid for a state banquet. Each guest was provided with an extensive menu, and each course would be complemented by a carefully chosen wine.

Noel and Chloe ordered the same dishes, on this occasion onion and thyme leaf soup, followed by Blackwater salmon, and for the main course slow-roast farm pork with chilli, fennel and coriander. Perhaps, when it was all over, there would be time and space for dessert.

Noel watched the man who was both his host and his client sitting across the table from him. Lord Renfield ate very little and spent most of the time talking to Carole, on his left, or to Karl Langer, on his right. He talked with considerable animation, particularly to Karl. But in one unguarded moment, he stared across at Noel, who could see the hopeless despair in the baron's eyes.

Chloe kept her eyes on Jessica Renfield, sitting on Karl Langer's right. What a pretty, natural girl she was! She was young, and as yet had nothing of her mother's great sophistication, but there was something very appealing about her. She talked animatedly to Karl, who was clearly very taken with her.

The main course was over by nine thirty, and Jessica excused herself and left the table. Her mother's eyes followed her. Chloe heard Lord Renfield say, 'Where's she gone?'

His wife replied, 'She says she has a migraine coming on. She's gone to lie down. I'll give it twenty minutes, and then I'll go up to check.'

* * *

Jean Lewis stood on the far side of the room, watching the proceedings. She'd had no part to play in the catering and could afford to enjoy herself, admiring the dresses of the bejewelled lady guests. Ah! Girlie had got up from the table and was making for the door. Probably one of her violent headaches, poor lamb. Now Lady Renfield was getting up, no doubt to see if Girlie was all right. After all, she was her mother.

But no. Jean watched as Lady Renfield crossed to the far side of the room to talk to a young man in evening dress. Who was he? She really must get some distance glasses. Now he was getting up and following Lady Renfield somewhere. What were they up to? Well, best mind her own business. She'd go upstairs now and see how poor Jess was getting on.

But before she could take a step, a shot rang out from somewhere on the floor above, followed by a piercing scream. Everybody in the great room was dumbstruck, as though observing a silence for someone who had just died.

Lord Renfield pushed back his chair and stood up. 'Jess, Jess!' he cried, and made for the door. Karl Langer swiftly followed him. Noel and Chloe were not far behind.

They found Jessica cowering against the wall outside one of the bedrooms. Her white silk dress was covered in blood. Lord Renfield hugged her close, leaving the others to venture into the bedroom. At that moment, his only concern was for his daughter. They were all aware that everything downstairs had stopped. The party was over.

Noel Greenspan went into the bedroom. It was a very old chamber, with a four-poster bed, still with its original hangings and antique furniture. The bed had not been slept in. The room reeked of gunpowder. Lying beside the bed was the body of a young man in his early twenties. He had dyed his hair emerald-green. He lay on his back, his eyes open, his arms outstretched. A handgun lay at his side. He had been shot in the chest, and a pool of blood was widening around his body.

'Nothing must be touched until the police get here,' said Noel.

They went out on to the landing. Jessica was now sitting on a chair, sipping a glass of water. Her father was still in attendance, but there was no sign of Lady Renfield.

'I was on my way to my room,' Jessica was saying between sobs. 'I heard a noise in Lady Clarissa's Chamber and went in. He was standing there, with a revolver in his hand. I don't think he recognized me. He just said: "It was his fault. It was all his fault." And then he — he shot himself in the chest.'

'You said he didn't recognize you,' said her father. 'Did you recognize *him*?'

'Yes. He was a waiter in a pub in town called the Victoria Arms. He seemed a kind-hearted lad . . . Oh, Daddy, please can I change out of this bloodstained dress?'

Jean appeared on the landing and folded Jessica in a loving embrace. 'Come on, love,' she said, ignoring the others. 'Come on, Girlie, old Jean will see to you.' She led Jessica away.

They went downstairs. It was time for the police to take charge.

* * *

Eleven thirty, and all the guests had gone. The police had descended on Renfield Hall, sirens blaring. First the SOCO team, there to secure and investigate the scene of the crime, and then DI French, accompanied by DS Edwards. Lord Renfield had ushered the two detectives into the oak parlour, still in its festive array, and had asked Noel and Chloe to join them.

'These are friends of ours who are helping me on a research project, French,' he said. 'I should prefer them to stay here.'

'We know Mr Greenspan quite well,' said French, nodding to the detective. 'He's welcome to stay, provided he observes the usual protocols in situations like this.

'So, at just after ten thirty,' he continued, 'a man by the name of Lewis rang us at Jubilee House to tell us that someone who was not a member of the family had committed suicide here at Renfield Hall.'

'That's right. Lewis is my butler.'

'I see. Now, the people who secure and examine the scene are still upstairs, and I shall learn a great deal about this incident from them later. What I want to know at the moment is what you yourselves witnessed.'

'We witnessed nothing, Inspector,' said Lord Renfield. 'We were all downstairs in the great salon when we heard the shot. My daughter—' French held up his hand to interrupt Renfield.

'Yes, I know you were downstairs, sir. But I want to hear your account of what led up to the discovery of the body. For instance, are you able to tell me the exact time that you heard the shot?'

'It was about a quarter past ten. I can't be sure of the exact time. My daughter had left the table just a few minutes before, and as soon as I heard the shot I went to find her. Mr Greenspan and Mrs McArthur were with me. Jessica — my daughter — was standing outside the room covered in blood. Lying on the floor of the room was the body of a young man.'

DS Edwards looked up from his notebook.

'Did you touch the body, sir?' he asked.

'Certainly not. My concern was entirely for my daughter. I took her out into the passage and tried to comfort her.'

'Did any of you recognize the young man? Had he been a guest at the dinner?' asked French.

'Good God, no! A boy with green hair? I should think not.'

'Was that room your daughter's room?' asked DS Edwards.

'No. Jessica's room is further along the passage. She heard a noise in Lady Clarissa's Chamber and went in. I don't know why they call her that. She was never "Lady Clarissa". She was Clarissa, Lady Renfield. Why do people get these things wrong? Anyway, the boy was standing there, she said, with a revolver in his hand. She called it a revolver, but girls are not expected to know much about handguns. Then she said he shot himself.'

'Hmm . . . Where is Lady Renfield?'

'I don't know where she is. She may be with Jessica. God knows, the poor child is in need of her mother at this time.'

'And this boy with the green hair,' said DS Edwards. 'Did he say anything? Or did he just shoot himself?'

'He said, "It was his fault. It was all his fault." That's what Jessica told me. Obviously, Sergeant, I'd no idea who he was talking about.'

Noel Greenspan had been watching him while he was speaking and had caught once again that expression of wild despair in the nobleman's eyes. He had come to him in Canal Street to seek help when it seemed that his right to the Renfield title and estate could be in dispute. The man who had raised the question, Guy Lavender, was dead — murdered. Had that been Lord Renfield's doing? Was it Renfield who had arranged that vicious mugging, but thinking that it had been ineffective, had then resorted to murder? Was that why he was apparently undergoing the tortures of the damned at this moment?

'How is your daughter bearing up, Lord Renfield?' asked DI French. 'It must have been a horrifying experience for her.'

'How kind of you to ask. She's coping quite well. A guest who is a doctor examined her and gave her a sedative. I know you will have to interview her to hear from her own lips what happened, but I hope that will keep until tomorrow.'

'Of course. DS Edwards will return tomorrow to listen to her account. We'll leave you now, sir, and continue our investigation.'

'Oh, there's one more thing I should mention,' said Renfield. 'You asked us whether we recognized the boy, and of course we didn't. But my daughter did. She said he was a waiter in a public house called the Victoria Arms.' He saw the glance that the two detectives exchanged. 'You know the place, do you?'

'Oh, yes, sir. It's a favourite haunt of Oldminster's gay community.'

'What! So that's the kind of dive that fellow Alan Lavender takes my daughter to! And now this wretched boy ends up dead on one of my bedroom floors!'

They saw Renfield flush with anger and clench his fists.

French thought: *The man's at the end of his tether. Some birthday party this has been!*

'Glyn,' said DI French, 'have a look downstairs. Pay particular attention to entrances to the house from the rear. I doubt if this poor boy came in by the front door. I'll go up now and see what Dunwoody's come up with.'

Upstairs, the SOCO team had finished their work. Dr Dunwoody was sitting on the end of the four-poster bed. He held his bloodstained hands in front of him, like a surgeon waiting to scrub up.

'What have you got to tell me, Ray?' asked French. 'One witness in this house claims to have seen the decedent commit suicide.'

'Very likely, Mr French. Poor lad! He looks no more than twenty. He was shot in the chest at point-blank range. The powder stains show that the muzzle of the gun was pressed against his chest. So it could certainly be suicide. I'll give you a fuller report tomorrow, after I've opened him up.'

'Anything else?'

'Yes, the gun was a Spanish Astra A-60. A point 32. Quite a nice semi-automatic pistol. Made in the sixties. I'm sure that you'll find the decedent's prints on the butt and the trigger.'

'I didn't know you were a gun man.'

'Oh yes. I was attached to Special Branch before I came to hide down here.'

Sergeant Edwards came into the room. He was slightly out of breath.

'I made a quick recce of the whole ground floor, sir, and there are six doors that you can use to get in or out of the place. Four of those are still unlocked, maybe to let the caterers get their stuff in and out. It's a massive place, sir.'

DI French glanced at his watch. 'It's well after midnight,' he said. 'Let's get this body down to Railway Street Mortuary and get ourselves home.'

* * *

Jessica woke with a start. What time was it? As though in answer to her question, a clock somewhere in the house struck three. How had she got here? Who had removed her clothes and put on her nightdress? Memories of the evening's events flooded back and she shuddered. She threw back the bedclothes and sat on the edge of the bed.

Jean. It was good, kind Jean who had soothed her and put her to bed. There had been no sign of her mother. That poor boy! What could have driven him to do such a terrible thing? What was it that he'd said? *It was his fault. It was all his fault.* What had he meant by that?

What had happened to Karl Langer? Had he stayed in the house, or had he insisted on leaving? Jessica would have to wait until breakfast to find out the answer to that question.

She still felt so shaken by the ordeal and was sure she wouldn't get back to sleep again. Perhaps half a glass of her father's brandy would do the trick. Feeling for her bedroom slippers, she ventured from her room. In the half-light thrown across the great staircase she groped her way downstairs to the entrance hall. She could make out the vague shapes of familiar pieces of furniture and heard the heightened ticking of clocks.

Her father kept his most expensive brandies in the old, disused cellar at the far end of the house. With money so tight these days he didn't want guests being served the premium stuff, and so quite literally couldn't afford to have it in the main cellar, where the serving staff would have been coming and going. But after the night Jessica had had, only the best would do.

As she stepped inside, she reached down to switch on the brass lamp that usually rested in the doorway. But it wasn't there. Giving a small huff of impatience she went back into the hall and switched on the main light, so that it would shine through.

Her screams of anguish and horror awakened the whole house. She screamed without ceasing until she collapsed on the floor in the merciful oblivion of a dead faint.

11. DR THORNHILL'S MINISTRY

It was four o'clock in the morning. Everybody at Renfield Hall was deeply tired, so that the proceedings in the oak parlour seemed unreal and dreamlike. Sergeant Edwards sympathized. It was not every family that witnessed two violent deaths in their home in a single night.

Lord and Lady Renfield, sitting in the window embrasure, were clad in dressing gowns. Lord Renfield seemed dazed and subdued. His wife was deathly pale, trying as hard as she could to suppress an uncontrollable trembling. Fred, their butler, was standing by the empty fireplace. Edwards noted that Jean, Fred's wife, was not there. A tired but clearly excited young police surgeon stood beside him.

When news of a second violent death at Renfield Hall had reached Jubilee House, Sergeant Edwards, who was working the eight to eight shift, had phoned Inspector French at home. French was in bed and had no intention of leaving it. He told Edwards to go to Renfield Hall and make a preliminary investigation. He could ring up young Dr Grimwade and take him along, as Dunwoody was due to be in London first thing in the morning. Edwards had heard the inspector's wife enquiring sleepily who it was. 'It's Glyn Edwards. He has to go out to an incident. Go back to sleep, Moira.'

Before interviewing the family, he had gone with Dr Grimwade, one of Dr Dunwoody's young recruits, to view the body. Grimwade had briefly examined the corpse and declared that the victim's skull had been crushed by a blow from a heavy brass table lamp. He estimated the time of death as being between ten o'clock and midnight.

'I gather that Miss Renfield discovered the body?' said Edwards. 'I'm so sorry to think that she should have been twice in the shadow of death on the same night. Lord Renfield, you've seen the body of the young man lying on the floor in your cellar. Were you able to identify him?'

'Yes, Sergeant. It was the body of Alan Lavender, the nephew of Guy Lavender. I have no idea what he was doing down there. Nobody even uses that cellar. And more importantly, he wasn't invited here.'

Suddenly, they all heard the sound of a vehicle drawing up in front of the house, the glow from its headlights passing across the uncurtained window. DS Edwards looked out into the dark and saw a gleaming private ambulance drawn up on the forecourt.

'Lord Renfield,' he said, 'do you know anything about this ambulance? Who's it for? Who's ill? Is there something that you've not told me?'

'I'll tell you, Detective.' Karl Langer, still in evening dress, had appeared at the door. 'Miss Jessica Renfield has suffered a very serious relapse. Seeing that boy shoot himself was trauma enough. Seeing her so-called boyfriend with his head smashed in drove her over the edge.' There was a moan of anguish from Lady Renfield, but no one reacted to it.

DS Edwards felt his hackles rising. This was the rich Yank who was also supposed to be hanging out with Jessica Renfield. There was an edge of arrogance to his voice that he did not like.

'And who might you be, sir?' he asked.

'My name's Karl Langer. I'm a friend of the Renfield family.'

'And was it you, sir, who summoned this ambulance? Let me remind you that you have no jurisdiction here. I would advise you that Miss Renfield should be removed to the Princess Diana Hospital in Oldminster, where she can be provided with a police guard until such time as she can be questioned. She will have to make a statement—'

'She's virtually in a coma,' said Karl Langer. 'I've no doubt your hospital is very fine, but I've arranged to take her immediately to a private sanatorium. Lord Renfield has already agreed to this. I'll let you have full details of where I'm taking her.'

'Will you indeed? If you do anything of the sort, it will be with my permission. You and your ambulance will wait until Dr Grimwade, the medical examiner here, has examined Miss Renfield and informed me about her condition. Unless, of course, you are a doctor yourself?'

Karl Langer turned white with anger but said nothing.

That should put the arrogant sod in his place, thought Edwards. He was the key player in a little conspiracy to whisk that poor girl away from the scrutiny of the law. Well, they could all wait until Grimwade had conducted his own examination.

When Dr Grimwade returned, he confirmed the truth of Langer's diagnosis, though he stopped short at using the word 'coma'. Edwards told the American that he could proceed, once he had given all necessary details to the PC on duty at the door.

Karl Langer treated Edwards to a disarming smile.

'Thank you, Detective,' he said. 'I take your point about jurisdiction, and I'm sorry that we had to fall out. The trouble is, you see, I kinda like to do things *my* way.'

* * *

Detective Inspector French felt guilty about staying in bed and leaving a murder enquiry to his sergeant, so he made sure he was early in his office at Jubilee House well before DS

Edwards got in at seven thirty, in order to sign off from his shift at eight. He'd procured some buttered toast and coffee from the canteen, because he knew that Edwards would have had no breakfast. He saw the sergeant's eyes light up as he came into the office.

'Sit down, Glyn,' said DI French. 'Toast there, coffee there. We'll not talk about Renfield Hall until you've strengthened the inner man.' He removed his old-fashioned rimless glasses, took a tissue from a box on his desk and began to polish them. The worst thing about having a baby late in life was involuntarily sharing all your possessions with a compulsive little hoarder. Betty had commandeered his glasses that morning, and the lenses were covered with sticky, milky fingerprints.

French watched his sergeant making away with the toast. Edwards was coping manfully by himself while his wife was away in Southbourne, visiting her mother, who was recovering from an operation. The trouble was that she'd been in Southbourne now for close on three weeks, and French wondered whether the man was feeding himself properly.

'Right, sir,' said Edwards, taking a tissue from the box and wiping his hands. 'Thank you very much for that.'

French glanced at the clock.

'You're due off at eight and back on days tomorrow. Go home and get some rest.'

'If you don't mind, sir, I'd like to work on this case for a few hours more. Both the Lavenders were killed in the same way — bashed over the head with a heavy table lamp. Are we looking at some kind of vendetta against the Lavender family?'

'A vendetta? I thought it might have been Lord Renfield who did away with Guy Lavender. He had that row with him in his shop, and then, as you know, a very respectable woman was sure that she'd seen him loitering around Wyvern Court soon after the murder. But I'm not sure now. Vengeance against uncle and nephew . . . What did they have in common? Did they have any mutual friends? Alan, the nephew, belonged to the artists' fraternity, I expect, but they've always seemed quite harmless to me.'

'I'll look into it, sir. Was there anything of interest in Guy Lavender's flat that might point to associates?'

'Nothing,' said French. 'There were some letters kept in a tin box, but they were all from his sister and his mother, chatting about holidays and suchlike. He kept a sort of diary, but it was all about book purchases and sales, with notes on value and profit. Nothing compromising, nothing of real interest at all.'

'A sister. Maybe she could tell us something about Guy's friends and associates.'

'No, I'm afraid she died long ago. Melinda, her name was. She was Alan Lavender's mother.'

DS Edwards was silent for a moment. *They've all gone now*, he thought. *The uncle, the sister and the sister's son. All gone to a better place, free from sorrow, free from pain.*

'What are you thinking?' asked French.

'I'm thinking of that lad who shot himself last night at Renfield Hall. The lad with green hair. What was his name? I don't think we established that last night. But Miss Renfield said that she knew him and that he worked at the Victoria Arms. Let's go down there now, sir, and ask some questions.'

* * *

The big tattooed barman at the Victoria Arms stood behind the bar, polishing glasses. It was too early for any customers to have made their way through the drab streets behind the train station. He stopped what he was doing when DI French showed him his warrant and asked him a question.

'A lad with dyed green hair? Yes, that's Colin McDonald. He waits at the bar here a couple of nights a week. What's he done?'

'He hasn't done anything, Mr . . . er . . .'

'Ham. Cecil Ham. Colin's a good lad, so if he hasn't done anything, Mr French, what do you want with him?'

'He's dead, Mr Ham. He committed suicide last night at Renfield Hall, that big mansion on the B6 near Abbot's Grayling.'

Cecil's expression remained inscrutable, but his eyes filled with tears. He lifted the counter flap and came out into the empty bar.

'Come into the back room, gents,' he said. 'We can talk there. Suicide? Poor boy. We were all very fond of him here.'

He led them into a room that was part office, part store. There was a roll-top desk bulging with papers and invoices, a stack of plastic beer crates and four sagging armchairs placed in a semi-circle in front of an old-fashioned kitchen range. A large poster on one of the walls advertised the previous April's Pride march. An uncurtained barred window looked out on to a depressing yard.

'Suicide?' Cecil Ham repeated, after the three men had sat down. 'Well, perhaps I'm not surprised. He'd not been coping at all since Leslie died.'

'Leslie Blackmore?'

'Yes. He was a quiet, gentle lad who worked on the stalls in the wholesale vegetable market in Napier Street. Leslie died in the Princess Diana a few weeks ago. A Wednesday, it was. He was only twenty years old. He died of an overdose, I believe. He came from Birmingham originally. His parents rejected him when he came out at eighteen, and he ended up here. Everybody here at the Victoria Arms clubbed together to give him a decent burial at Mount Road cemetery.'

'Didn't his parents come to the funeral?' asked DS Edwards.

'No. Not they. I've a feeling his mother would have come, but his father was the dominant figure at home and wouldn't hear of it. A friend of mine who lives near them in Birmingham told me that.'

'Tell me about these two young men, Mr Ham,' said DI French.

'Colin and Leslie were more than just friends. They were inseparable. Leslie was what you might call the faithful one

— he only had eyes for Colin. But Colin McDonald was promiscuous by nature. He couldn't help it. But he was careful — you'll know what I mean. Be that as it may, he was utterly rocked by Leslie's death.'

'We've got more news for you, Mr Ham,' said DI French. 'Alan Lavender, Guy Lavender's nephew, was also found dead last night at Renfield Hall. Like his uncle, he'd been bludgeoned to death.'

Cecil Ham sprang up from his chair with an oath.

'So Colin did for both of them? He must have been crazy. *Both of them?*'

'What do you mean, Mr Ham? Why should Colin McDonald have done for either of them? If you know something that we don't—'

'It's not for me to say anything more, Mr French, but I'll put you in touch with someone who'll tell you all you need to know about Leslie Blackmore and Colin McDonald. His name's Dr Joseph Thornhill, and he's a kind of unofficial medical adviser to some of the men who come here to the Victoria Arms. People who'd fight shy of their local doctor will go to him with their troubles.'

Ham scribbled an address on a piece of paper and handed it to French.

'He should be in his surgery at this time of morning,' he said. As the detectives left the Victoria Arms they heard him mutter, 'So Colin did for both of them? What a tragedy.'

* * *

Dr Joseph Thornhill's surgery occupied a corner house in a red-brick terrace of Edwardian dwellings near the wholesale vegetable market. A stout, middle-aged man with a straggling moustache, he was about to open his morning surgery, but said he could spare them half an hour. He sat behind his table, which held a computer and printer, a wire basket full of cardboard folders and one of those sleeve affairs for taking blood pressure, the name of which no one can spell or pronounce. Thornhill listened without interruption until French had finished telling him about the two deaths at Renfield Hall, and then he spoke.

'Patient confidentiality is a supremely important concept, Mr French,' he said. 'However, with two of my patients dead, it's going to be my sad duty to break that confidence.'

'Were both Alan Lavender and Colin McDonald your patients?'

'Not Alan Lavender, no. But his uncle Guy was, and so was Colin McDonald. These men — some of them will confide their deepest concerns to me, rather like confessing to a priest. Usually, their confidences are sacrosanct, but in this particular instance I realize that I must speak out.

'I had another young patient, a boy called Leslie Blackmore, who died recently in the Princess Diana Hospital. He came to see me some weeks ago and told me that Guy Lavender, the bookseller who was murdered last month, had paid him handsomely to have sex with him. Apparently, this had occurred over eighteen months ago, before he'd met and fallen for Colin McDonald.'

Dr Thornhill opened a filing cabinet and removed a cardboard folder, from which he removed a single sheet of paper which he placed on his table. He referred to it every now and then as he told his story.

'I don't like to speak ill of the dead, but sometimes it's necessary. Guy Lavender had insisted on unprotected sex, assuring Leslie that he was "clean". But he wasn't. He was HIV positive. Or at least, that's the way it seems.'

'You mean he had intercourse with that young man,' DS Edwards cried, 'knowing that he could be delivering a death sentence?'

Dr Thornhill sighed. He picked up the sheet of paper, glanced at it and threw it down again.

'It's not as simple as that, Sergeant. It's possible that Guy Lavender didn't know that he was infected at the time. Some people with the HIV virus can show no symptoms for years, yet continue to transmit the virus.'

'So when Leslie Blackmore told you what had happened,' said DI French, 'wasn't it your duty to confront Guy Lavender?'

'I tried to, but Lavender had left the country for the Frankfurt Book Fair, and by the time he came back, I had left for my annual holiday in Florida.' Dr Thornhill blushed. 'I should have done more, but I didn't. I wrote Lavender a letter—' he held up the sheet of paper that he had consulted — 'but I never sent it. I have over six hundred patients in this practice and no assistance from temps. Besides, though I'm quite sure Leslie was telling me the truth about Guy Lavender, and that he hadn't had unprotected sex with anyone else in all the time leading up to him meeting Colin McDonald, it would only be his word that Guy Lavender was the person who transmitted HIV to him. I would have been able to do no more than urge Guy to get himself tested, to refrain from unprotected sex and to inform anyone he'd been intimate with that he'd tested positive.'

So that was it, thought DS Edwards. Whether Guy Lavender really was the one to infect Leslie Blackmore or not, that's what Colin McDonald would have believed. Therefore, when his boyfriend Leslie died, Colin had got revenge by murdering both Guy and his nephew.

The doctor concluded his tale.

'It wasn't HIV that killed poor young Leslie Blackmore. He succumbed to something more insidious than that. He convinced himself he was dying and could think of nothing else. He stopped all physical relations with Colin and withdrew from everyone and everything he ever loved . . . and found he couldn't live with the fear and the shame of it all. He dosed himself with pills, desperate for an out, and died in hospital a few weeks ago.'

'You've been very helpful, Doctor,' said DI French. 'I gather that you're a specialist in this field?'

'No, not at all. This is an ordinary NHS general practice. But I feel that I have a ministry — if that's not too pompous a word — to gay people. You see, I once—' He stopped abruptly, and looked at his watch. 'Oh, ten minutes to go. Time to tell you of a personal experience.

'Many years ago, when Aids had just come to public awareness, I attended to a young clergyman, one of the first people in England to contract the disease. He was a charming, devout man, a curate in a northern town — I won't say which — and a graduate of Oxford, or maybe it was Cambridge. When he died, aged thirty-two, he was buried in a steel cabinet soldered shut, and the undertakers wore white anti-contamination suits. You wouldn't have thought that he had once been a human being. It was that experience that helped me realize that I was here to treat and cure people if I could, not turn my back on them through fear or ignorance.'

* * *

Dr Thornhill had given them the address of Colin McDonald's lodgings. He had occupied two basement rooms in a decaying house beyond the railway sidings. The door was opened by an unshaven man in vest and shorts, who regarded them with bleary eyes.

'Police? I don't have nothing to do with the police. This is a 'spectable house. So he's dead, is he? There's another dollop of rent gone. Who'll clear his things out?'

The man took them down to the basement and left them alone. Colin McDonald seemed to have led a hand-to-mouth existence in the two damp basement rooms. There was a table, a couple of chairs, a television set and a one-bar electric fire. A set of shelves held a few books. A kitchenette was separated from the room by a curtain. It was quite tidy, but there was little in the cupboards except a box of cornflakes and an open bag of sugar.

In the second room the bed was unmade. Beside it was a chair, holding an alarm clock, which had stopped. The wardrobe held quite a good selection of clothes. Searching through these, Glyn Edwards found a folded sheet of paper in the inside pocket of a thin nylon bomber jacket.

'Sir,' he said, 'here's the poor lad's suicide note.'
It was brief and to the point.

It was me that murdered Guy Lavender. I thought I wouldn't care, but I can't live with the guilt. I gave him a good kicking in the street, but that didn't stop my rage. I went round to his flat and bashed his head in with a lamp. He infected my friend Leslie Blackmore with HIV, like his life was worth nothing. I was left to watch poor Leslie die. I don't want to live without him. Goodbye, Mum and Dad, and my sister Violet.
Colin McDonald.

'So that's it, Edwards,' said DI French. 'Two murders solved. He was beside himself with grief, and must have assumed that Alan Lavender was somehow in league with his uncle. Tragic, really — tragic for all concerned. So he had a family somewhere. I'll put somebody on to tracking them down.'

'I don't dispute the suicide note, sir,' said DS Edwards. 'But why was it here, in that jacket? Why didn't he take it with him when he went to Renfield Hall? And what was he doing there at all?'

'I don't know, but we'll find out. We'd better get back to the office. There are other matters we need to deal with as well as this Renfield Hall business. By midday, if we're lucky, we'll have the results of his autopsy.'

DS Edwards did a final rummage through a pile of clothes on the floor of the wardrobe and found a laptop with a power lead coiled around it. It was an old IBM model, with serial and parallel ports but no USB.

'Take it back with you to the office, Glyn,' said DI French. 'Then get yourself home. It's long past your bedtime.'

'Yes, sir, you're right. I'll go now and catch a few hours' kip. But I'll come back in later this afternoon. This case is bugging me, and I want to have a good look at this laptop. It may yield something of value.'

* * *

'She's back,' said Carole Renfield. 'I thought we'd got rid of her after that seance, but she's back again. What are you going to do about it?'

Mrs Gladys Osbourne shifted uneasily. If she handled this wrong, this formidable woman could become a nuisance.

'You'll realize, Lady Renfield, that I know who you are now, so you'll probably mistrust anything else that I tell you. But it is my duty to tell you that the troubled spirit appeared to me some days after your visit and repeated very earnestly that she wished you no harm. I saw her spirit form, standing over there by the china cabinet.'

'What did she look like?'

Mrs Osbourne smiled and shook her head.

'I've seen the picture of Lady Clarissa in that guide book to Renfield Hall. She looked like *that*.'

'I don't care what she says, Mrs Osbourne. She unnerves me. Normal folk don't see these dreadful things. And now she's started talking to me, but although I can see her lips move, her words come out of my mouth. I'm terrified that my husband will hear me. This is all in strictest confidence, of course.'

'Naturally, Lady Renfield. Have you attended any of those meetings I suggested to you?'

'No. I want to be rid of her. She's been hanging around Renfield Hall for over two centuries. Can't you help me to get rid of her?'

At last! Here was a way to be shot of this woman without doing her any harm.

'If that's what you really want, then I would suggest an exorcism. You evidently regard Lady Clarissa as a malignant entity, and of course you may be right. "For oftentimes, to win us to our harm, the instruments of darkness tell us truths, win us with honest trifles, to betray us in deepest consequence." Shakespeare had very deep insights into these matters.'

'An exorcism? We're Church of England. We don't know any priests who would do that sort of thing. Anyway, my husband wouldn't allow anything like that.'

'You can perform an exorcism yourself,' said Mrs Osbourne. 'You would need to lock yourself in the haunted room and carry out a few simple rituals. If the spirit is malign, it will be banished from your house, and will be unable to attach itself to your personality.'

'What are these rituals? Will I have to dress up in some ridiculous garb?'

'That will be quite unnecessary. I will give you the name and address of a spiritualist exorcist, who will tell you what to do and give you the various things necessary for the performance of the ritual. His name is Abraham Sylvester, and he lives at number eight, Gosfield Park, on the far side of the race course. He will charge you a modest sum, and tell you all that you need to know.'

Lady Renfield rose from the chair where she had been sitting and put the suggested donation on the table.

'Thank you, Mrs Osbourne,' she said. 'I'll see this Mr Sylvester. I want that censorious bitch out of my house. An exorcism sounds just right for me.'

When Lady Renfield had gone, Mr Osbourne came in from the next room.

'Any luck?' he asked.

'Yes, I've got rid of her to Abe Sylvester. But I'm worried. She hears herself talking as though she was the departed spirit herself. That could mean—'

'I know,' said her husband. 'I don't like the sound of it either. I'd advise you to write an anonymous letter to Lady Renfield's doctor telling him what you fear. I think we've a duty to do that. Tell him that you're a medium, but that you don't want to reveal your identity. You could go out to Binford and post it there.'

'I'll do that,' said Gladys Osbourne. 'Meanwhile, Abe should be able to keep her at bay by selling her one of his do-it-yourself exorcism kits.'

Mr Osbourne sighed. 'Sometimes I get sick of the whole business, Gladys. I wish we'd tried to make more of a go of the tobacconist's. At least we were earning an honest penny.'

'Yes, and not much more! This medium business pays much better, so you just be content and attend to your allotment. Anyway, we're well rid of that odious woman.'

12. DOUBTS AND REVELATIONS

True to his word, DS Edwards arrived back at Jubilee House just after four o'clock. DI French handed him the result of the autopsy on the body of Colin McDonald. It confirmed that the cause of death was a single shot to the chest discharged from a semi-automatic pistol. Death would have been instantaneous.

'We can be quite sure now that it was Colin McDonald who murdered Guy Lavender,' said French. 'Forensics sent up a report of their findings while you were away. Black cotton fibres were found caught on the inside bolt of the sitting room of Guy Lavender's flat in Wyvern Court. They suggested that McDonald wore gloves — black cotton gloves — to ensure that he left no fingerprints. The SOCO people found those gloves thrust into a bush in the grounds of Wyvern Court.'

'Granted the murderer wore gloves, sir,' said DS Edwards. 'But did Forensics come up with anything more positive? How can we prove it was Colin?'

'They did,' said French. 'McDonald had drunk a glass of water in Guy Lavender's kitchen, presumably after committing the crime, and his DNA was found on the rim of the glass he'd drunk from. So there it is. Case closed.'

DS Edwards went into his own cubbyhole of an office, plugged in Colin McDonald's laptop and booted up the aging machine. It was running Windows 7, which made life easier for anyone frustrated with the odd ways of Windows 10. There were a few video games, and one of those free word processors, but not much else by way of software.

Most of Colin's emails were entirely innocuous messages from friends, making appointments to meet in one or other of the cafés in the town centre, mixed with junk mail from various online stores.

And then he found something that made him sit up. It was a message from someone who was clearly using an alias. That would be a little problem for Forensics to solve. Having read the email, DS Edwards hurried back to DI French's office, carrying the laptop with him.

Hi Colin,

Alan Lavender knew all about his uncle's fling with Leslie — along with the sordid details of how he became infected with HIV. All because he didn't want to use protection. Guy always loved to brag . . . and how Alan laughed when he heard his uncle's exploits. The Lavender men are all the same, you see. No regrets and no remorse. Take it from a friend who knows first-hand. Uncle Guy taught his worthless artist nephew everything he knew.

Come to Renfield House on the evening of 10 October at eight o'clock. Come to the kitchen door, and someone will take you to a place where Alan is being held by us. Bring a gun. The Lavender men should be made to pay for what they've done. To Leslie, to me and who knows how many other victims.

'No name, sir,' he said. 'But the prelims show that it was sent at 11.00 p.m. on the eighth. Someone at Renfield Hall was out to lure Colin McDonald there on the night of Lady Renfield's birthday party.'

'Well, whoever's behind this, it seems our anonymous sender knew exactly what to say to get Colin riled up and ready to kill. We need to pay the Renfields a visit about all of this,' said DI French. 'Shake things up a bit. Put the wind up them again, you know? I was going to outline a theory about what happened, but after the lunch break today I found a note left on my desk from Freddie Fusspot. He wants all details of the case, including notebooks, sent to him upstairs. He's already sensed there's going to be trouble with the chief constable and Lord Renfield's other friends, and he's naturally rather vexed that our killer or killers managed to trash Lady Renfield's birthday party. He'll be down here at half past five.'

* * *

Superintendent Frederick Philpot was not a detective, and partly compensated for this by ensuring that his uniform was immaculate. Most of the personnel at Jubilee House, the headquarters of the Oldshire County Police, seemed scruffy and untidy when compared to his magnificence. He was a stickler for protocol and 'going by the book', qualities that had earned him the nickname 'Freddie Fusspot'. For all that, he had a keen eye and an alert mind, so when he erupted into DI French's office, he and DS Edwards were both prepared to listen very carefully to what he said.

'I'll start my commentary on this case,' he said, 'by issuing a verbal rebuke to you, DS Edwards. You should have resisted that American's strident disregard of your orders and insisted on Miss Renfield's being taken to the Princess Diana Hospital. Mr Karl Langer may be as rich as Croesus, but he has no standing here. Don't let anything like that happen again. Do I make myself clear?'

'Yes, sir.'

'Very well. Now, I'll begin my interpretation of the facts with that email that you sent up to me with the notebooks, et cetera, and the message summoning Colin McDonald to Renfield Hall. Note the date specified for him to go: the tenth of October. The writer would have known that on the

143

evening of that particular day, the house would be full of people — guests, household staff and caterers.

'"Bring a gun," it says in the email, suggesting that the writer knew that Colin McDonald would know where to obtain one. You'll need to follow that up, French. And so he came at eight o'clock to the kitchen door of Renfield Hall. Do you agree with me so far?'

'Yes, sir.'

'Very well. This young man is friendless and alone, and filled with self-hatred. He had killed Guy Lavender, but was clearly not a killer by nature. Someone — we'll come to whom later — met him at the kitchen door and took him up to Lady Clarissa's Chamber. I think that they told him to stay there until they brought Alan Lavender up to the haunted room to receive his sentence.'

Superintendent Philpot treated them to a confiding smile. DS Edwards thought: *He's telling us how brilliant he is and waiting for our admiration.*

'But this young man,' Philpot continued, 'burning with hatred for those who'd caused his friend's death, was not content to wait there. Once alone, he left the bedroom and went downstairs to the cellar. I think that he, too, had written an anonymous note, designed to lure Alan Lavender to a specific room in the house. Why? Because he had no intention of shooting Alan Lavender. The noise of the shot would bring everybody running. No, he chose the same instrument of death as he had used on the uncle — a table lamp.

'And so he did the deed and slipped back to Lady Clarissa's room. When the person who had admitted him to the house came for him, he would tell him that he had already executed Alan Lavender. However, as fate would have it, it was not our unknown conspirator but Miss Jessica Renfield who came into the room. By now, Colin McDonald was devoured by guilt and remorse — as I said, he was not a killer by nature. When he saw that beautiful, innocent young woman come into the room, he snapped. "It was his fault. It was all his fault," he cried. Of course, he meant Guy

Lavender. And so, in the firm grip of fear, guilt and remorse, he used the pistol to commit suicide.'

The superintendent, who all this time had been sitting in DI French's chair, leaned back and smiled.

'So, officers,' he said, 'what do you think?'

'Who was the accomplice in the house, sir?' asked DS Edwards.

'The accomplice? Well, almost certainly someone from the gay community. It could have been somebody employed by Mayfair Cuisine or anyone who could grab a tray and pose as a waiter. That's why the birthday party was chosen for the murder.' He stopped and looked keenly at French.

'I know, French, that after Guy Lavender was killed, your suspicions fell on Lord Renfield — silencing Lavender over this inheritance business. But I think you'll agree with me now that the whole wretched affair has its genesis somewhere in Oldminster's gay community.'

'But why stage the whole thing in Lord Renfield's house, sir?' asked DS Edwards.

'Well, Sergeant, Renfield was the initial prime suspect for Guy Lavender's murder. That, along with a houseful of party guests, would've made for a very large pool of suspects for us to investigate.

'Now, the press are outside, baying for information. Will you address them, French, or will I? They're entitled to some sort of statement.'

'Well, sir,' said French, 'I know that DS Edwards will agree with me that you've given us a brilliant theory as to what happened in this case. So perhaps—'

'Excellent! I'll go out there now and give them a story for the evening papers.'

Superintendent Philpot swept out of the room, and French turned to Edwards. 'What do you think?'

'Well, sir,' Edwards replied, 'it was quite impressive, in its own way. Maybe he's right, and we've just got a bit of mopping up to do — the gun and so on. But then again, maybe he's wrong, so for the moment I'm keeping an open mind. Lord

Renfield detested Alan Lavender, and he turns up bludgeoned to death in Renfield's house. He was a rival for his daughter's hand, whereas he wanted her to marry into money and solve his own problems. I've always had my suspicions of the noble lord, sir, and I happen to know he's in cahoots with Patrick Gorman. It's rumoured that they cooperated on various dodgy deals when they were both in the army, years ago. And I know that you don't exactly regard him as a fine specimen of upright manhood. Do you think that Renfield was at the scene of Guy Lavender's murder, sir? That witness was pretty positive.'

'Well, I'm not saying she was wrong, but what about Colin McDonald's note of confession, and the fact his DNA was on that drinking glass in Guy Lavender's home? It seems unlikely to me that it would be anyone other than Colin.'

'Hmm, the sighting still seems a mighty coincidence to me, sir. And I'm thinking about that gun, the one Colin McDonald used to shoot himself.'

'These low-life characters know where to get a gun if they want one, Glyn. You know that yourself. McDonald probably bought it off a dealer in a pub. Freddie Fusspot wanted me to investigate that, but I'm not going to. It's what they call "wasting police time".'

DI French consulted his watch and got up from his chair. 'I've got to go, Glyn,' he said. 'Traffic want to talk to me about a new madcap scheme that the city council's thinking of introducing. It's a contraflow system in Springfield Vale, which will result in utter chaos. I'm leaving Alan Lavender's murder with you.'

When French had gone, DS Edwards sat in his guvnor's chair and began to recall the dramatic details of Alan Lavender's death. Everybody at Renfield Hall had been devastated by the horror of two unnatural deaths in one night. All of them, he included, had been looking through tired eyes. Little wonder: on the second occasion, it had been four o'clock in the morning.

Had anything significant remained in his memory from that time?

People in dressing gowns. Lord Renfield, stunned and subdued. And his wife, Lady Renfield. He recalled that she'd been unable to control the trembling that shook her whole frame. And later, she had moaned in anguish. What had that meant? All this was telling him something that he still couldn't grasp.

And there was something troubling him about the presentation of Alan Lavender. Something to do with young Dr Grimwade, the medical examiner. Before Edwards had interviewed the family, he had gone with Grimwade to view the body. They had stayed in the cellar just long enough to ascertain the probable cause of death. He had looked down at the body of Alan Lavender, noting the crushed skull and the pool of blood surrounding the head like an obscene halo. That had been sufficient at the time, but now he recalled something else.

Alan Lavender had been wearing evening dress. He had been a *guest*. Yet didn't Lord Renfield say that Alan wasn't welcome there? So who invited him?

Edwards suspected it was Jessica Renfield — after all, she'd have wanted him on her arm, and she wouldn't have necessarily informed her father, knowing his distaste for the boy.

So then what of the email that Edwards had found on Colin McDonald's laptop? Was that message a fraud, designed to mislead the police? Somebody at Renfield Hall could have sent it.

Come to the kitchen door, and someone will take you to a place where Alan is being held by us. Bring a gun, and avenge poor Leslie's death. Well, Colin had had a gun and had used it to terrible effect upon himself. But had he really brought it with him? Or had somebody at Renfield Hall *given* it to him?

Someone will take you to a place where Alan is being held by us. Freddie Fusspot had suggested that this 'someone' could have been one of the waiters from Mayfair Cuisine, another member of the gay community conniving at Alan's murder. Sheer speculation. When Mr French came back from Traffic

147

tomorrow, he'd let him know that Alan Lavender had been a guest at Lady Renfield's party, and they would take things from there.

* * *

A couple of days after the fateful birthday party, Noel and Chloe received an invitation from Karl Langer to dine with him at the Escoffier. When they arrived, it was to find that Karl had booked an intimate private dining room on the first floor. During the excellent meal they talked about the events of the last few days, which gave Chloe the opportunity to ask a question.

'What has happened to Jessica? Poor child, she suffered a complete physical and mental collapse.'

'She did,' said Karl. 'No girl should ever have had to witness two violent deaths. I was sorry for the poor deranged lad who shot himself, but I've lost no sleep about the other fellow, Alan Lavender, I can tell you. He had it coming to him — he was a twister and a fifth-rate Lothario. He posed as Jessica's boyfriend, but he never loved her.'

The three of them fell silent. Karl's brows were knitted in a frown of anger. Coffee was served, and the mood gradually lightened.

'Where is Jessica now?' asked Noel.

'She's at the Mendelssohn Clinic, a private sanatorium on the far side of Chichester. She's receiving the best possible treatment there from specialist physicians and psychiatrists. And there she stays until she's restored to health. And when she *is* restored, I will personally restore her to her parents. Lord Renfield is at one with me on this.'

'Is she allowed visitors?'

'Not as a general rule, but that was partly why I invited you here tonight. Would you care to visit Jessica and see what progress she's made? I kinda like you both, and I'd be happy to ferry you down to the clinic sometime this week.

Now how about some brandy to go with this excellent coffee? They've got a bottle of Louis Treize here.'

* * *

The Mendelssohn Clinic nestled at the foot of a wooded ridge in one of the more secluded areas of Oldshire. Five miles from the nearest village, it could be reached only via the twisting B13 road. Its buildings had been designed by a prominent Art Deco architect of the 1930s, with the intention of soothing people whose psyches had been damaged by trauma of all kinds. Karl Langer drove Noel and Chloe there on the following Monday, 16 October.

It was very soothing and peaceful inside, with all the floors and corridors covered in oatmeal carpet. The nurses wore the attractive uniforms of the 1950s, with white caps and pale blue dresses, their ranks indicated by the colour of the snake-buckled belts that they wore. They were met in the reception area by the proprietor of the clinic, who had been alerted by phone to expect their arrival.

Dr Felix Mendelssohn, a stout, bald-headed man wearing an unbuttoned white coat, was carrying a number of case files and looked quite desperate to be elsewhere.

'I'm pleased to meet you, Mr Greenspan, and you, Mrs McArthur,' he said, shaking hands with both. 'I'm a little late for a case conference, but here's Matron Callaghan. She'll conduct you to Miss Renfield's suite. I hope you'll both stay to staff lunch. Perhaps I'll be able to talk to you then.' An impressive woman in traditional matron garb appeared from a side room, and Dr Mendelssohn all but bolted along the facing corridor.

The matron led them along a sunlit corridor and admitted them to the suite of rooms that had been reserved for Jessica. There was no medical paraphernalia in sight. Jessica was lying back in a reclining chair, clad in a suit of lounge pyjamas. She appeared to be asleep. A paperback book had fallen from her hand to the floor. Karl Langer took one of her hands gently in his and kissed her lightly on the forehead.

'Karl? Is that you?' she asked sleepily as her eyes opened. Noel saw that she was having difficulty focusing. He also noticed the pulsating of a vein in her right temple. She was young and resilient, but it would take a long time for her to recover completely from the traumatic events she had endured.

Jessica pressed a switch, and the chair whirred into an upright position. She smiled at her visitors, and when she spoke her voice was light but firm.

'Oh! I remember you. You were at Mummy's party. I remember speaking to you, Mr Greenspan, at dinner, before my migraine came on. How do you do, Mrs McArthur? I'm afraid we didn't have much time to socialize, because . . . well, because of what happened. Karl, show Mr Greenspan the library and the music room while I have a chat with Mrs McArthur.'

Evidently, the convalescent girl wanted to speak to Chloe alone. For one anxious moment she imagined that the girl was going to say, 'Please help me. I am being held a prisoner here!' and was relieved when Jessica said, 'This is a wonderful place, Mrs McArthur. There are psychiatrists here who can strip your mind clean of its subconscious terrors and bring you healing. It's all done by talking, but they direct the talk so cleverly that you find yourself seeing all kinds of things in a different light.'

'So you are starting to recover, are you, my dear? *Really* recover, I mean.'

'Yes. But I received such violent shocks that day that my body was affected, and I needed treatment from ordinary doctors as well. I was unconscious for thirty-six hours.'

'Mr Langer brought us here to see you today,' said Chloe. 'It was so very kind of him.' Would the girl take the bait?

'Oh, Karl has been wonderful. You've no idea . . . I used to snub him and try to make him angry so that he'd go away.

But I don't want him to go away now.' Jessica's pallid face was suffused with a sudden blush.

'I think I'm falling for him. But don't tell him, will you, Mrs McArthur?'

'Do please call me Chloe. No, I won't tell him, Jessica, but then, I don't think he'll need to be told.'

'Oh, Chloe, we Renfields are such frauds . . . Karl's too good for the likes of us. But I got rid of him just now because I wanted to talk to a woman, someone who's not going to make a fuss. I've come to terms with what happened to Alan — that crazy boy killing him. But I can tell that Karl knows something about Alan that I don't. He's found something out, and I want to know what it is. I thought you might be able to find out for me.'

Chloe sat still for a moment, thinking back to something that Karl Langer had said when they had dined together. *Alan had it coming to him because he was a twister and a fifth-rate Lothario. He posed as Jessica's boyfriend, but he never loved her.*

'Yes, Jessica,' she said, 'leave it to me. I'll find out what that secret was.'

* * *

They accepted Dr Mendelssohn's invitation to lunch, which proved to be a cheerfully simple meal served in the clinic's cafeteria. When it was over, Chloe contrived to be alone with Karl while Greenspan and the psychiatrist talked shop.

'What a well-manicured lawn!' she exclaimed. 'Do let's take a walk around it, Mr Langer.' They found a way out onto the path and began their stroll through the well-tended gardens.

'Mr Langer,' said Chloe without preamble, 'when we dined together the other night, you said something very interesting about the late Alan Lavender. "He had it coming to him, because he was a twister and a fifth-rate Lothario. He posed as Jessica's boyfriend, but he never loved her." What did you mean by that?'

Karl Langer frowned, and for a moment Chloe thought that she had appeared too intrusive. But Karl's reply soon put her at her ease.

'He was my rival for Jessica's affections, Mrs McArthur,' he said. 'And I'm not given to putting up with rivals. But I set my spies on him to see what he got up to, and it soon emerged that he made regular visits to London. Well, one of my folks took to following him and found that he had another woman friend who lived in a little house in a place called Maida Vale. Yes, ma'am. I kid you not about this.'

'A girlfriend? And yet he was going out with Jessica?'

'Yes. Only it turned out that she wasn't a girlfriend. They were married in a registry office in London three years ago. My man found that out. So Alan Lavender, my rival, was contemplating a spot of bigamy. He was supposed to be a great lover, despite the fact that he looked like a refugee from the boondocks, but he had his eyes on what he imagined was Jessica's fortune. Well . . . I could have told him some things about it that would have sent him scampering back to Maida Vale. But that's another man's business.'

'*Married?*'

'Yes, ma'am. And when his uncle was murdered by that young hood, Alan inherited a very tidy sum. My agents found all this out, you understand. He knew that he'd never be allowed to marry Jessica. So he planned to take his money and return to his wife in Maida Vale, though I don't think he'd have stayed with her long.'

'So there's a young woman in London who never knew that her husband had another marital prospect afoot in Oldminster. Well, won't she inherit his money?'

'She will, and I've already undertaken to see that she inherits the lot. I think it's about three hundred thousand pounds. Maybe more. She deserves it, too, according to my agents. She's a decent young woman who works in a café to make ends meet.'

Karl Langer suddenly flushed with anger.

'One of my people found out something else about our fifth-rate Lothario. His wife — she has a name, damn it . . .

Lucille. When Lucille fell pregnant, he bullied her into having an abortion. That was when he had high hopes of "marrying" Jessica. Lucille and her baby had suddenly become a nuisance. And that's why I didn't shed any tears over his death.'

They walked back into the warm and cheerful clinic. It was time for them to return to the Church Eaton Hotel.

'Karl,' said Chloe, using his Christian name for the first time, 'you must tell all this to Jessica. She knows that you're holding something back, and it will hurry her healing if she is allowed to hear the whole truth about Alan Lavender.'

'You really think so?'

'Yes, I do. Tell her as soon as you can. Telling her will help exorcize some ghosts.'

* * *

'No, no, Renfield,' said Lord Renfield's solicitor, 'it just won't do. You must face facts and cut your coat according to your cloth.'

Frank Renfield looked at the man who held his future happiness in his hands. Adrian Radcliffe-Reynolds looked thoroughly at home in his blue pinstriped suit and pristine white shirt. His tie contrived to look like that of Winchester College, but he'd once told Renfield that he'd bought it at Tie Rack. A well-nourished, frowning sort of man, he'd performed miracles in the past. But now, it would seem, the age of miracles was over. He had even refused a glass of sherry.

'That birthday party of Carole's cost £6,580. How do you intend to pay for it? Mayfair Cuisine will tender their bill at the end of the month. You have £2,345 in the bank.'

'Can't you arrange an advance with Solomon's? They've been very good in the past.'

'Solomon's won't deal with you anymore. They've written off a debt of £634 to clear their books of you, which was extremely decent of them. Evidently a title talks, even in these times.' Was that a smirk? Surely not.

'Your long-term debts are accruing loan interest daily, and together they amount to over two million pounds. I very much fear that some of the longer-term creditors will foreclose this year. If that happens, then you'll be declared bankrupt. And you'll lose all this.'

'What am I to do?' Renfield despaired. Did he sound as broken as he felt?

'You must sell this place. Didn't Goldstein offer you three million for the house and land? Make a clean break, Renfield. Buy a smaller property in Chichester. There are some very fine properties for sale there at the moment. Yes, a clean break. One more month like this and you'll be utterly ruined.'

When the solicitor had gone, Frank sat back in his favourite chair in the library and forced himself to face up to reality. Jessica had to marry Karl, and sooner rather than later. She was falling for him at last, and no wonder. Maybe fortune was beginning to favour him? With Alan Lavender gone, Karl had no rival for Jess's affections. Bishop Poindexter had suggested that a lavish wedding in Oldminster Cathedral would bring a lot of bookings to the city's hotels, thus boosting the local economy . . .

He was dreaming again. It would suit him down to the ground if they could be married quickly and without fuss in the local registry office, if that would bring Langer's fortune nearer to him. Because the moment that Karl and Jess were married, Frank proposed to confess his dire financial state to his son-in-law, who would feel obliged to bail him out.

This house, his ancestral home and seat of the barony, was beginning to lose its lustre. It was stained with the blood of those two young men. Adrian Radcliffe-Reynolds was right. It had become a millstone around his neck. He could convey Renfield Hall to Karl by deed of gift, if necessary, knowing that after his own death Jess would succeed to the title as Baroness Renfield in her own right, so that there would be barons of Renfield at Renfield Hall in perpetuity. And plenty of money to let them live properly as aristocrats.

But he was afraid of Carole. Any suggestion that they should move to Chichester would be met with such a fierce outburst of rage that he would be utterly overwhelmed. Any counter-arguments from him would sound like mere bluster. Yes, he was afraid of her, afraid of what she would do, and of what she may have done. She had been tearful and overwrought, and he'd put it down to the shock of Jessica's breakdown. She'd never been a religious woman, but he knew that she had been seeing a spiritualist recently. Why would she do that? Jean said that she'd started to talk to herself. Sometimes she'd hold conversations with people who weren't there. If this bizarre behaviour continued, he'd make her go to the Mendelssohn Clinic for some proper medical treatment.

It wasn't only Carole who made him afraid. After his angry visit to Guy Lavender in his bookshop he had wondered whether he could swallow his rage and do a deal with him. He recalled that eventful Tuesday, 26 September, when he had left the British Legion Club and walked down to Wyvern Court. He had found the front door of Guy Lavender's flat open, and on entering had seen the bookseller lying dead on the floor with his skull crushed by a heavy table lamp. He'd recoiled in horror and left Wyvern Court as quickly as he could. Fortunately, he'd been wearing gloves — he always dressed meticulously — so he knew that he'd left no fingerprints. Evidently, someone had seen him leave, but he'd had no trouble in denying it. Oh, well. Soldier on.

* * *

DS Glyn Edwards sat at the table in Alan Lavender's flat, reading through the few letters that the dead man had left lying about the untidy living room. What would happen to his possessions? As far as he knew, all his family were dead. Maybe Mr Cantor would be able to find some distant relative to inherit his things. But wait! Karl Langer had discovered that Guy was already married, so his effects would go to his wife. He'd no liking for Langer, but the young millionaire could certainly get results.

There were several letters from Mr Cantor, Alan Lavender's solicitor. Some were opened, others still sealed, because they'd arrived after Alan's death. There was very little of a personal nature — no 'love letters' from Jessica Renfield. But what was this? A letter, still in its opened envelope, and written on the crested notepaper of the Renfield family.

My dear boy,
You will have received the parcel from the tailor by now. Bring the enclosed invitation with you. I can promise you a very rewarding time later on the tenth.
All my love. C.

This was Alan's invitation to Lady Renfield's birthday party, the letter that she had written to lure him to his death. He could well imagine the activity implied for a 'very rewarding time'. He would take the letter away and put it in the file relating to the murder of Alan Lavender. And when Mr French had finally broken down the chief constable's resistance to causing scandal, he would personally arrest Lady Renfield on a charge of murder.

13. AT THE MONKSHEAD COUNTY ASYLUM

On Friday, 20 October, Lance Middleton QC, freed from his work in Europe, arrived in Oldminster, and Noel met him at the station in his Ford Mondeo. With much puffing and panting, accompanied by a monologue detailing the woes of travelling by rail, he managed to get into the car while Noel put his luggage in the boot. In less than twenty minutes they had arrived in Wellington Square.

'You'll be staying the night with me, but we're going to have lunch at Chloe's,' said Noel Greenspan. 'And then we'll discuss this whole business of Lord Renfield and his inheritance. I've taken all the relevant documents over to Chloe's. It'll save going back to my place. You won't want to move for an hour after Chloe's fed you.'

'I don't know why you two don't move in together, into your house. It's a superb property, and if you let a decent designer loose on it, it would be an ideal home for you two. Save all this dashing across the square. You might even get married.'

'Oh, shut up, will you? Can you imagine someone like Chloe marrying a man with a face like mine?'

'Yes. Your facial affliction is only temporary. It will pass.'

'Well, I can't. I wouldn't dare ask her. Anyway, we're going to hers because she's decided to serve a substantial lunch to satisfy your gourmet's appetite. Did you know she was a cordon bleu cook? At this very moment she's slaving over her new gas-fired Aga.'

They crossed the square, and Noel let himself into Chloe's house with a latchkey. She appeared briefly at the kitchen door to say hello to their friend, and within a quarter of an hour ushered both men into the dining room of her apartment. Lance's round, clean-shaven face bore a smile of anticipation as he tucked his napkin under his chin.

The lunch began with a light consommé, followed by grilled sirloin of beef, accompanied by mushrooms, tomato and battered onions, served with a mixed salad, and concluded with a baked apple and raisin cheesecake. It was accompanied by one of Sainsbury's choice Merlots.

'Chloe,' said Lance, when he had eaten all before him and drunk his third glass of wine, 'that was quite superb! It's always so civilized here. It's like being in a Trollope novel. Or do I mean Thackeray? This square has its own particular charm, too. You know, you and Noel really should—'

Noel firmly interrupted.

'The time has come, Lance,' he said, 'for us all to adjourn to Chloe's kitchen, where you can examine the various documents in this business of the Renfield inheritance. Chloe and I have already reached a conclusion on the matter. Now we want your expert lawyer's slant on it.'

'On the way here from the station, you told me that you've been commissioned by Lord Renfield to look into this. Are you going to make it all come out in his favour? Or are you going after the truth?'

'We're going after the truth,' said Noel. 'You know that already, Lance, so stop being frivolous. As for Lord Renfield, I don't think he cares anymore, one way or the other. He's had a terrible amount of trouble recently, poor man. So come, let us show you the documents and tell you all that we know.'

They sat at a big, scrubbed table in the kitchen, and Noel gave their friend a concise account of the claims made against the Renfields concerning their rights of tenure, the murders of Guy Lavender and his nephew Alan, and the spectacular suicide of Colin McDonald at Renfield Hall.

Lance listened with rapt attention and then asked to see the evidence that they had assembled. He read the letter from the dismissed librarian Jethro Evans to Charles Blazey and rapidly scribbled something into a small notebook that he took from a pocket. He pulled a wry face but made no comment.

Noel handed him the letter that Guy Lavender had sent to Lord Renfield. He glanced through it and then put it aside in something like disgust. 'Nothing to do with it,' he muttered. 'It's just a crude attempt at blackmail. Let's stick with the eighteenth century. What else have you got?'

'I have what might be called the official version of Lady Renfield's death,' said Noel. 'It's from the *Bow Street Intelligencer* for the twenty-fifth of June 1784.'

'Ah! Now we'll be able to see the facts in the case,' said Lance. 'This is more like it.'

Noel handed him the photocopy he had made on his visit to London.

Noel and Chloe watched Lance as he read the account, occasionally muttering something aloud that had made a particular impression upon him.

'Hmm . . . "Ran frantick", did he? . . . "Lying abed, much troubled with the toothache" . . . I know the feeling. "He seemed out of his senses, his eyes rolling wildly". Well, well . . . Rushed up the stairs, violent altercation, scream of anguish . . . "He felled me with a blow" . . . And he was found unfit to plead? This Timothy Reid?'

'He was. And then he was taken to the Monkshead House of Refuge, where he stayed until he died.'

Lance Middleton said nothing for a while. He sat back in his chair, staring out of the window. His lips still moved as though he were recalling the wording of the account.

'I don't like the sound of it,' he said at last. 'It's all too glib. Glib footmen, glib prose. Were footmen so articulate? There's a whiff of conspiracy there. Anything else?'

'I have a photocopy of the will of the fifteenth Baron Renfield,' said Noel. 'You'll find that very interesting, I think.'

In the Name of GOD, Amen

Last Will and Testament of Me, Frank Renfield, Baron Renfield of Abbot's Grayling, in the County of Oldshire, Nobleman.

I give devise and bequeath all of which I die possessed, saving the excepted bequests herein below devised, all properties, moneys and expectations, to my son and heir, the Honourable George Renfield, Infant at Law.

EXCEPTING THAT

I give and devise to all and several my household servants, the sum of £10 each.

And to the Parish Church at Abbot's Grayling the sum of £50 absolutely.

And to Matthew Grace, formerly my swine-master, and to John Forbes, quondam cow-keeper, the sum of £500 each, in recognition of their singular and devoted faithful service.

Witness my hand, this 31 July 1812

Frank Renfield

Witnessed by:

Augustus Bywater, Solicitor and Commissioner for Oaths

Edward Grant, Surgeon

'Oh, dear me, yes. Five hundred pounds? That was a tidy fortune in 1812. Those two men, Grace and Forbes, were like King Duncan's servants in *Macbeth*. They were suborned. I need to think . . . There's something in all this paper that gave me a sudden idea. I'll recall it in a minute.'

Chloe showed him the copy that she had made of the entry in the parish registers of St Paul's at Paul's Cross.

February 13, 1826. John Forbes. Gentleman Farmer. Aged 72. Funeral paid for by Lord Renfield of Abbot's Grayling. £7 8s 6d. Buried in churchyard.

'Yes,' said Lance. 'From footman to gentleman farmer. It's all pointing to a conspiracy. This Timothy Reid was to be what our American cousins call "the patsy". He was to be framed for a murder that he did not commit. Mind you, that's only a theory. We need to probe further . . . Ah! I've remembered what it was! Timothy Reid was confined to the House of Refuge at Monkshead. In later times, this became the Monkshead County Asylum, and I happen to know that its ruins are still standing. A good number of these places were simply abandoned, and Monkshead was one of them. Let me remind you of Enoch Powell and his game-changing contribution to all this. He . . . Chloe, do you still have any of that Blue Mountain coffee that you served last time I paid you a visit? A steaming brew at this juncture would be most welcome.'

'Beware of that particular indulgence,' said Noel. 'You will end up like Mr J. Alfred Prufrock: "I have measured out my life with coffee spoons."'

'I don't know this Mr Prufrock,' said Lance, 'and I can't imagine what he meant by saying that. You have some peculiar friends.'

Chloe switched on the percolator. After they had all refreshed themselves, they settled down to hear what Lance had to say about Enoch Powell.

'There used to be madhouses in the eighteenth century and later,' Lance began. 'They were private establishments, and people would approach the proprietor to arrange for a relative to be admitted, after examination by what they called a "mad doctor". Some of these madhouses were very good, others were abominable. There were also asylums, partly funded by an imposition on the rates and supported as charitable institutions, and your House of Refuge at Monkshead would have been one of these. The name "asylum" defined what these places were supposed to be: safe havens for the mentally afflicted, who could be prevented from doing harm to others and to themselves by being confined to these establishments.

'There wasn't much legal control of these places until the 1840s, when the state began to acknowledge its duty to regulate and inspect.'

'Are you going to get to the point soon?'

'Yes, Noel. It was from the 1840s onward that the system of public asylums developed. A great deal of money was spent on building new asylums, often palatial places, and the re-establishment of older foundations, which were provided with new, impressive buildings. A great deal of good work was done in these places.

'And then, in the 1950s, came the introduction of antipsychotic drugs. Patients could be kept calm, their hallucinations and delusions banished. People began to question the need for physical confinement, especially as the asylums were becoming overcrowded, and suggested other solutions.'

'Care in the Community,' said Chloe.

'Exactly. And that brings us to the Right Honourable Enoch Powell MP. In 1961, when he was Minister of Health, he declared that mad people should no longer be kept in great isolated institutions but should be cared for in special wards opened in the public hospitals. He made an impressive speech on the subject — as you know, he was very good at making speeches — and what he said sounded the death knell of the asylums. Most of them have now been converted into luxury flats, while others have quite literally been left to fall down.'

Lance Middleton poured himself another cup of coffee but made no attempt to drink it. He sat silently at the table, brooding over what he had told them.

'Yes,' he continued at last, 'they were all closed down, and their occupants turned out, more or less to fend for themselves. It was really to save money, of course. And so that cruel, heartless concept, "Care in the Community", was brought in. The mentally afflicted, drugged and dazed, were sent home to cope as well as they could with the occasional visit from a "carer". My own . . . But there, friends, I mustn't bore you with my favourite hobby-horse. The point I'm making is that the Monkshead House of Refuge became the Monkshead County Asylum. It still stands, and I'm quite sure that a visit there will unearth further proofs that Timothy Reid was the victim of conspiracy.'

* * *

The Monkshead County Asylum lay hidden in a dense wood, reached by trekking from the nearby village across uneven fields and along rutted tracks skirting fields of root crops. It was an enormous, red-brick Victorian Gothic building of three main storeys and attics, its roof line broken by pinnacles of stone and rusting cast iron. It was a total ruin, and the three researchers had to negotiate a series of wooden barriers to reach the front door, which was gaping open. One entire section of the building to the left of the entrance had been burnt out, its mullioned windows gaping and bare. Trees had begun to grow on the roof. All the windows in the right-hand side of the frontage had been broken. Above the door was an inscription carved in sandstone:

Monkshead County Asylum
Opened by HRH Prince Alfred, Duke of Edinburgh
1878

They stood on the overgrown forecourt, looking up at the dilapidated building.

'They were just abandoned,' said Lance Middleton. 'They were conceived as belonging to a dead, ignorant age.

They didn't bother to salvage anything of value — just emptied out the staff and patients and left these places to rot. They were state property by then, you see, and therefore belonged to no one. The arrogance of the 1960s was unbelievable. Shall we go in?'

The dark interior of the asylum had been thoroughly vandalized. Doors had been torn from their hinges and lay on the broken-tiled floors. Fires had been lit. What Lance said proved to be true: rusting iron bedsteads had been overturned in the wards, and there were trolleys, kidney bowls, bedpans and other medical paraphernalia littering the floors. Light fittings had been wrenched from the ceilings and left on the floor. It was chilling, too, to see old-fashioned wooden filing cabinets, their drawers pulled open, and still crammed with files of case notes. Everything had been abandoned when the brave new world of the sixties beckoned, in this case with Enoch Powell at its head.

Chloe heard herself whisper, 'Why have you brought us here?'

'I brought you here,' said Lance, 'because this building replaced that of the old House of Refuge. If we delve deeper, we should find the cellars, which were often used as record rooms. They almost certainly left the archives there, though of course they may already have been plundered or wantonly destroyed. But it will be worth looking.'

They advanced further into the wrecked building. In some rooms the floorboards had been ripped up, leaving the rotting joists exposed. Making their way through heaps of rubbish, they found the stone stairs leading down into the basement. It took them half an hour to clamber over heaps of fallen timber and plaster, but eventually they came into what was obviously a very old, pre-Victorian cellar. Sure enough, the ancient records were there. A line of old wooden cabinets had been torn open, and their contents strewn on the impacted clay floor. At this level, water had seeped in from some underground culvert, and many of the documents had long ago turned to dried pulp.

'I suggest we take as much of these papers as we can hold,' said Noel Greenspan. 'As you said, Lance, they no longer seem to be anybody's property, so finders keepers.'

They had brought powerful torches with them and were able to collect a considerable pile of old files and letters, many of them, as they could see, from the eighteenth century.

'How are we going to carry all this lot back up the stairs?' asked Noel.

'In these large black bin bags which I brought in this satchel,' said Chloe. 'That's thanks to my Guide training. "Be prepared."'

They filled three of the bags with the entire collection of documents and began to haul them back up the stone stairs. Apart from rats, and the occasional inquisitive cat, they were the only living things in the dead building.

That evening, Chloe's kitchen was converted into a dry-ing-out chamber for the masses of paper they had rescued. On returning from Monkshead they had consumed sand-wiches and coffee, and set to work on bringing some order to their finds. They listened to the humming of the Aga, and the ticking of the kitchen clock as they worked in silence.

'There's an awful lot of Victorian stuff,' said Noel at length. 'Letters of enquiry, things like that. "Will you accept my feeble-minded nephew" . . . "Dear Sir, I hear that the new convulsive therapies are highly effective" — Ugh! "Estimate for the installation of the electric light" . . .'

'Eureka!' cried Lance Middleton, waving a water-stained envelope in the air. 'This is surely it! This is the proof you've been searching for. Look!'

The envelope was marked in a copperplate hand: *In re. Timothy Reid*. It contained two documents, one written out on sheets of old-fashioned foolscap paper, the other a letter, still with its wax seal attached. Lance spread out the documents on the kitchen table, anchoring their curled ends with items from the cruet and the knife box. All three then sat down at the table to read the evidence that Lance had found.

DEPOSITION of TIMOTHY REID, Gentleman, a Lunatick, Given to Dr George Peterson, a Master in Lunacy, 3 March 1789.

Proem. The petitioner, in this his third application, insists that he is sane, and has been all along. He was committed to the Oldminster House of Refuge at Monkshead, in August 1784. He is very well read and writes a good hand. He speaks without going frantick, and is courteous in his bearing. However, most of the physicians who have examined him are unanimous in believing that he is quite insane and must be held fast.

By me John Fisher MD, Barber-Surgeon at the Monkshead House of Refuge.

Item. We have omitted here some general observations and narrative made by the Petitioner, as they are much as those recorded in earlier applications.

Petitioner. I had been brought a note earlier in the day from Matthew Grace, a footman at Renfield Hall, telling me that a member of the family had called and was like to threaten Lady Renfield.

(*Questioned.* Did the note give the name of the family member? *Petitioner.* No, sir. But I knew who it must have been. *Questioned.* Did you really? And where is this note? *Petitioner.* I left it at my house, but on returning, found that it had gone.)

Petitioner. I made haste on foot, the distance being no more than a mile, though the road was pitted with ruts and holes. Eventually, I gained the gates of Renfield Hall and made my way to the porter's room near the entrance to the house. There I found Matthew Grace, aforementioned, and another man, also a footman, sitting on a bench, talking to each other. They looked up as I entered and sprang to their feet. You see, sirs, in those days I was still really a gentleman and treated as such, not confined as a lunatick to such a place as this. 'God be praised, Mr Reid, sir,' cried Grace. 'There's nothing that we could do — our station forbids it. But you, sir, can stop that scoundrel. He's with Lady Renfield now, and he's brought a new will for her to sign. You know what that portends, sir.' The second man — I never knew his name — added his supplications to those of Grace. 'Go, master,' he said, 'and stop him. Take one of these candles, and go up to my lady's chamber.' I said nothing, but did as the man bade. I knew that it was the nephew of Lord Renfield, at that time absent with his son in the Plantations, who had come once again to frighten Lady Renfield into giving away her son's inheritance.

(*Questioned*. You say, 'once again'. Has this nephew threatened her before? *Petitioner*. Yes, sir. On at least three occasions to my certain knowledge. Frank Renfield was a dissipated wastrel and gambler, rendered desperate by debts that he could not pay.)

(*Questioned*. So what did you do?)

Petitioner. I bounded up the great staircase and so to Lady Renfield's chamber. I flung the door open, and Renfield turned to face me with a snarl of rage. The fellow was little more than a beast disguised in the fair form of a young man, much of an age as I myself was then. 'Curse you, Reid!' the miscreant cried. 'You have no business here. I am desperate, do you hear? I am in the shadow of the gallows. I tell you that her ladyship there will sign this will or never rise from that bed alive.'

The good lady sat up on her pillows, and frail as she was, I saw the look of haughty defiance on her face. She was one of the Steynforths of this county, a proud family, whose ancestors fought at Agincourt. She would show no fear of such as Frank Renfield. 'You may rant and rave as much as you will,' she said, in a firm voice, 'but I will never do anything to deny my son his birthright. Go your ways, wretch. There is nothing here for you.'

It was then that I saw the pistol in his hand. I sprang forward to disarm him, but my action was too tardy. There was a crash and a flash, and Lady Renfield fell back dead on her pillows. O cursed day! It will go down in the annals of infamy. Thursday, 24 June 1784. I had been deafened and momentarily blinded by the discharge of his pistol, and he had rushed madly from the chamber. I followed, but was prevented by the two footmen, who stood barring my way.

(*Observed*. Here the prisoner shed tears, but soon controlled himself and continued his narrative).

The footmen were holding fat leather purses, and I knew at once from their expressions that Renfield had suborned them and made them agents in his wicked conspiracy. I told them that I would alert the watch and inform the thirdborough of what had happened.

(*Questioned*. And you maintain that all this is true, and that the present baron, Frank Renfield, is a usurper and murderer? *Petitioner*. I do. It is the truth. He had intended all along that I should be charged with Lady Renfield's murder. I ask you now that justice should be done to me and the weight of the law fall upon that wicked man, whose evil deeds should not go unpunished.)

End of Timothy Reid's Petition.

A Note by the Master in Lunacy, written here in his own hand, 3 March 1789. I asked the Petitioner whether he was well housed and treated, and he said he was. I told him that our decision would be delivered to him on the 5th inst., and he was taken away to his lodging.

'It's a totally different version of what happened in Renfield Hall on the day of the murder,' said Chloe. 'And it reads so very convincingly. Taken together with the other evidence we've collected, it surely proves Timothy Reid's innocence.'

'Well, it may look like that,' said Lance cautiously, 'but we need to tread carefully. I've been looking at this other document. It's a letter that could throw a spanner in our particular works.'

There was no address given at the top of the letter, but it was dated 25 March 1789.

Sir, I have received yours of the 22nd inst., for which thanks. I can oblige you readily with the details that you solicited. I was present with others at the examination of Timothy Reid, a Petitioner of the Third Instance, on the 3rd March this current year. You tell me that you have seen the account of that interview in the public records, and that you are also aware of what has been done in the case.

There was little truth or reason in Reid's narrative, which had all the chilling persuasion of a subtle madman. Lady Renfield was indeed shot dead on the date specified, but at that time Frank Renfield was away in London. Enquiry was made at the time as to the Petitioner's circumstances, and it was found that he was heavily in debt. Lord Renfield, the fourteenth baron, was visiting his plantations in Jamaica and had taken his son Ralph with him. Both died of malaria in the epidemic at Kingston there, some three weeks after the murder at Renfield, without ever knowing that Lady Renfield had been slain.

Mr Frank Renfield duly succeeded to the title and estates as the fifteenth Baron Renfield and is happily still with us. The Petitioner, Timothy Reid, was taken up and charged soon after the murder but was declared unfit to plead by reason of insanity. I saw no reason to challenge that verdict, and Reid will remain under restraint in the House of Refuge at Monkshead, in the County of Oldshire.

By me: George Peterson MD, Master in Lunacy.

'There spoke the law,' said Noel Greenspan, 'and Timothy Reid was condemned to live out his days in an asylum.'

Lance pointed to a line of writing written in pencil by another hand at the foot of the letter.

Timothy Reid died, deluded to the end, on 25 May 1794. Rotting of the lungs.

'So what's to be done?' asked Noel. 'I've been acting on Lord Renfield's behalf, as you know. If I tell him that Timothy Reid's version of events was not accepted by the authorities of his day, I'm sure he'll be both pleased and relieved. But on the other hand—'

'On the other hand,' cried Chloe, 'poor Timothy's account could well be true. It reads so convincingly. And who is this Dr George Peterson MD, Master in Lunacy? Why should we take his word on the matter?'

'Well, of course, he was an expert in such things—'

'Was he indeed, Noel? Or was he another powerful member of the conspiracy to see Timothy Reid locked away for a crime he didn't commit? A fellow conspirator with Matthew Grace and John Forbes? Do you remember those "fat leather purses"? They would have contained gold guineas. Why shouldn't this Dr Peterson have had a share in the loot?'

Lance Middleton clapped his hands.

'Well said, Chloe,' he cried. 'I was inclined to agree with Noel, but now I'm not so sure. I'll look into this Dr Peterson — I know where to find any records of office-holders of his sort. But as well as that, I'll take all this material to my friend Lord Dangerfield, who's an advocate in the Chancery Division. He's the best man to give a sensible ruling in this case. I'll leave for London tomorrow and beard Dangerfield in his den in the Rolls Building. I'll contact you as soon as I know anything useful.'

14. THE TRAP

It was Tracey Potter's misfortune to be received at the kitchen door of Renfield Hall by the lady of the house herself. Tracey had just turned sixteen and had left school that summer with two GCSEs. She'd got a job as a shelf stacker at Robinson's supermarket but hadn't stayed long. That supervisor had had it in for her. She'd not been late *every* morning, and she really had been sick for two weeks in August.

Anyway, she'd got the sack, and her dad had belted her for it. Her dad used to come to parents' evenings and he'd say, 'If our Tracey gives you any trouble, give her a clip round the ear.' Most of the teachers were gormless dopes and would look at her dad as though he'd crawled out of an apple.

She'd lasted a week at Thorne's ironmongers. That was because Mr Thorne couldn't keep his hands to himself. He thought she'd be anybody's for a packet of fags, but she wasn't that kind of girl. Anyway, her dad would murder her if she did anything like that. Finally, when her dad was getting fed up with her hanging around the house all day, her friend Shona told her to try to get kitchen work at Renfield Hall. Shona's dad had the occasional pint with Fred Lewis, the Renfield's handyman or whatever he was. Shona said that Mr Lewis was a very nice man.

But on the fatal Monday morning when Tracey Potter knocked on the kitchen door of Renfield Hall, it was opened by Lady Renfield herself.

'And what can I do for *you*, miss?' she said, surveying the girl standing nervously on the doorstep from top to toe. Tracey found herself dumbstruck. The lady was very beautiful and wore lovely clothes, but she had a tumbler of gin in her hand and was what her dad called 'half seas over'. She was stumbling about on high heels. Fancy wearing those in the house! Perhaps she shouldn't have come.

'Well, speak up!' cried Lady Renfield, taking a swig of gin from the tumbler.

'I've come to ask if there's any work going in the kitchen, miss—'

'Miss? You stupid girl. Don't you know who I am? I'm Lady Renfield, and your sort of people call me "my lady" when they address me. Didn't they teach you anything at school? So you want to work in the kitchens here, do you?'

'Yes, my lady.'

'Well I'm sorry to tell you — what's your name? I suppose you've got a name?'

'Tracey, miss. I mean, my lady.'

'Yes, it would be, wouldn't it? Tracey. Or if not that, Stacey, or Lacey, or some other daft bloody thing. Well, Tracey, there's nothing for you here. We'll be employing many more staff very soon, God willing, but you won't be one of them. Is that your best dress?'

'Yes.'

'Well, it's very nice, but it's too tight for you. Or rather, you're too tight for *it*.' Lady Renfield laughed, hiccupped and had another sip of gin.

'Stop eating junk food, and then maybe you'll slim down to fit it. Where did you buy it?'

'From a shop in Binford.'

'Well, I buy all my dresses in Paris. Like this one I'm wearing this morning.' Lady Renfield staggered and clutched the door post to steady herself.

'I suppose you've got a spotty little boyfriend? Only the spotty ones would bother looking at you, because all the really pretty, slim girls don't go after spotties. What does your father do?'

'He's out of work at the moment, my lady, but—'

'Oh, I see. Another bloody scrounger. Fred! Jean! Where are you? What are you crying for, Tracey, or Stacey, or whatever your name is? Ah! Fred. There you are. See this girl off the premises, will you? She got the wrong one today when she met me. I can see through them. Let them wash the pots and they run off with the silver. Get her out of here! Right off the grounds and into the road! I hate her. Spying on me . . . Where's Jean? I want to lie down.'

Fred Lewis walked quietly beside the sobbing girl as he escorted her off the premises. He put an arm round her shoulder and could feel her trembling. He'd heard most of Carole's cruel raving. No child should have to put up with that.

'Take no notice, love,' he said. 'Lady Renfield's not well. She doesn't mean half the things she says.'

The girl stopped on the path, and the face that looked up at him was that of a scorned woman.

'Oh, yes she does, Mr Lewis. She's a cruel witch, and I hate her. My dad works hard as an asphalter on the roads, and when he's working, he turns up every penny to Ma. And anyway, she needn't give herself airs and graces. I know something about her that would cook her goose if I told.'

Very gently, and confidingly, Fred asked her what she meant.

'What is it you know, love? You can tell me. I'll keep your secret.'

'It's about a young man. The one who was murdered in your house. She was seen snogging him in some kind of pantry in that kitchen of yours. Why should I protect her? You heard the things she said to me, and about my dad. I hate her.'

He saw the girl safely off the premises and made his way slowly back to Renfield Hall.

* * *

173

Tracey Potter went to Shona's house and told her friend the whole story. They sat on the sofa together, drinking orange squash. Shona was only fifteen. She wore a denim jacket covered in badges and an artfully frayed mini-skirt of the same material, and had painted each of her fingernails a different colour. Her mother often said that her Shona was not as daft as she looked.

'I hate that woman,' Tracey concluded. 'I should get the law onto her.'

'So she was kissing that guy who was killed, and her husband a lord, an' all?'

'Yeah, she was.'

'Who told you?'

'D'you know Kenny Stott? Well, he got taken on by those people who arrange parties. I forget what they're called. He was there in the kitchen, getting fresh wine glasses, when he saw them together. He told Janet Pike, on the condition that she told nobody else, so she told me.'

'Well,' said Shona, slurping down the last drop of squash, 'why *don't* you have the law on her? Get your revenge on the stuck-up cow. Like in that film on telly last night. *Don't Mourn for Sandra*. We only saw half of it because Dad wanted to watch footer.'

'What do you mean, have the law on her?'

'I mean the police station. Go and tell them what she said to you, and then tell them about her and that Alan Lavender snogging in the pantry. I don't know whether it's against the law, but at least it'll start people talking. Would you like a piece of cake?'

'Yes please. What would I have to do? I'd be scared. Will you come with me?'

'All right. There's no need to be afraid, you haven't done nothing. We'll go as soon as we've eaten this cake.'

* * *

DS Edwards looked at the two teenage girls who had been ushered into his office by the front-desk constable. They sat on two chairs in front of his table, shoulders hunched, hands parked under their thighs. The constable had whispered, 'Something to do with Renfield Hall, Sergeant, so I thought I'd bring them up to see you.' They looked terrified — probably regretting venturing into a real police station.

'What can I do for you, girls?' he asked. 'I can't spare you more than five minutes.'

They looked at each other, hoping that the other one would speak first.

'Go on, Tracey,' whispered Shona fiercely, 'tell him what happened at Renfield Hall this morning. And tell him about the infidel . . . the indifel . . . the snogging in the pantry.'

Tracey took a deep breath and blurted out her story. When she had finished, DS Edwards treated her to a friendly smile.

'You haven't made all this up, have you?'

'No, sir. Cross my heart and never say die. You won't tell my dad I've been here, will you? He'll give me a leathering if you do.'

'Your secret's safe with me, Tracey. Now then, what were the names of the two friends you mentioned? I need to write them down.'

'Kenny Stott and Janet Pike.'

'Right. Good. What you've told me might be very important, so please don't tell anyone else about it.' He scribbled something on a piece of paper and handed it to Tracey. 'Take that downstairs to the canteen, and they'll give you both a cup of tea and a sandwich.'

Well, well, said Edwards to himself when the delighted girls had departed. Kissing and cuddling in the pantry on the night of the birthday party, to which Alan Lavender seemed to have been invited as a guest, only to become a victim of murder. How long had *that* been going on? By all accounts, the late Alan Lavender was a young man of goatish disposition. He'd been a bad lad, with a wife in London, a girlfriend in Oldminster and a titled lady as a sideline.

But that titled lady had been his girlfriend's *mother*. What kind of a woman did a thing like that? Why had she invited him to her party, making sure he wore evening dress, so as to blend in with the other male guests? Had Frank Renfield found out and murdered him? Had Jessica? I mean, really, how had Lady Renfield expected to keep her husband and daughter from seeing him?

Edwards began to recall the events of 10 October. For the moment, he let his visual imagination take priority over his skills in rational detection. Still vivid in his mind was the scene in the oak parlour.

Lord Renfield had looked shocked and bewildered, like a man unable to grasp what was happening in his own house. When questioned, he had given a halting account of what had occurred after they had heard the shot. He'd gone to find his daughter, and the girl had given an account of what had happened. A young man — Colin McDonald — had shot himself in front of her. He could see the father in his mind's eye, comforting his daughter, and he could imagine Noel Greenspan and his secretary Chloe McArthur joining him on the landing. One vital family member was absent from the scene. *Lady Renfield*. Wouldn't it have been instinctive for a mother to see if her daughter had come to any harm? A shot, followed by general panic, but no thought in her mind that her own child might have fallen victim to a killer?

Glyn Edwards let his inner vision move on to his second visit to Renfield Hall, in the cold small hours of the approaching day. At four o'clock in the morning, who did he see now? Lord and Lady Renfield sitting together in their dressing gowns. *He* was still cowed and subdued, yielding precedence to that American businessman, Karl Langer. *She* had been as pale as death and trembling with fear. What had she witnessed? Or what had she *done*?

On Edwards' first visit, Jean Lewis had been very much in evidence, making her presence known and fussing over Jessica Renfield because her mother wasn't there . . . Now, in the second interview, Jean had been missing. Wherever she was, it was probably something to do with Lord Renfield's daughter, who was also absent, in a most terrible condition after her second shock of the night.

Young Tracey Potter's story suggested that Lady Renfield had taken to drink. Was that to drown sorrow or guilt? DI French was in London but would be back tomorrow. It was time for them to interview Lady Renfield and ask her more than a few pertinent questions. Meanwhile, there was a little job waiting for him to do.

* * *

'So, Kenny,' said DS Edwards, 'you saw something nasty going on in the pantry at Renfield Hall. You'd better tell me about it.'

Kenny Stott blushed, more with anger than embarrassment.

'Trust girls not to keep a secret,' he said glumly. 'Janet Pike promised not to tell anyone.'

'Girls have their own logic, Kenny,' said DS Edwards. 'Of course Janet Pike promised not to tell anyone, but "anyone" didn't include her best friend, and it was the friend who told us.'

'Who was it?'

'That's privileged information. Or to put it another way, we don't rat on our informers. So come on, don't be shy. Tell me what it was you saw going on in the pantry. It could be important.'

Kenny Stott told him. Even allowing for the lad's enthusiastic embellishments, it was clear that Lady Renfield had bestowed a very passionate kiss on the late and apparently unlamented Alan Lavender.

* * *

Jean Lewis sat in the kitchen at Renfield Hall, enjoying a cup of tea. Would Frank ever pay them this month? They could both earn a steady income working in a garden centre or in Robinson's supermarket, but some idiotic idea of loyalty kept them in thrall to the Renfields. Fred was fiercely loyal to Frank, and she was devoted to Girlie. So they stayed. But it would be nice to have some pay this week.

It would be all right if Carole wasn't there. She dressed beautifully, and was beautiful herself, but she was also a drunken hussy. Frank didn't seem to notice, but this woman, with her haughty manner and her airs and graces, had slept with her own daughter's boyfriend. She had sneaked into Chichester to buy those clothes for her fancy-boy, Alan Lavender, so that he could come to her party. She had betrayed not only her husband but her daughter, too.

Wait! That's who it was that she'd picked up from the table at the birthday dinner and taken off somewhere. Jean hadn't been able to see clearly at the time because she didn't have her glasses. *It was him.* It was that Alan. And that poor young girl had come to the door looking for work, only to be sent away with a flea in her ear. But she'd told Fred that Carole had been kissing Alan Lavender in the pantry — *her* pantry! Some lad working in the kitchen had recognized him. But why, out of all the young men Lady Renfield could have had an affair with, had she chosen her daughter's boyfriend?

Oh, God, of course . . .

Tomorrow, when Jean went into Oldminster, she'd go to see that detective sergeant — what was his name? — Edwards. It was time to tell what she knew, or suspected, to the police.

* * *

'Wouldn't you like to stay with your sister for a while, Carole? You're starting to look quite ill. A change of air would do you good.'

Lord and Lady Renfield were having breakfast in the kitchen on the day following Tracey Potter's disastrous inter-view with Carole.

'It's no wonder I'm all to pieces, Frank, living as I do in a slaughterhouse, and with my only child confined to an asylum—'

'Hardly that, my dear,' said Frank Renfield, looking up from his *Times*. 'It's a care facility, and she'll be with us again in a week or so. Earlier than that, possibly. So, what do you say? Would you like a break?'

'It's very kind of you, Frank, but I think I'll stay here. I'm more and more convinced that Jessica's going to do the right thing and marry Karl, and then all your troubles will be over. Don't worry about me. I'm — I'm all right.'

Fred came into the kitchen, bringing the morning's post, which, as usual, he handed to Frank, who put down his paper and turned his attention to the letters.

'Two for you, my dear, and three for me. These two are bills . . . Really, that fancy grocer of ours is becoming a trifle impertinent. Better switch to Tesco.'

'Tesco requires upfront payment,' said Carole, drily. 'I've got a letter from one of those Scots firms that sell you slabs of best beef, and an invitation to open a garden fete to raise funds for the Royal British Legion. I might accept that. It's for the end of December.'

'Matthew Grace, the gardener, respectfully begs that I'll pay him the fee I owe him. I really must oblige him. Hello, here's a letter from Colonel Laxton. What can he want? I've already given him £50 for SSAFA. He . . . well, well. I'll go and smoke a pipe in the library and peruse this further, I think.'

Although it was only nine o'clock, Frank Renfield poured himself a glass of brandy and settled down in his favourite chair to read what Colonel Laxton had written.

My dear Renfield,

I have received a very interesting letter, sent by courier, from someone I know in the Home Office, a man who is also an agent of MI6. In view of the increasing danger to our security as a nation from external influences (which had better not be named in this letter), he is recruiting a team of ex-army officers to act as observers, each to be assigned to a specific part of the country. It is to be arranged on a county basis, with an overseeing role assigned to the Lord Lieutenant and the Chief Constable in each case.

Would you be prepared to join this team? My contact mentioned you specifically by name as a highly respected former officer and a member of the country's old aristocracy. An emergency meeting has been called for this coming Friday, 27 October, at the Old Mill, Greycote, Sussex. It will start at noon, giving the participants from both Oldshire and Sussex time to make their way there.

I have been told that there will be a very generous remuneration, paid quarterly, for those who agree to serve on the team.

Do not tell anybody about this meeting. Do not acknowledge this letter, and bring it with you when you arrive at Greycote. Secrecy at this stage is absolutely essential.

Sincerely yours,
William Laxton, Col.

Well, well. This was an offer Frank couldn't refuse. He'd be proud to serve his country once again, and a quarterly cheque would certainly come in handy. When he got there, he'd introduce himself to the Johnny on the desk as 'Major the Lord Renfield'. That'd make them sit up . . .

To Frank's surprise, he found out that Greycote had its own railway halt, and that he could reach there in just over an hour by taking a train to Chichester and another train from there directly to Greycote. He would do as Laxton said and tell nobody — not even Carole — what he intended to do. He'd just say that he would be 'away on business' on Friday and leave it at that.

* * *

Frank Renfield arrived at Greycote station just as half past eleven was striking from a church tower partly hidden by a line of elms. Greycote itself proved to be a hamlet of red-brick cottages surrounded by naked fields of black earth. The halt was unmanned, but a short walk brought him to a pub, where the landlord told him that the Old Mill could be found at the end of a lane just opposite; he'd get there in under ten minutes. The landlord had called him 'sir' and had accompanied him to the door to point out the lane. Frank was conscious of the fact that he looked out of place in this deep rural setting. He had dusted off his old British Warm, and was wearing a black bowler hat and tan leather gloves. He'd consciously adopted this persona of a retired regular officer to impress the people he was going to meet at the Old Mill.

It was a bright chilly morning, and the lane, overhung by gnarled trees, was damp underfoot. In a matter of minutes the Old Mill came into view. It was built of old rustic brick, and the mill wheel, half collapsed and decayed, still clung to one of the walls. The stream that had once provided power to the mill had long ago been diverted from its original bed, which was now overgrown with stunted shrubs and nettles.

The door to the mill stood open, and Frank entered a sort of anteroom, where a young man in black jacket and trousers greeted him. He was a nondescript sort of fellow, who spoke quietly and respectfully.

'Major the Lord Renfield? Welcome to the Old Mill, my lord. I believe you have something to give me?'

Ah! This was more like it. Someone who knew how to address him properly and who didn't think he was demeaning himself by doing so. He took Colonel Laxton's letter from his pocket and handed it to the young man.

'Thank you, my lord. Please go through now to the conference room.'

Frank Renfield did as he was told, and the young man closed the door behind him. The room was bare of any furniture except a deal table and two chairs, one of which was occupied by a middle-aged man with a round, fleshy face, a stubbly chin and watery grey eyes. He wore an old-fashioned belted mac, buttoned up to the neck, and, rather incongruously, white cotton gloves.

Frank began to feel uneasy. Where were the others? And then he saw that there was a heavy army pistol lying on the table — the same model of pistol he'd been issued during his army years. He made a move towards the table, but the man picked up the pistol and pointed it at him.

'Sit down, Captain Renfield,' he said, 'and listen to what I'm going to say. First, there is no hush-hush meeting of security personnel here today. That letter, purporting to be from Colonel Laxton, was written by *me* and was designed to appeal to your vanity and your greed. You cut a real dash sitting there in all your finery, but I know what a craven-hearted fellow you really are.'

'Wait!' cried Frank. 'I know who you are! You're Private Porteous. You served with your twin brother in the Oldshire Light Infantry. What do you want with me? Why have you lured me down to this wretched place?' His voice quavered. 'Are you going to murder me?'

Victor Porteous looked at him with a grim smile. He waved the pistol about, but Frank saw that his finger was not yet on the trigger.

'It would be an execution, not a murder,' he said in a quiet, cultured voice. 'You're guilty of the murder of my brother, by preventing another man from rescuing him when he was swept away by that raging torrent. Do you remember? Do you acknowledge your guilt?'

'Guilt? Why should I feel guilt? Your brother leapt onto the pontoon before his platoon commander had given the order to do so. In fact, that order would never have been given — the weather conditions were too bad. Corporal Gorman prepared to dive in after him, but I ordered him not to do so. I would have lost two men instead of one—'

'I saw you smile! You hated both of us because we couldn't measure up to your idea of what a soldier should be. You were glad that Alexander died.'

'No, Porteous, you're wrong. And you saw no smile. I tell you, I was near to tears. The decision I made was what any other commander in the field would have made. That's what you have to do when you're an officer. But I can tell you this: I've been haunted by that scene ever since. It's a nightmare that never leaves me.'

Frank Renfield caught Porteous's glance and saw that his eyes were flickering with indecision. What would the unstable fellow do? If he pointed that pistol at Frank once more, Frank would overturn the table and put up a fight for his life.

But when it came, Porteous's reaction was totally unexpected.

He gave a long, drawn-out sigh. 'Very well,' he said. 'You've given me your excuses after all these years, and I'm inclined to believe what you've told me. Goodbye, Captain Renfield. I'll leave you now to the judgement of God.'

Frank Renfield said nothing. He hurriedly left the room, noting that the nondescript young man was no longer there, and made his way to the railway halt. Since his arrival, the hamlet of Greycote had come to life, and there were a number of people about. He waited for a quarter of an hour before the little diesel train arrived and stopped when he signalled the driver. He sank back gratefully in his seat. It had been a disturbing experience, but had finally laid to rest one of the ghosts that had haunted his life for more years than he cared to remember.

* * *

Abraham Sylvester sat in the back room of his curio shop, listening to Lady Renfield as she described the infestation of her house by her murdered predecessor. 'Infestation' had been his own word, not hers, and it seemed to have gone down well.

The back room was divided from the shop by a bead curtain, and was crammed with all manner of crystal balls, planchette boards, Pierrot dolls and rather ugly pieces of Chinese furniture. Old lamps hung from the ceiling, which was stained with smoke, and a glass cabinet held some sets of tarot cards and what appeared to be a pickled baby in a sealed glass jar. Sylvester and his visitor sat facing each other in silver-sprayed basket chairs.

Abraham Sylvester wore an embroidered silk dressing gown and a tasselled cap. He could have looked ridiculous in this garb, but his haughty expression along with his waxed beard and moustache made his visitors immediately stand in awe of him.

'We call it an infestation,' said Abraham Sylvester, 'because the spirit entity takes on the characteristics of a germ, poisoning not just its surroundings, but the person to whom it attaches itself — you, in this case, Lady Renfield. But, as Mrs Osbourne knows, there are ways of driving these spirits away.'

'Should I have consulted the vicar?'

'No, because vicars don't believe in these things. One or two of them may go through the motions of saying a few prayers in your house, but their hearts are not in it. I will give you the means of performing an exorcism that will rid you and your house of this trapped entity.'

He opened a drawer in a cupboard and brought out a sealed packet, a small brass bell and a slim booklet, the contents of which were printed in English and Latin.

'When you judge the time to be right,' said Sylvester, 'go into the haunted room that you've described to me and light there as many candles as you can find in the house. Place them on the mantelpiece, the window sill and around the bed. In that sealed packet is a quantity of incense and some discs of charcoal. Heat the charcoal over an open fire or gas burner, then place it in a metal dish. Sprinkle the incense on it, and the room will be filled with a beautiful fragrance. You should then lie on the bed and read aloud the prayers in that booklet, either in English or Latin, it doesn't matter which. After each prayer, ring the little bell. When you have finished, say the Lord's Prayer quietly.'

'Is that all? How much will it cost?'

'There is no charge for these things, but a donation of twenty pounds would be welcome.'

'Well,' said Lady Renfield, 'I'll try it. What if it doesn't work?'

Abraham Sylvester smiled.

'It has never been known to fail,' he said. 'But if it fails in your case, then I will give you your money back, and you will have to let Mrs Osbourne know at once. At *once*, Lady Renfield.'

When Carole had gone, Abe Sylvester phoned Mrs Gladys Osbourne.

'Glad? It's me. I've given her an exorcism kit. Let's hope it works — it's amazing how effective these things can be if the client has sufficient faith. But I've told her that if nothing happens, she's to contact you at once. You've found out the name of her doctor, haven't you? If the phantom won't go away, then it's a doctor she needs, not us.'

15. SUSPICION

Lance Middleton's voice came crackling into Noel Greenspan's phone. 'Can you hear me? There seems to be cosmic interference today. I've got some very interesting news—' A meaningless babble followed.

Noel began to walk around the office in an attempt to improve reception. Why hadn't the idiot used a landline?

'Where are you?'

His friend's voice suddenly resounded loud and clear.

'I'm walking down New Fetter Lane towards Holborn Circus. I've just come from a meeting with Lord Dangerfield at Lincoln's Inn. He looked into that business of Dr George Peterson MD, Master in Lunacy. He really *was* a villain. He was caught taking bribes from what they called "interested parties" to have a sane man committed to an asylum. All this happened long after poor Timothy Reid had died in the House of Refuge.'

'So Peterson could have stitched up poor Timothy! What happened to this Peterson?'

'Well, he was sacked, disbarred and sentenced to five years hard labour. Evidently that didn't agree with him, because he died in prison two years later.'

'I see,' said Noel. 'So it's more than a mere possibility that Peterson took bribes from the Lord Renfield of the day to have Timothy Reid committed for life. So what happens now, if anything?'

Little inarticulate sounds of caution came through the phone. Noel knew that Lance the friend had been replaced by Lance the QC.

'Look, it would be injudicious to say any more about this over the phone. Can I come down to see you both tomorrow afternoon? Monday? There's a train at two forty. I shan't require feeding.'

'Come by all means. We'll contain ourselves in patience until we see you.'

* * *

Lance Middleton arrived, fussing and chattering in his usual manner, late on Monday afternoon. They sat in the kitchen, where Chloe had brewed Lance's favourite Jamaican coffee. He looked hugely excited and ever so slightly supercilious.

'I am wondering how best to explain matters to you,' he began. 'Legal stuff can be quite obscure to the layperson. This coffee is exquisite. When I come here, I feel that I've come home.'

'The best way of telling us how matters stand,' said Noel Greenspan, 'is just to tell us, without any shilly-shallying nonsense. So come on: spit it out.'

Chloe tried and failed to contain a shout of laughter. Lance, to his credit, treated them to a good-humoured smile.

'Very well. After I'd discovered those facts about Dr George Peterson MD, Master in Lunacy and monumental rogue, I trailed them in front of my friend Lord Dangerfield. He was very interested in the legal possibilities of a trial of succession and asked whether he could borrow my notes for a day or two.

'Now, it so happened that the secretary of state for justice, who is also Lord Chancellor, was in the house at the time and overheard what Dangerfield said. He thought that any judicial questioning of the Renfield inheritance had some validity and sent everything off to a special ad hoc committee that sits in the Chancery Division of the High Court.

'I very soon heard from someone I know on that committee that the case was gathering momentum, and sure enough, that very afternoon I received a letter by courier from the Garter Principal King of Arms asking for full details not only of my investigation, but of your own researches into the matter.'

'How did they know about our researches?' asked Noel.

'Well, somebody told them. Probably Dangerfield.'

'And how did *he* know?'

'He knew because *I* told him. And then, late yesterday evening, another courier turned up at Lincoln's Inn with a writ of summons from the Judicial Committee of the Privy Council, in which I was admonished, and advised, and many other things, to hold myself ready to appear before them and answer all questions that they may put to me honestly and truly and so forth. They're all in it together. They intend to sound each other out on the question of Frank Renfield's right to his title and land, and then reach a legally binding judgement. This is all very hush-hush, you know. Nothing that I've said must be repeated outside these four walls.'

They were silent for a while, considering what all this activity meant. Noel thought, *Will Frank Renfield actually be demoted to commoner and his title be given to Tim Reid?* It would create a furore in the press, and no doubt in the House of Lords. The deposition of a peer through no fault of his own would be unprecedented in the annals of English law. Only football would drive it to a hidden corner of the news.

Noel recalled a Hercule Poirot story in which Poirot's investigation was an utter disaster. When charged with this, he'd replied, 'True, it was not one of my more striking triumphs.' Noel felt like that about Lord Renfield. The peer had come to him for reassurance, but all that Noel could tell his client was that he was done for.

'Well,' said Lance Middleton, 'I suppose I'd better get back to London. There's a train at seven twelve.' He sounded as though all the cares of the world were on his shoulders.

'Nonsense,' said Chloe on cue. 'You must stay to dinner. And then you can go across the square and camp out with Noel. It's lamb casserole for dinner tonight.' Lance visibly relaxed.

'How very kind! In fact, I brought a small valise with me containing some night things and so on, in case — but yes, thank you. How very kind!'

'So the Privy Council are after you,' said Noel. 'Are you going to be imprisoned in the Tower?'

'No, no,' said Lance. 'As a matter of fact — should I tell you? It's a close secret, and if anyone finds out that I told you, I'll be ruined. Finished.'

'Tell us,' said Noel. 'Cut the hyperbole.'

'I saw the Lord Chief Justice only this morning. He's in on it, too. He told me that they intended to pass the buck by the clever strategy of announcing that it was their belief, after examining all the evidence, that Timothy Reid was the true and rightful heir to the Renfield title and estate, but that the issue must be decided by an appeal from the claimant directly to the Queen, an appeal which would be instantly granted. House, land and title would be given to the Reids.'

* * *

'I was so standoffish towards you, Karl,' said Jessica Renfield, 'but I was always afraid that I'd fall for you, and I thought that I was in love with Alan. How could I have deceived myself like that? He was *married*. And he'd forced his wife to abort her baby. Mother was right all the time.'

'So it was just because you were afraid that you were falling for me?' Karl asked. 'That was the only reason for it?'

Jessica blushed. She had never spoken disparagingly to Karl about her father, but this morning, the morning of her departure from the Mendelssohn Clinic, was a time for confessions. Karl, following her around as she collected items to pack, had suddenly proposed. She had stood quite still while he went down on one knee and produced a little black

189

box from his pocket. She opened it and gasped in awe at the diamond engagement ring that it contained. Ever her father's daughter, she had thought, *It must have cost a fortune!* The writing on the lid showed that it had come from Van Cleef & Arpels of New York.

Then he'd asked her to marry him. When she had burst into tears he had swept her into his arms and comforted her as though she was a little girl. That was when she professed her own love for him and accepted his offer of marriage.

He had slipped the ring onto Jessica's finger, and she had resumed the frantic packing as a means of hiding her joy and her guilt. That was when he had started asking her questions about her previous attitude towards him, each enquiry accompanied by an amused satirical smile.

'Come on, tell me. Was that the only reason you were cold towards me?' he pressed.

'No, there was another reason. Daddy . . . my father was using Renfield Hall as a trap for you, with me as the bait. It was disgusting. Daddy's on his uppers, and he thought that if he could persuade you to marry me, you'd bail him out. It was horrible. Can you imagine how I felt about that, Karl? Even now, on this wonderful morning, I wonder whether you had the slightest hint of what was happening.'

Karl Langer laughed, and once again enfolded her in his arms.

'Of course I knew what was happening, darling,' he said. 'I knew all along what your father was up to, but I was happy to assume the role of a simple American boy being duped by the subtleties of English aristocrats. Yes, I knew that your father was after my money — or after some of it, at least. And I tell you, I didn't care! I loved you, and I liked your father, and despite his mercenary motives, I know that he likes me. He never had a son, and I've felt over the last year that I've begun to assume that position, more or less. I don't know whether he realized that, but it's the truth. So once again, let me assure you that I don't care! I always intended to bail Lord Renfield out. I want a father-in-law who's free from debt. And your mother, too. I've never taken to her, Jess, but I've seen what grief and anxiety are doing to her. She'll never recover from the shock of those two violent deaths in her own home, but I'll do what I can to see that she comes to no harm.'

It was agreed by all parties that the wedding of the Honourable Jessica Renfield and Mr Karl Langer would take place in Oldminster Cathedral at the end of November. The Bishop of Oldminster, the Right Reverend Jeremy Poindexter, would officiate, and Mr Karl Langer would be invited to become one of a select band of special patrons of the Cathedral Fund. Miss Renfield would be given away by her father, Lord Renfield. The best man would be the groom's brother, Mr Lincoln Langer of New York. The groom's parents, Mr and Mrs Langer, would attend.

Invitations to the wedding would be sent to the leading luminaries of the county, and a reception would be held in the Oldminster Guildhall, by kind permission of the Lord Mayor and Common Council of the City of Oldminster.

* * *

Jean Lewis leant against the cold Victorian range in the kitchen of Renfield Hall and admired her newly painted fingernails. Hawaiian Pink, the girl in Boots had called it. Well, it was a change from the violent red that she usually favoured. 'It makes your hands look like talons,' Fred had complained. Maybe he was right.

The boss's breakfast was on the gas hob at the far end of the kitchen — bacon, fried egg, sausage and tomatoes. As soon as she heard him coming downstairs she'd brew his tea and make him some fresh toast.

She'd never forget the morning he'd come breezing into the kitchen, all smiles, to tell her that Jess was going to marry Mr Langer. She'd seen the joy of relief in his face and knew that his financial troubles were over. Would he keep them on? Maybe. He'd always been kind to her, because he knew how much she cared for his daughter.

Something was up with Lady Renfield though. Something in her mind. Very beautiful she was, and always well turned out, but *he* was terrified of her. Those two had rubbed along together well enough for years, but even now they were quids in, she couldn't manage a smile for him, the sour-faced cow.

Here he was now!

'Good morning, Jean,' said Lord Renfield. 'How are you? It's a nice day for November, isn't it? Firework day tomorrow! Has the paper come?'

'I'm very well, thank you, sir. The paper is there on the table, by your place. Fred will bring in the mail presently.' She added, suppressing a cruel smile, 'Is Her Ladyship not coming down?'

'No, she doesn't want any breakfast today. I expect we'll see her at lunch.'

Jean began to make Lord Renfield's toast while the electric kettle was boiling. Her Ladyship! Frank was too good for her. She gave herself airs and graces, and admittedly she came of good stock, but her father had been a mere baronet — not a true aristocrat, like Frank. There'd been no money there, either.

There was something up with her. Not only was she drinking, swigging gin out of the bottle, but she was still talking to herself. Fred despised her, and so did Jean. It was all she could do to be civil to Lady Renfield. She'd lusted after that handsome lad Alan Lavender, and betrayed her husband and daughter. Obviously Lady Renfield was still very active in that department, though the poor old guvnor looked past anything of that kind these days.

Jean had gone shopping in town a few days ago and had visited the delicatessen in Abbey Flags, the road where Mr Lavender's bookshop had been. Whoever it was who got Mr Lavender's money hadn't wasted any time in selling up and moving on. The bookshop had gone. It was now Gill's Organic Juice Bar. Well, *that* wasn't going to last long!

Here was Fred with the morning's mail.

Jean deposited a plate of buttered toast on the table, fetched the teapot and left Frank to enjoy his breakfast. It was time to give the entrance hall a good brushing. Now that he was in the money, perhaps he'd employ a couple of girls to help with the housework full time. It was not as though—

Dear God! What was that? Lord Renfield's anguished cry of despair echoed from the kitchen into the hall.

* * *

The morning's mail had brought a formal letter from the Lord Chancellor, informing Frank, Baron Renfield of Abbot's Grayling in the County of Oldshire, that his title was considered to be held in defect and should rightly belong to Timothy Reid, Esquire, residing in the same county. It would be for the said Timothy Reid to claim his right, and when he did so, the title of Baron Renfield would be his entirely, as would the house called Renfield Hall, and the estate attached thereunto. Frank would revert to the common title of Esquire, and so would be addressed as Mr Frank Renfield.

His cry was one of despair but also of rage. He was to be denied his rank of aristocrat just as the old business of Private Porteous had been settled, and he had been pulled back from the brink of bankruptcy. And . . . Oh God, Jess would not inherit the title that was to be taken from him. Why had he ever asked that man Greenspan to look into the matter? What would Carole say when he told her?

His family's past was beginning to destroy him. There had always been rumours that his ancestor, another Frank Renfield, had gained his title through murder. But it was only a story, because someone else had killed Lady Clarissa and had been locked away for life. What if the old rumour, though, were true? *The mills of God grind slowly, but they grind exceedingly small.* Was this latest blow to his pride part of an act of retribution emanating from the bloody past?

It was time to pull himself together and go and talk to his future son-in-law, Karl Langer. If he reacted badly to the news that the Renfields were to become commoners, he might decide not to marry Jess after all. And so the nightmare would return.

As Frank rose from the table, Fred came into the kitchen. He was as white as a sheet.

'Sir,' he said, 'there are three policemen at the door, demanding to see you.'

He knew Detective Inspector French and Sergeant Edwards, but the third man, in the uniform of a superintendent, was unknown to him. It was this man who spoke first.

'Are you Frank Renfield?'

'I am. And who may you be?'

'I am Superintendent Saville of the Sussex Constabulary. Frank Renfield, I have here a warrant for your arrest on the charge that you did, at Greycote, in the county of Sussex, on 27 October 2017, discharge a pistol at one Victor Porteous, so that he died, and that you did murder him. You do not have to say anything, but it may harm your defence if you do not mention when questioned something which you later rely on in court. Anything you do say may be given in evidence.'

'You may pack a small bag of essentials, Lord Renfield,' said DI French, 'and then you must accompany us to police headquarters.'

Half an hour later Frank Renfield left Renfield Hall, the sobs of Jean and Fred's blustering threats against the police echoing in his ears.

* * *

'I'm afraid there can be no doubt about it,' said Superintendent Saville. 'Renfield arrived at Greycote at eleven thirty on the 27 October — eight days ago. He was seen by the landlord of the local pub, who directed him to a property there called the Old Mill. This had been purchased two months ago by a man called Victor Porteous, a Londoner, who had recently retired as a private investigator and had bought the property with a view to restoring it as a residence for himself. Porteous was "camping out" in the place, and there were ample means of establishing his identity.

'Renfield was seen entering the Old Mill. He was also seen leaving it after a stay of half an hour. He was readily recognized by his formal dress and his bowler hat. He left the village immediately by the next train.'

'Perhaps he knew this man, sir,' said DI French, 'and was simply paying him a visit. He may have been murdered after Lord Renfield left the premises.' Superintendent Saville smiled and shook his head.

'It's no good, French,' he said. 'I know he's one of your Oldminster people, a local bigwig and all that, but it won't do. They have a particularly alert PCSO at Greycote, and it was he who called at the Old Mill soon after Renfield had left the village. He found Mr Porteous lying back dead in a chair. He had been shot through the right temple. There was no sign of a weapon in the room.

'A search of the bushes surrounding the Old Mill was made, and a recently discharged army-issue pistol was found. Now before you tell me that it could have been anybody's pistol, it was easily traced by its engraved number. It was the pistol issued to Lord Renfield when he was commissioned into the Oldshire Light Infantry. Renfield's fingerprints were found on the trigger.'

'Well, sir,' said DI French, 'I'm more sorry than I can say. Did your investigation find any definite link between Lord Renfield and this Porteous?'

'Yes. Porteous had written a letter to a fellow detective, a man called Noel Greenspan—'

'Greenspan? He lives here, in Oldminster. He's very well known to us.'

'Well, in this letter, which obviously he'd never had time to post, Porteous told this Noel Greenspan that he feared for his life and was convinced that Renfield would kill him in order to prevent him from revealing a grave crime that Renfield had committed. He said that Greenspan would

195

understand what he meant, as it had to do with the meeting they'd had in London on 20 September.'

'We'll get Greenspan here, sir,' said French, 'and find out what took place at this meeting in London. It's very good of you, Superintendent, to share all this information with us. This crime took place on your patch, and the investigation belongs to the Sussex Police. Are you at liberty to tell me what Lord Renfield has said in his defence?'

'He said that he'd received a letter, ostensibly from another retired officer, a Colonel Laxton, inviting him to join a new security group that MI6 was forming. He was to meet the other members of the group at the Old Mill for a briefing. When he got there, he found Porteous waiting for him, urging him to confess to professional negligence in allowing Porteous's brother to drown. He said the two of them came to some sort of accommodation and he left. It was a cock-and-bull story if ever I heard one. He claimed that Porteous had been wearing cotton gloves — why, I can't imagine. There were no such gloves on the dead man's hands. He said that he'd been received at the mill by a young man, a sort of civil servant, who'd made him surrender the letter from "Colonel Laxton". Very convenient, that. No, there was some dark secret in Renfield's past that he wasn't going to allow to come to the light of day. He hunted that man down and killed him.'

Superintendent Saville got up.

'I'll leave you now, if I may,' he said. 'I don't want to miss my train. It's eight days since the murder, and Renfield's trial will start at Chichester Crown Court on Monday the thirteenth. Everything we've discovered has been submitted to the CPS and to the defending counsel. Some family friend of Renfield has secured the services of Sir Julian Hallett QC for the defence. Very impressive, but I don't see what he can do. This is an open-and-shut case.'

'I bet that "family friend" is Karl Langer,' said DS Edwards when their visitor had gone. 'The Renfields are practically bankrupt, or so I've heard, but Karl's made of money.'

DI French sprang from his chair and moved restlessly about the office.

'I don't believe any of this,' he said. 'Lord Renfield was suspected of killing Guy Lavender just because he'd had a little public row with him. Now he's accused of murdering this Victor Porteous, just because he had some kind of contretemps with *him*. And on top of that, a gaggle of legal experts are saying that he's no right to his title and estate. What's it all about? Is it class prejudice or what? Do *you* think Lord Renfield's a murderer?'

'No.'

'Let's get Noel Greenspan and Chloe McArthur over here. Let's hear what this mysterious meeting in London was all about. Superintendent Saville's a sound man, as far as I can judge, and I'm not going to interfere with his investigation. But we needn't sit here doing nothing. Any new facts that come to light we can pass on to Sussex. Let's not waste any time. Get Greenspan here.'

* * *

'And that's the whole story, Inspector French. We were hired first by Guy Lavender to delve into the facts of the Renfield inheritance, and then, the day after Lavender was killed, Lord Renfield came to us with the same request. We amassed a considerable body of evidence showing that Frank Renfield's title and lands were secured by criminal acts by one of his ancestors. The matter's now out of our hands, as various legal luminaries have taken up the matter, though of course we retain an interest in the outcome.'

It was the afternoon of the same day. Noel Greenspan was in his office when DI French phoned him, and he was more than happy to go to Jubilee House immediately. He and Chloe had both decided that the police needed to know of their activities involving Guy Lavender and Lord Renfield, so French's summons was welcome. 'This Victor Porteous — what can you tell me about him?' asked DI French.

'Like me, he was a registered private detective. He was very successful in his early days and had rather plush offices in Mayfair. But in recent years he'd moved to a more modest location in Islington. When Guy Lavender hired us to look into this business of Lord Renfield's title, I immediately thought of Victor Porteous, because I knew that he had a strong personal grudge against him and might have been useful in helping our investigation. So Lavender and I went to see him.'

Noel Greenspan stopped speaking and looked rather embarrassed. DI French waited patiently for him to continue.

'Well, Inspector French,' said Noel, 'it was a mistake. The smart, go-ahead man I'd known fifteen years ago had degenerated into a sort of cunning tramp. His physical and mental decline were terrible to witness. However, he told us a tale about his time doing National Service, a very sad and harrowing tale that put Renfield in a very bad light.'

Noel told the two officers the story of the disastrous army exercise.

'It had preyed upon his mind,' he continued, 'and become an obsession — a need for revenge. I began to fear for Renfield's safety, though I said nothing of this to him. Guy Lavender was my client at that time, and what I learned was to be retained for his advantage.'

'Very nicely put,' said DI French. 'When you accepted Renfield as a client, you should have told him all this. That's a bad mark against you, Greenspan. However, Porteous's story was true, and Lord Renfield readily admits to it. The general feeling in Chichester is that Renfield found out where Porteous was living, went there and killed him, on the principle that dead men tell no tales.'

'My researches—'

'Your researches are all very well, Greenspan, but this is a murder case and now remains in the province of the police. By all means use your researches to throw light on that inheritance business — you might like to communicate with Lord Renfield's counsel, Sir Julian Hallett QC, through the retaining solicitor, Edgar Friedlander & Son. They have their offices somewhere near Lincoln's Inn.'

'I'm sorry that we've fallen out over this matter, Inspector—'

'No, we haven't fallen out, Greenspan. It's just that I thought you needed to have your knuckles rapped for not informing your client about something of first concern to him. So I'm going to tell you something now that may be relevant to your case. I'm telling you in strict confidence, and you must not quote me as the source. Lady Renfield had been having an affair with Alan Lavender, her own daughter's boyfriend, and it was Lady Renfield who smuggled Alan into Renfield Hall to be present at her birthday party. As you can imagine, DS Edwards and I are making fresh enquiries about what may have happened that night when Alan was killed.'

Inspector French got up from his desk and looked out of the window.

'This is a horrible business,' he said. 'Renfield's suffered so many blows recently, and this charge of murder caps the lot. I hope he's acquitted, but I have my doubts.'

* * *

'There's a visitor for you, Renfield.'

It was the period called Recreation, when remand prisoners were allowed to exercise in a cheerless cavern of a room with yellow distempered walls and flickering overhead lights. You could walk about, read newspapers or play draughts. Most of the prisoners preferred to stand around talking to each other. They were guarded by four uniformed warders, one of whom approached Frank Renfield as he was preparing to read an old copy of the *Daily Mirror*. It was stamped 'HM Prison, Lea Hill. Not to be taken away.'

'A visitor for me, Mr Weaver? Who on earth can it be?'

'Well, I don't know, do I?' said the warder. 'Go into the interview room and then you'll see who it is, won't you? Or you can stay here and I'll tell him to push off.'

Who could it be? What would they think of him, wearing this denim suit and a tieless shirt?

In the interview room, a solitary visitor sat at one of the tables. A warder stood stiffly nearby. As Renfield sat down at the table, the warder said, 'No touching. No passing of objects either way. You have ten minutes before the end of Recreation.'

Frank Renfield looked at his visitor. He'd never seen him before in his life. A little man in a loud check suit, he wore thick glasses, and he had the red, swollen and pitted nose of an alcoholic. Who on earth was this fellow? Maybe they'd got the name wrong.

'Hello, Frank,' said the man, 'how are you? Are you bearing up in here?' He suddenly lowered his voice. 'I'm going to ask you some questions. Just answer them. Never mind who and what. When you saw this Victor Porteous, what was he wearing? Lower your voice when you answer me. Try to look sad, as though you're talking about some family matter.'

'He was wearing an old-fashioned fawn mackintosh, buttoned up to the neck. Oh, and for some reason he was wearing white cotton gloves.'

'White cotton gloves. Did you see a gun? A pistol?'

'Yes. It was an army-issue weapon. According to the police, it was my pistol, with my fingerprints on the trigger. But I didn't shoot him. He was the one waving it around.'

'You knew who he was, though.'

'Oh yes. I knew who he was. Let me tell you—'

'No, Frank. Just answer the questions. What did he look like, this Victor Porteous?'

'Well, he had a round, flabby face, and watery grey eyes. He looked in need of a shave.'

'And what was the young man like? The one who met you at the Old Mill?'

'He was just a young man of twenty-five or so. Nothing special about him. He was wearing a black jacket and black trousers. He looked like a junior civil servant. He spoke quietly and addressed me by my title.'

The visitor motioned to the warder that he wanted to leave.

'Chin up, Frank,' said the nameless man, 'I'll tell the wife that you sent your regards. Cheerio.'

Who in God's name was that? thought Frank Renfield as he was escorted back to the recreation room. Whoever he was, he had a definite purpose in coming. He'd had a few visitors — a tearful, frantic Jessica; Fred, who'd told him that whatever he'd done, he'd stand by him; and Noel Greenspan, who'd already seen Karl Langer, and who together had briefed counsel. Carole couldn't bear the thought of seeing him in prison garb and had stayed away. Well, he wouldn't have wanted her to witness his shame.

A bell rang, and Recreation ceased. Time to return to his room, to await whatever fate had in store for him. The simple room reminded him of a platoon corporal's billet in an army barracks, except that with this particular room, you were locked in for the night.

16. ON TRIAL FOR MURDER

The trial of Frank Renfield began on 13 November in Chichester Crown Court. The judge was Mr Justice Hartley-Moore. Sir Julian Hallett appeared for the defence. Prosecuting for the Crown was David Pendry QC, a barrister with a formidable reputation for getting his man.

Frank Renfield, brought up into the dock from the holding cells, pleaded not guilty, and the trial began. He sat between two policemen and let his thoughts wander to his home and family while the judge delivered his opening address. He felt numb and curiously detached from the proceedings. His counsel had urged him to be optimistic and to make a good impression in court by not slouching in the dock. He no longer cared what impression he made.

He'd rather enjoyed the accounts of his life and career given in the *Daily Mirror* and *The Sun*, and the pictures of him being hustled into a police van, a blanket over his head. He was fast becoming a household name. Fellow prisoners had taken a shine to him as a real, classic killer, and had begun to call him 'mate'. What would he get if they found him guilty? Twenty-five years? They'd have to lodge an appeal if it came to that.

David Pendry began his examination. He regarded Lord Renfield with unbridled scorn. Was it true that he was desperate for money? Was it true that he might soon lose the barony to which he was not entitled? Answer yes or no. Frank did as he was told. Was it true that Victor Porteous, a licensed private detective, had threatened to reveal Renfield's dastardly behaviour towards Porteous's brother Alexander, leading to the young man's death by drowning? And had he then determined to silence the man who could reveal his heartless behaviour to the world? He was quite accustomed to violent death, wasn't he? Murder had been done in his own house.

And so it went on. He would answer yes or no, but would not demean himself by stammering out explanations.

Witnesses were called. The man who kept the pub in Greycote and three other men from the village who could identify him as the man who had asked his way to the Old Mill, and who had been seen later hurrying away from the scene of murder. The exhibits were shown to the jury — Frank's army pistol, the letter written by Victor Porteous saying that he feared for his life. That part of the trial was over far sooner than he'd expected. It was now the defence's turn.

Sir Julian Hallett QC began his defence with an account of Lord Renfield's distinguished army career, his public work as a magistrate, his chairmanship of many worthy societies. He dwelt on the fact that Lord Renfield had suffered the trauma of one suicide and one murder committed in his own home on the same night, a trauma which the learned counsel for the prosecution seemed to hold against him. The prosecution had produced Lord Renfield's army pistol. He would have more to say about that later. As for the letter written by Porteous and left lying in open sight where it could be conveniently found, it was, as evidence, not worth the paper it was written on.

Sir Julian now called witnesses. Colonel Laxton entered the witness box to pay tribute to Lord Renfield's avid support for SSAFA. Cross-examined, he said that he had no connection with any kind of hush-hush organization. He was just a retired army officer, with a continuing interest in all things military. He was surprised that Lord Renfield had fallen for what must have been some kind of hoax.

To Frank's surprise and alarm Fred Lewis appeared in the box and began a rambling eulogy of his employer, which counsel failed entirely to stop. When Fred was finished, he bowed to the judge, who bowed back. Fred then left the box.

'Call Patrick Gorman.'

What? For the first time that morning, Frank Renfield paid full attention to the proceedings.

'My lord,' said David Pendry, 'I have had no notice of this witness. Learned counsel is not playing fair.'

'Well,' said Mr Justice Hartley-Moore, 'what do you say to that, Sir Julian? Are you playing tricks on us?'

'My lord, this witness only presented himself at my chambers yesterday morning. I had to put various things in motion, including giving instructions to the police at Greycote, and have had no chance to acquaint learned counsel for the prosecution of this witness's testimony, but I must advise you that it is vital to the triumph of justice here today.'

'Very well, I'll admit it. But I don't much care for this kind of thing. Carry on.'

Frank Renfield watched as Patrick Gorman entered the witness box. He was very smartly dressed in a navy-blue suit with the regimental tie. What on earth was he going to say? What *could* he say?

'You are Patrick Gorman of Atlee Buildings, Oldminster?'

'Yes, sir.'

'Mr Gorman, I should like you to tell your story to my lord and the jury as you told it to me yesterday.'

Gorman made no attempt to look at the prisoner in the dock. He stood upright and earnest as he gave his evidence.

'My lord and jury,' he began, 'I have known Major the Lord Renfield for many years and had the honour of serving under him in the Oldshire Light Infantry. He was a captain then and a fine company commander. I was present with him on the day when Alexander Porteous was drowned. He had jumped onto a moored pontoon before the order to do so was given, and he was swept away by the raging current in the river and drowned.'

'So it was his own fault, Mr Gorman?'

'It was, sir. It was also a great tragedy. When I saw that Alexander Porteous was going to drown, I prepared to jump into the river and make an attempt to save him—'

'You prepared to jump into the river?' the judge interrupted. 'That was very brave of you, Mr Gorman. Pray continue.'

'Thank you, my lord. You see, it was my duty as I saw it to save one of our men from death. I learned that kind of ethics from my company commander, Captain — as he was then — the Lord Renfield. But the captain, seeing that the case was hopeless, ordered me to desist. You see, he didn't want two useless deaths that day. That's what I call bravery, my lord — an officer's decision takes great courage, because he alone bears responsibility for his own acts.'

'My lord,' said David Pendry, 'this is all very well, and perhaps it clears up this business of what Captain Renfield did or did not do. But what has all this to do with the matter in hand? Learned counsel for the defence seemed to hint at some dramatic revelation.'

'You did, you know, Sir Julian,' said the judge. 'Are we going to get it?'

'We are, my lord. Mr Gorman will now tell you what he did on Friday, 27 October.'

Patrick Gorman glanced briefly at the prisoner in the dock and then began his evidence. Frank Renfield listened in bewilderment as his old army crony proceeded to prove his innocence.

'My lord and jury, as I said, I have known Major the Lord Renfield for many years. As I told you earlier, he was an outstanding officer, but like many of his class, a bit of an innocent when it came to believing what people told him. So when a mate of mine who works at Oldminster train station told me that His Lordship had bought a ticket to Greycote for Friday morning, I knew I'd have to go after him to see that he came to no harm.'

'Why should he come to harm by going to Greycote?'

'Well, you see, my lord, I knew all about Victor Porteous and his threats against Lord Renfield from our army days together, and over the years I've kept an eye on Porteous's comings and goings. Me and a few mates, including the man who works at the railway station. I'd been told a few weeks ago that Porteous had bought this rundown old mill at Greycote, and I wondered why he'd done that, him being a Londoner and all. So when I was told that His Lordship was going to travel down there, I decided to follow him and see that he came to no harm.'

'The more I listen to you, Mr Gorman,' said the judge, 'the more I like you. You seem very loyal to the prisoner. May I ask why?'

Patrick Gorman blushed, and once again glanced briefly at Renfield.

'Things weren't easy for me, my lord, when I left the army, and Lord Renfield was very, very good to me. I won't go into details, but more than once he pulled me back from the brink of ruin. There weren't many ways in which I could repay his kindness, but looking out for him was one of them. And so I went down to Greycote by an earlier train and waited near the Old Mill to see what would happen.'

'This was on 27 October?'

'Yes, my lord. It was a cold, bright day, and I was able to conceal myself in a tangle of bushes that grew beside the mill. Now, I can't be exact as to times, but eventually Lord Renfield appeared on the road above where I was hidden. He was wearing his British Warm greatcoat and a bowler hat, every inch the officer and gentleman.

'He knocked on the door and was admitted by someone inside. He was in there for no more than twenty minutes or so, and then he came out again, looked around him and hurried away down the road. It was then that I heard a shot.'

There was a stir in court, and the judge called for silence. Everyone now gave their full attention to the upright and loyal ex-soldier standing in the witness box.

'I went into the Old Mill and found Victor Porteous lying back dead in a chair. He was seated at a table, and there was an empty chair facing him. A heavy pistol was still clutched in his right hand, but even as I took in the scene, his fingers relaxed and the pistol dropped to the floor.'

Sir Julian Hallett QC now wrested the examination of the witness back into his own hands. He'd allowed the learned judge to have his say; now it was his turn.

'A shocking sight, Mr Gorman, I have no doubt. Could you describe the dead man in a little more detail?'

'Yes, sir. He was a round-faced kind of a man, who could have done with a shave. He was wearing an old mackintosh buttoned up to his chin and white cotton gloves.'

'And when you saw the condition of this dead body, Mr Gorman, did you draw any specific conclusion?'

'My lord, I object,' cried David Pendry QC. 'The witness's conclusions are not evidence.'

'I know, I know,' said the judge. 'But in this instance, it'll do no harm, I'm sure, to hear the witness's opinions about what he saw. After all, he was there, and we weren't. You may answer the question, Mr Gorman.'

'Yes, my lord. It was very obvious to me that Victor Porteous had committed suicide.'

'Now, as you were going to leave the Old Mill,' said Sir Julian, 'something else happened, didn't it?'

'Yes, sir. I heard a noise in the little anteroom and hid behind an inner door that led into a big room full of broken-down old machinery. I stood there and watched a man come into the room where the body was lying. He was a young, ordinary-looking chap wearing a black jacket and black trousers and, like the dead man, he was wearing white cotton gloves. I watched as he carefully picked up the pistol from where it had dropped from Porteous's hand, wrapped it in a handkerchief and put it carefully in his pocket. Then he pulled the white cotton gloves from the dead man's hands and put them in his pocket as well. I noticed that he'd become ashen-faced and had started to tremble. I don't think he'd seen many dead bodies.'

'And what did you do then?'

'I made myself scarce, sir. I'd gone there to keep an eye on Lord Renfield, not to involve myself in a suicide that was being dressed up to look like murder.'

David Pendry QC cross-examined, but with little enthusiasm. He felt that Gorman's testimony would sway the jury very decisively in Renfield's favour. Julian Hallett then called a Dr Danvers as his final witness. Danvers was a clinical psychiatrist who had treated Victor Porteous on a number of occasions and had felt that he was on the verge of being committed to a special hospital.

'Porteous had become obsessed with this story of an injustice towards his brother,' he said. 'This obsession had grown into a monomania, an *idée fixe*, as the French call it. In time, his daily life had narrowed down from a successful detective practice to a sort of vagrant, obsessed with seeking revenge on Lord Renfield. I say vagrant, but in fact he was not short of money.'

'Can you give any credence to the evidence of the witness Gorman?'

'Yes, I can. Suicide as a means of framing someone for murder is not unknown, and it is a frequent fantasy of patients confined to certain hospitals. I can give you documentary evidence of two such cases under my own care.'

'I should now like to call the jury's attention to this business of the white gloves,' said Sir Julian Hallett. 'Why was the dead man wearing white gloves? The answer, ladies and gentlemen of the jury, is so that his own fingerprints would not appear on the trigger of the pistol! The young man had been hired to retrieve the weapon and hide it where the police would find it. Notice that he, too, was wearing white cotton gloves. Why? Because that pistol was the property of

Lord Renfield, and it had his fingerprints on it. Of course it had! They were anxious to leave them there in order to incriminate him.'

Sir Julian turned and picked up a plastic folder from the desk.

'Acting on my suggestion, my lord, the local police at Greycote made a further search of the grounds at the Old Mill, and there, concealed in a crevice in an old garden wall, they found these — two pairs of white cotton gloves! My lord and jury, I rest my case!'

Mr Justice Hartley-Moore, in his summing up, made much of Lord Renfield's public service. He recommended the jury consider very carefully the remarkable evidence given by Patrick Gorman and the medical evidence of mental states furnished by Dr Danvers. Gorman's evidence very effectively proved Lord Renfield's innocence. The police must now try to establish the identity of the young man dressed in black, who had probably been hired by Porteous to arrange for his suicide to look like murder. He was tempted to instruct the jury to find the defendant not guilty, but he would leave it to their common sense to bring in their own verdict.

The jury unanimously found Frank Renfield not guilty of murder.

* * *

Two days later, Frank Renfield sat in his library, consoling himself with a glass of brandy. He was profoundly thankful that he had been found innocent of Porteous's death, and was even able to feel a modicum of pity for the wretched madman. How could he ever repay Gorman's loyalty and care in following him to Greycote and witnessing what he did?

Fred and Jean were, for some reason, ecstatic. Fred kept asking him was there anything he wanted, and Jean had begun to sing lustily as she hoovered the whole house.

Carole looked as though she was on the verge of a breakdown. She was drinking more heavily than ever, and she seemed to be seeing and hearing things as she staggered around the house. Jean looked after her and saw that she was fed, but she was doing that for Jessica's sake. Carole had abdicated her role as chatelaine of Renfield Hall.

There was a sudden commotion in the hall. Voices were raised, and in a moment the door was flung open and Timothy Reid burst into the room, defying Fred's attempt to introduce him properly.

'Frank,' he cried, 'what is all this nonsense? I got a letter today from some flunkey or other inviting me to assume your title and steal your house! I've never been so offended in my life. Do they think I'm a parasite, depriving another man of his rights?'

'I got a letter too, Tim, on the same day as I was arrested for that murder. No doubt you saw the story in the papers. Anyway, I honestly don't give a damn about it all anymore. Apparently all you have to do is tell the Queen—'

'I'll tell the Queen nothing! I didn't think it was possible to feel so angry. Linda's the same. You don't think — you don't think that I had anything to do with this?'

'Of course not. So you're going to let sleeping dogs lie?'

'I'll have nothing to do with it. I don't care what may have happened in the past. I'm not interested. It's just a silly lawyer's game. I've already talked to my solicitor in Oldminster, and he says he'll draft what he called an Instrument of Renunciation, which I will sign. That will bury the whole rotten business for good and all. I say, Frank, are you all right? Steady on!'

Lord Renfield, twentieth baron of that name, had burst into tears.

* * *

Karl Langer called at Renfield Hall that evening and stayed to dinner. Jean, conscious of the fact that the young American would soon be Lord Renfield's son-in-law and the husband of Girlie, had contrived to produce a very satisfying meal, which Fred had served with renewed panache. Lady Renfield had asked for a tray in her sitting room. It was becoming rare these days to see her in the dining room in the evenings. Jess was staying for a few days with an old school friend in Chichester.

Earlier in the day, Lord Renfield had cornered Fred in the pantry, where he was unpacking groceries. 'There are going to be vast changes here soon, Fred,' he'd said. 'I hope to be able to live more like a peer of the realm than I've been able to for some years now.'

Fred thought, *Is this the end for Jean and me?*

'But I hope you and Jean will agree to stay with me, Fred. I wouldn't fancy carrying on if you two weren't about the place.'

Choking back tears, Fred had addressed his employer correctly for the first time. 'Of course we'll stay, my lord,' he'd said. 'And the feeling's mutual!'

After dinner, Lord Renfield and Karl retired to the library for their usual brandy. Karl thought, *He's looking younger, and his face isn't as ravaged as it used to be. He's a man who saw himself about to fall into a bottomless pit and was pulled away from the brink just in time.*

No talk of money had passed between them, but Renfield must have known that he, Karl Langer, would save his future father-in-law from ruin.

'Karl,' said Frank Renfield, 'I can't stand this place anymore. I never thought I'd say that, but it's true. Renfield Hall was sucking the life-blood from me. It was like . . . like a sinister idol, making terrible demands upon me. Carole was a victim, too. She was more fanatical about this place than I was. It's . . . She's . . .' His voice trailed away, and he sat holding his empty glass and staring into space.

'What are you going to do? I'm here to help you, if I can. You know that, Frank.'

Lord Renfield appeared not to hear. He seemed to be looking at something far away, beyond the confines of his ancestral home. Finally, he roused himself and spoke.

'There's a beautiful old house, Karl, a place called Stanton Old Place, which until a few weeks ago was the seat of the Steynforth family. The Steynforths were relatives of my mother's family, and I spent some very happy times there as a boy. Their son Robin and I were at school together. They were a far more ancient family than the Renfields. You can see their family vault and monuments in the church here, together with those of the Reids.'

Something stirred in Karl Langer's soul. Here was another fascinating glimpse into the old aristocracy of England.

'What kind of a place is this Stanton Old Place?' he asked. 'Would I like it?'

Lord Renfield laughed. 'Oh, yes, Karl, you'd like it. It's a beautiful black-and-white-timbered Tudor manor house, with old-fashioned gardens in the Elizabethan style. Knot gardens and so forth. It's not as big as this place, but big enough. And now John and Marjorie are planning to sell up and emigrate to Canada.'

Frank Renfield got up from his chair and brought a magazine from the library table. It was a recent copy of *Country Life*. 'There you are,' he said. 'It's being advertised for sale in one or two of the posh magazines.'

'"This exceptional historic property, lying in a secluded valley twelve miles from the ancient cathedral city of Oldminster, stands in its own park of three hundred acres,"' Karl read. 'Hmm . . . They want £5 million pounds for it.'

'That's mere fantasy,' said Frank. 'They'll be lucky to get three. I believe the estate has gone to seed over the last few years, but that's the kind of house I'd like to live in now. It's a happy place. Renfield Hall . . . it's stained with blood. With suicide and murder. It's got to go, no matter what Carole says. She's . . . She's not well, but she won't let me call a doctor.'

'But she'll be well enough for the wedding?'

'I don't know. When Fred showed her that vile letter from the Lord Chancellor, she seemed to have a fit — a real fit, you know. He thought she was going to die. No, Karl, she's not well. Not well at all.'

'Why don't we buy this Stanton Old Place?' asked Karl. 'We won't give them five, but we could run to three, or maybe a little more. Perhaps you and I could look it over? Ride the cars down there and see what shape it's in.'

'Ride the cars?'

'Yes, you know, go via the railroad. I suppose there's a depot there? Then you could put this place on the market, and we could all go to live at Stanton — you, me and Jess. And Lady Renfield, of course, if she'll come.'

Frank's voice was unsteady. 'Do you really mean that, Karl?'

'Yes, of course I do. The more I think about it, the more I like the idea. And besides, I don't think Renfield Hall will be good for Jess either, after what she's had to witness. No, don't say anything, Frank, and for Pete's sake keep a stiff upper lip! Let's pour out some more brandy and drink a toast to our new life.'

* * *

'England is a strange country,' said Karl Langer. 'As well as a queen, you've got a king. But he isn't really a king, he's a King of Arms, and he, in cahoots with a few other solemn lunatics, decide to hand a man's titles and property to someone else, entirely on their say-so. That, friends, couldn't happen in the States.'

Karl was relaxing with Tim and Linda Reid in the Reids' private quarters in the Church Eaton Hotel and Spa. It was the slack period following lunch, and there was time to talk.

'Well, Karl,' said Tim, 'it's not going to happen here in the UK, either. I've already seen to that. Frank Renfield and I have always got along well together, and no lawyers' fantasy was going to make me steal my kinsman's rights and property. This may be a strange country, but it's not as awesomely daft as that. Not in practice, anyway.'

'This place is doing well, isn't it?' said Karl. 'This hotel, I mean.'

'We're doing very well,' said Linda. 'It's hard work, but Tim and I enjoy that.'

'Have you thought of expanding?' asked Karl. 'All businesses need to grow.'

'We do have ambitions,' said Tim, 'but we're realists, too. You have to crawl before you can walk.'

'I'm thinking of investing in the hotel business,' said Karl. 'My American companies are all tech-based, although I have a large investment portfolio in real estate. But I'd like to form a company that could bring together some independent hotel outfits here in the UK. I'm thinking of places that may have become run down through lack of investment, which could be turned round to high-quality accommodation.'

Tim shifted uneasily and glanced at his wife.

'You're not thinking of buying us out, are you?' he asked. 'Because we're not for sale.'

Karl laughed. 'No, nothing like that,' he said. 'But I've seen what you've achieved here at Church Eaton, and the clever things you've done to attract custom, particularly from the States. Jessica and I intend to spend most of our time in England, but for several months of the year we'll have to be in New York and California. We have a lot of conferences with big companies and government agencies, and I'd sure like to hold some of those meetings here, in England. This would need some high-class entertainment in exclusive surroundings, well away from London.'

'What are you saying?' asked Tim.

'I'm saying that I have my eye on a very desirable property here, in Oldshire, a place where you could let your genius run riot. Let me invest in your company. Put a manager in here and embark on a new venture in partnership with me.'

'You'd invest in us?'

'I'd invest in your talent. I tell you I've got the ideal place. The man who owns it doesn't know yet that he's going to sell it to me, but he will. Yes, sir. I kid you not.'

'And where is this place?' asked Linda Reid.

'It's called Renfield Hall,' said Karl, laughing. 'Frank's sick of that bloodstained place and wants to make a move. So I'll offer him four million pounds for it and listen to his sigh of relief as he accepts.'

The Reids were only half listening. They were whispering excitedly to each other, and Karl could make out some of the things they were saying. 'The Renfield Hall Hotel and Spa . . . There are sixty acres, so . . . The Renfield Hotel, Spa and Golf Course . . . Limousines to ferry guests from Heathrow . . .'

'We'll need to register a new company,' said Karl, 'and offer its shares on the market. Let's call it the Reid Group. We can appoint Frank as Honorary Chairman, if you like.'

But the Reids were not listening. 'Masked balls in the autumn . . . Tudor banquets . . . A ghost trail from the hall to the cathedral . . .' And so it went on. There would be no stopping Tim and Linda Reid now.

17. PHANTOMS

'She planned it down to the last detail,' said DS Edwards.

It was 20 November, just one week after Frank Renfield's acquittal. Lord Renfield was the talk of the town and something of a local hero. He had faced a suicide and a murder in his own home, and had then been accused of murder himself.

The *Oldshire Gazette* had brought out a special edition with Frank's portrait and a chronicle of his life. Half a page was devoted to Patrick Gorman and the dramatic evidence that he had given to prove Lord Renfield's innocence.

Frank's story had been interwoven with an article on the coming marriage of Mr Karl Langer and the Honourable Miss Jessica Renfield in Oldminster Cathedral. Originally planned for the end of November, it had been rescheduled for 9 December.

At Jubilee House, though, DS Edwards and DI French were engaged in a much grimmer business than celebrating a local hero and his daughter's forthcoming marriage. DS Edwards had never accepted Superintendent Philpot's assertion that Alan Lavender had been murdered by Colin McDonald. He was now outlining his own theory, which he presented to DI French as fact.

'Sir,' Edwards continued, 'I've put together a sort of timeline concerning Lady Renfield's doings on the night of the party. At about seven thirty, she admitted Alan Lavender to Renfield Hall at what's called the garden entrance. Nobody saw her do so, but that's what must have happened, as a short time later she was seen by a witness, whom I later interviewed, locked in a passionate embrace with Lavender in a pantry adjoining the kitchen.'

DI French uttered a little sound of disgust but said nothing.

'There was more to it than that, sir,' said DS Edwards. 'Jean's nephew, a young artist called Jerry Carter, actually witnessed Lady Renfield and Alan Lavender having sex together. He told his aunt, who then told me.'

'They had some choice names for people like her in Victorian times,' said French. 'What was it they would have called her? An "abandoned woman". She's certainly that.'

'Yes, sir. Alan Lavender was wearing evening dress,' DS Edwards continued, 'so he would have blended in very well with the other male guests. He liked to give the impression that he was a scruffy, badly dressed oaf, and in many ways he was. A tuxedo would be an ideal disguise, if you get my meaning.'

'Hiding in plain sight,' said DI French.

'Yes, sir. I think that Lady Renfield told Lavender to make himself scarce until dinner, when he was to take his seat at one of the tables in the dining room, away from the family. With reference to that particular point, Jean Lewis came to see me and told me some very damning things — damning to Lady Renfield, I mean. She asked me to keep what she told me to myself, though she must have realized that communications of this kind must be shared with other police officers.

'Jean Lewis was able to ascertain that Lady Renfield bought a suit of evening clothes, together with a shirt and tie, from a gentlemen's outfitters in Chichester, and that she later posted these items to someone else. It's reasonable to assume that these items were intended for Alan Lavender, who was to come to Renfield Hall as a guest.'

'Why did she invite *him*, of all people?' asked DI French. 'I thought she hated him because he was after her daughter, who she wanted to marry that Karl Langer, your friend with the ambulance. But then, you've told me that she—'

'I'll come to that presently, sir,' said Edwards. 'Bear with me for a moment. Once Lady Renfield had successfully smuggled Lavender into the house, she was able to go and join her family. That would have been at 7.50 p.m. Presentations followed at 8 p.m., but lasted only half an hour. I don't know what happened to Lady Renfield then, and it's only a guess on my part that she admitted Colin McDonald to the house and took him up to the haunted room. She'd have spun him some yarn in order to keep him there until she needed him.

'Jean Lewis also states that she saw Lavender seated at a table during dinner, and that after Jessica left the table with a headache, she saw Lady Renfield lead Alan from the dining room. I suggest that she took him to the disused cellar.'

'So far, Glyn, your theory has been very persuasive. So what happened next?'

'Everything suddenly went wrong, sir. The shot rang out. Lord Renfield rushed out to check that his daughter was all right. He was followed by Noel Greenspan and Chloe McArthur. And from that moment onwards nothing was seen of Lady Renfield.'

'Greenspan has been to see me,' said DI French. 'He told me a great deal of interesting things about the Renfields and their family history. It was quite true, apparently, that official attempts were going to be made to deprive Renfield of his lands and title, and hand them over to the Reids, but nothing came of it.'

'I should think not,' said DS Edwards. 'That was simply a lawyers' game that went too far. I don't know how that man keeps sane. He's been fighting off bankruptcy for years, and on top of that, he's had to cope not only with suicide and murder in his own home, but his own trial for murder. A lesser man would have collapsed under the strain.'

'I know. I still think he's a bit of a rogue, Glyn, but he's certainly had more than his fair share of troubles to contend with. Anyway, Sergeant, you've given an excellent résumé of the case. I think you'll find Mr Philpot won't tie our hands when I've told him. Lord Renfield's married to a very clever and designing woman. But *why*? Why did she do all that? What was the point of all this to-ing and fro-ing, and playing hide and seek?'

'Jean Lewis saw the point, sir. She saw right through the elaborations to the crux of the matter. The Renfields were facing financial ruin. The solution to their dilemma was for Jessica to marry Karl Langer. But Jessica thought she was in love with Alan Lavender, so Alan Lavender had to die.'

'You think—'

'I think that when Lady Renfield took Colin up to the haunted room, she gave him that gun — why not? Her husband had been a professional soldier, and probably had more than one souvenir. Or perhaps she got it from some other source. It's not as easy for a man to obtain a pistol "on the street" as Mr Philpot seems to think, and Lady Renfield would not have left anything to chance. When she judged the time right, she would have taken Colin down to the cellar, where he would shoot Alan Lavender dead in revenge for the death of his friend Leslie Blackmore.'

'But Alan Lavender had nothing to do with Leslie Blackmore's death.'

'I know, sir, and she was taking a gamble that Colin would have believed what she said about Alan in that email — that Alan had laughed when he heard of his uncle's plan to infect Leslie with HIV. I mean, it's a pretty outlandish claim. Her gamble could well have paid off. Of course, she'd no interest in what happened to Colin after that. She would have achieved her aim: her daughter Jessica could no longer marry Alan, because Alan was dead. But it all went wrong when Colin McDonald shot himself.'

'What did she do?'

'She knew that the sound of the pistol shot would bring Alan Lavender out of the cellar, so she got there before he could leave the room, and bashed his head in with the lamp. After that, sir, she was as free as the air.'

DI French got up from his chair and crossed to the window. He looked at the leafless trees in the town hall garden and saw that a thin rain had begun to fall.

'I'll apply for a warrant this afternoon, Glyn,' he said, 'and we should get it tomorrow. Freddie Fusspot will raise no objections when he's heard what I've got to tell him. Duty is duty, but I dread facing Lord Renfield with this bombshell. How do you tell a man that his wife's a murderess?'

* * *

'Jean,' said Lady Renfield, 'I never used to believe in ghosts, but I do now. They're gathering together here, in this house. I know what they want, but I'm not going with them.'

Jean Lewis felt a sudden chill around her heart. Lady Renfield was as elegant as ever and had not yet begun to neglect herself, but there were dark shadows under her eyes, eyes that never these days seemed to settle on any one thing. She was ill, but not in the body . . .

They had met that evening in the gallery, where Lady Renfield had been staring at the portrait of Clarissa, one of her predecessors as chatelaine of Renfield Hall. She appeared to be having a conversation with the centuries-dead woman, but it was a conversation in which she provided both voices. Frank's wife was mutating into some kind of grotesque ventriloquist.

'She's the worst of all,' said Carole, 'for ever preaching at me and telling me how wicked I am. I've had enough of her, and the others. I don't know who half of them are — they're shadows, and they don't speak. But *she* does. She never stops!'

Lady Renfield backed away from the portrait and staggered away along the passage. These days, she seemed to be permanently intoxicated. Frank either didn't notice or didn't want to know. He'd become totally absorbed in what would be his rosy future — his and Girlie's.

Lady Renfield suddenly reappeared.

'I'm going to exorcize that bitch,' she said, 'by burning some incense in her haunted room. Maybe later on tonight. Will you give me your arm to go downstairs? I'm not as steady as I was. I'm going to sit in the oak parlour to escape these phantoms.'

Jean felt a sudden surge of pity for Carole Renfield, the woman she detested. Within a couple of weeks she had degenerated from a confident woman to a disordered wreck. At this rate, she'd be quite unfit to attend her own daughter's wedding. She guided her down the stairs and into the oak parlour, where she left her sitting in one of the straight-backed Hepplewhite chairs that stood in the great window embrasure. Then she left her, but lingered uneasily in the hall.

* * *

As Carole sat staring at the window, now palled in darkness, she fancied that Clarissa, Lady Renfield was sitting in the chair opposite her. Even downstairs, she couldn't escape the attentions of the censorious bitch.

'You've stirred up all the devils in Hell,' said Clarissa. 'And you've woken *me* from the sleep of ages. The blood of that boy who shot himself was like a libation to Morpheus.'

Carole swallowed a scream of anguish as she realized that it was she who had spoken those words. The ghost — was it a ghost? — was speaking through her mouth. If anybody heard her, they'd think she'd gone mad. What was a libation to Morpheus? She didn't use words like that. Maybe she'd read it somewhere.

* * *

It had been one of those dreary, dark days in late November that threaten a storm and unleash it as the sun is going down to rest. Renfield Hall had been lashed with torrential downpours, roused by lightning and deafened by peals of thunder.

Frank Renfield sat in a chair at the far end of the room, thinking of the rosy future and enjoying the new-found luxury of a calm and untroubled mind. He had been smoking his pipe, but it had gone out, and he was falling into a fitful doze.

'It was none of my doing,' said Carole. 'I gave him the gun, but I intended him to shoot Alan Lavender dead with it, in order to avenge the death of his friend, who died of Aids. You didn't have that disease in your day, Clarissa. Or maybe you did, and you called it something else. I told him to bring a gun, but I was taking no chances. Sure enough, he came empty-handed, so I provided him with a gun myself.'

'Dear me!' said Lady Clarissa. 'I can see that you share the wickedness of my nephew, another Frank, who murdered me in that room upstairs where you brought the poor addle-pated lad. Well, Lady Renfield, the Good Book says that the wicked shall be turned into Hell.'

On the other side of the room, Lord Renfield was sitting up horrified in his chair.

'Guns were common enough in my day,' said Clarissa. 'Flintlocks, mostly. I gather they're not very easy to come by now. You wicked woman, where did you get it?'

Carole Renfield smiled in self-satisfaction.

'Well, I didn't get it from my husband, because the only gun he has is his old army pistol. I went looking for it, but it wasn't in his drawer. I think somebody must have stolen it, in order to frame him for that murder that he didn't commit. Damn them! Security in this house leaks like a sieve. We had a break-in last month, and a few things were stolen, but it wasn't worth reporting. Maybe Frank's gun was stolen then, by that man who tried to frame him for murder.'

'Keep to the point, madam. You're confusing me.'

'Very well. I got that gun from Nancy Grieve, the wife of one of Frank's old army friends. We were chatting in her dressing room one day, and I pinched it from her top drawer. I thought that was very clever.'

'The Grieves of Holt?' said Clarissa. 'We used to visit them occasionally, and we sometimes met at one or other of His Majesty's levees. Thomas Grieve came to see me just after that young man's blood had opened the doors of the tomb. He was one of my beaux, you know, in my tender years.'

Carole thought, *I remember reading all that about the Grieves of Holt in a history of the Renfield family in Frank's library. Am I just imagining this nagging ghost? Is it just my conscience? No, because I have no conscience.* Conscience is a word that cowards use, to keep the strong in awe. *Shakespeare said that, or Milton, or someone.*

'I planned it down to the last detail,' Carole boasted. 'You wouldn't have had the courage. I promised my husband that Jessica would marry Karl Langer and lift us out of penury, and I remained true to my promise. Incidentally, I very much resent your coming back from the dead like this. I think it's vulgar.'

'If you're so good at planning,' said Clarissa, 'you'd better tell me what you did, you shameless hussy.'

'The presentations lasted only half an hour,' said Carole, 'and while everybody stayed chatting in the library, I went to the kitchen door and admitted Colin McDonald to the house. I'd sent him an email, you know, telling him to present himself at eight o'clock. It was real penny dreadful stuff, all about avenging his friend's death.'

'In my day,' said Clarissa, 'a lady of title would not have behaved in that way.'

'Very likely not,' said Carole, 'but things are different these days. I took him upstairs and parked him in your room. If that offended you, I'm sorry. I don't believe in ghosts, as a rule, but I suppose I'm obliged to believe in *you*. I gave him the gun and told him to stay there until I came for him. I was going to take him down to the cellar when the time was ripe and get him to avenge his friend's death by shooting Alan . . .

'But it all went wrong when he shot himself, the silly fool! I had to act quickly. The house was in chaos, and while I longed to see if my daughter was all right, I knew I had to get rid of

Alan before he came out to see what the noise was all about. I went to the old cellar, where he was waiting patiently for me—'

'Why was he waiting?' asked Clarissa. 'I find all this very confusing.'

'He was waiting because I'd promised first of all to have sex with him, and then to persuade my husband to accept him as a potential son-in-law. That's what kept him there. He was a handsome young brute, you know, and his vanity became his undoing. And if that fool McDonald hadn't shot himself, I'd have brought him down later to shoot Lavender dead, like I told you. I would have been completely in the clear, the picture of injured innocence. But that was not to be. I was obliged to carry out the execution myself. He was waiting in the dark so as not to be discovered. Once I'd slipped in there with him and convinced him it was our time to be alone together, I picked up the lamp and smashed his head in with it.'

There came something like a moan from Lord Renfield, but his wife did not hear it. She was still in thrall to her spectral visitor, speaking her words as well as her own.

'What?' cried Clarissa. 'You murdered him? And worse still, you offered to engage in physical commerce with this fellow? I've heard enough. You shameless hussy! Your husband is sitting there, dumbstruck, on the other side of the room, and you dare to tell me such a thing in his hearing? Such matters were managed much better in my day.'

'I was terrified for some time afterwards,' said Carole. 'I couldn't stop trembling. But it soon passed. It was worse when Frank was told that he would lose his title. I nearly had a stroke when Fred told me that. I got my courage back, then. If it had happened, you see, I'd have got rid of the Reids myself. I'd have waited until they threw us out, and then I would have crept back one night, locked them in their bedroom and set fire to the house. But I didn't have to.'

Carole laughed, and it was a sound that made her husband's blood run cold.

'Isn't it time you were gone?' she cried. 'Don't you have to disappear on the stroke of midnight or something?'

Clarissa rose majestically from her chair, shook her head in sorrow and walked silently through the wall. Carole, ignoring her husband, walked unsteadily from the oak parlour into the entrance hall.

Frank Renfield sat in a sort of horrified trance. He had listened to her as she spoke in two voices, as though she were reading a play. It was as though there had been a third person in the room. Eventually, the stricken husband roused himself from his stupor and reached for the telephone.

* * *

Jean Lewis, concealed in a dim corner of the entrance hall, watched Lady Renfield as she paused on the stairs. She was talking to someone, although there was nobody there.

'Yes, I had sex with him many times. He was very good, you know, and it amused me to think that I was using sex to lure him to his death. What? No, I didn't. More fool Jessica for falling for him. Of course it wasn't incest. How could it have been? I hated him because he was a threat to Frank and me, and I used what means I could to get rid of him. I'll remove anybody who threatens my husband. But I see you're in livery. What are you, a footman? How dare you ask me these questions. What's your name? Does Fred know that you're here? Your name's John Forbes? Well, Forbes, know your place, and go about your business. I have an exorcism to perform.'

Lady Renfield continued on her way up the stairs.

It's as though she was speaking on the phone, thought Jean, trembling with fright. *You couldn't hear what the other party was saying. Oh God, she's gone mad! If they don't take her away, she'll do herself an injury. Or do something awful to us. Thank God, Girlie's still away.*

Lord Renfield, ashen-faced, came out into the hall.

'Jean,' he said, 'Her Ladyship has been saying the most dreadful things. I've sent for the police, and for Dr Hargreaves. Stay with me here in the hall until they arrive.'

* * *

Carole Renfield had carried out Abraham Sylvester's instructions and had filled Lady Clarissa's room with candles, some tall and fixed in old candlesticks, others mere tea lights arranged on the bedside table. She did not switch on the electric light. She had lit a fire in the old grate, and with some difficulty had managed to ignite the charcoal and had then used tongs to place it in a brass bowl. The atmosphere in the haunted room grew hot, and Carole coughed as the acrid smoke tickled her lungs. She placed the incense on to the glowing charcoal, and almost immediately the room was filled with a beautiful perfume.

Carole lay back on the ancient four-poster bed and opened the pamphlet that Sylvester had given her. She would read some of the prayers aloud and ring the little bell that the medium had provided. Would it work? Would it drive the spirit of that censorious woman away? So far, there had been neither sight nor sound of her. Carole opened the pamphlet, saw that the prayers were printed in a minute typeface and leaned over towards the candles on the bedside table to see them more clearly.

* * *

Downstairs, DS Edwards had arrived in answer to Frank's frantic phone call, accompanied by a uniformed constable. The warrant for Lady Renfield's arrest for the murder of Alan Lavender would not be available till the following morning.

The two officers sat in the oak parlour and listened as Frank Renfield told them all that he had heard. When he had finished, Jean Lewis added her story to his.

'My wife is in urgent need of medical attention, Sergeant,' said Frank Renfield. 'Whatever she has done, she is sick in her mind. I blame myself. I should have cared for her better.' Lord Renfield's voice broke, and he buried his face in his hands.

DS Edwards said nothing. In his opinion, Carole Renfield had driven herself to the borders of insanity through guilt and remorse, but it was for the law to decide whether she was sane enough to face a trial for murder. He felt almost smugly satisfied that his theory had been confirmed as true by the murderess herself.

'Fire! Fire!'

Fred Lewis appeared at the door, white-faced. As though on cue, the room began to fill with curling fronds of smoke. Edwards told the constable to phone the fire brigade, and with Frank Renfield following him, ran out into the hall. They made their way up the stairs and were confronted on the landing by a dense pall of smoke and the noise of crackling timbers. At the same moment, a violent explosion blew the door off the haunted room, and they saw that the old chamber was in the grip of a raging inferno.

'There's nothing we can do,' DS Edwards cried. 'We must leave the house until the brigade arrives. No, Lord Renfield, don't!'

Frank had dropped to the floor and was crawling towards the raging fire. In an instant he had disappeared from sight, only to reappear in less than a minute, crawling crab-wise out on to the landing and dragging the lifeless body of Carole Renfield with him out of the ruin.

It took the fire brigade nearly four hours to put out the fire. The walls in that part of Renfield Hall were of solid brick faced with stone, and it had been possible to contain the damage to three adjacent rooms on the landing. The rest of the great mansion was saved.

Once the story of Lady Renfield's death had reached the papers, both Mrs Osbourne and Abraham Sylvester came forward to tell the police about the do-it-yourself exorcism that had led to the tragedy. At the coroner's inquest, no blame was assigned to them. It had been a foolish act by Lady Renfield to light so many naked candles in a room full of tinder-dry furnishings and drapery. The firemen thought that the blaze had started because Lady Renfield had placed a number of candles too near to the curtains of the four-poster bed.

A post-mortem was carried out on her body, preserved by her husband from being calcined in the raging furnace of

Lady Clarissa's Chamber. She had died of smoke inhalation, having fallen to the floor of the room. No serious damage had been done to the body. However, on opening the cranium, the medical examiner had discovered a massive tumour on the brain. It was suggested at the inquest that much of Lady Renfield's unusual behaviour had been caused by this malignant tumour. It was also agreed by two other surgeons present at the autopsy that Lady Renfield would not have lived for more than six months if the fire had not so tragically taken her life. Verdict: death by misadventure.

* * *

Peer's Killer Wife Dies in Fire was the headline in the following Thursday's *Daily Mirror*. Lance Middleton threw the paper down in disgust. 'They've jumped the gun there,' he said. 'We don't know for certain that Carole Renfield killed anybody.'

Once more, the three friends were assembled round the kitchen table in Chloe's house in Wellington Square, and were lingering over coffee and a liqueur after dinner.

'Oh, yes we do, Lance,' said Noel Greenspan. 'DS Edwards had very cleverly proved that she murdered Alan Lavender, and his conclusions were confirmed by the wretched woman herself, who blurted out the truth while possessed by some delusion that old Lady Renfield had come back from the eighteenth century to make her confess. Lord Renfield heard it all, and so did Jean Lewis. Renfield called the police.'

'It's very tragic,' said Lance. 'What happened to her? Did she commit suicide?'

'The fire people think not,' said Noel. 'She'd filled the haunted room with candles — in order, apparently, to perform an exorcism — and it's thought that a draught caused the hangings of the four-poster bed to catch fire. The room was as dry as tinder. Lady Renfield must have died very quickly. No "care in the community" for her, poor woman. I wonder . . .'

'Wonder what?' asked Lance.

'Did the spirit of Clarissa really appear to Lady Renfield? A lot of people claim to have seen ghosts. Do you remember those words of T. S. Eliot in "Little Gidding"? "The communication of the dead is tongued with fire beyond the language of the living." Brain tumour or not, Lady Renfield may indeed have been visited by the ghost of her husband's ancestor, a visitation that resulted in her being "tongued with fire" in reality. What do you think, Lance?'

'I think you're talking a lot of bosh. I'd take anything that a poet said with a pinch of salt, myself.'

'Maybe you're right.' Noel Greenspan laughed. '*Of course* you're right. I must ration my poetry reading in future. Let the poor soul rest in peace. I suppose that Jessica's marriage has been called off for the duration?'

'No, it's to go ahead on the ninth,' said Chloe. 'Lord Renfield insisted, and Jessica thoroughly agreed. Noel and I have been invited. We're both rather touched by that.'

'I went to see Lord Renfield yesterday afternoon,' said Noel Greenspan. 'I was going to tell him all about our investigation, but he wasn't interested. All he could talk about was Carole. He was already planning to have her placed in the Renfield vault in Oldminster Cathedral. "She'll be there, you see, Greenspan," he said to me, "when Jess walks up the aisle on my arm." He's forgiven her everything. I've never seen such fidelity. It was really moving. But I sensed that he's relieved that she's gone.'

'I'm not surprised he feels like that,' said Chloe. 'Don't forget, she was devoted to him, too. She committed murder for his sake.'

'I think he'll rally, you know,' said Noel, 'especially as he and Karl are planning to relocate with Jessica to Stanton Old Place soon after the wedding. It will be a new beginning for Frank.'

'I managed to get Jean Lewis to come to tea here yesterday,' said Chloe. 'She told me some interesting things. Jessica loved her mother, but was always frightened of her.

Jean thinks she sensed that all was not well with her mother's mental balance. Carole used to beat her, even when she'd grown up. Jean had heard that there was supposed to be insanity in Lady Renfield's family, though it was only a rumour.'

'Lord Renfield told me that she seemed to be talking to someone who wasn't there,' said Noel. 'But she was talking in both voices. So, since you won't allow for a ghost, whatever she thought she saw was entirely in her head.'

'The poor woman was suffering from that undiscovered brain tumour that made her see and hear things that weren't there,' said Lance. 'Ghosts don't come into it. I've known cases like that. I've read about them in works on forensic jurisprudence. But we shall never know for sure.'

Lance finished his coffee and glanced rather helplessly at the percolator. Chloe poured him another cup of Blue Mountain coffee.

'And you've both been invited to the wedding?' he said. 'Well, that'll be very nice. I expect there'll be a grand reception. Still, one can't have everything in this life. I'll think of you both while I'm dining alone in Lincoln's Inn.'

'I'm sure we could wangle a place for you if you really want to come,' said Noel.

'Oh no,' said Lance, smiling rather sadly. 'I was only joking. I brought nothing but trouble and anguish to that family through my forensic snooping. If I turned up at that reception, I would truly be the spectre at the feast!'

* * *

It was nearing the end of the month. The remains of Lady Renfield had been laid in the family vault, where the Dean of Oldminster had read the committal service. Frank had descended into the vault, where he had glimpsed the ornate but crumbling coffin of Clarissa, Lady Renfield, which had been deposited there in 1784. There would be no memorial service, or 'celebration of her life', as the modern fashion liked to put it. Carole would remain alive in his heart for as long as she chose to dwell there.

On the afternoon of the same day, Lord Renfield had made his way to the British Legion Club.

'I've been through some very bad times recently, you know, Pat,' said Frank, a pint of bitter in his hand. 'And now that Lady Renfield has gone, I've decided to make a new start with Jessica and her husband-to-be at Stanton Old Place.'

'So you're moving out then, Major,' said Pat, staring moodily into his own pint. 'Does that mean that we'll not see you here in Station Street anymore?'

'Why ever not?' said Frank. 'The British Legion Club's the one place where I can relax. I've got true friends here, the type of men who wouldn't turn their backs on me if I was in a tight corner. Men like *you*, Pat. Besides, Stanton's only twelve miles from Oldminster — hardly the end of the world, you know. So I'll be dropping in here as usual when the fancy takes me, for a pint, a pie and a chat. But I was wondering . . . if anything unpleasant were to happen in the future — little things, you know, where I'd need a bit of help — could I still rely on you to give me a hand?'

'I'm always here for you, Major, you know that. You and I go back a long time.'

'Well, that's very satisfying. Neither you nor I go in for fancy speeches, Pat, but you know that I'll never be able to repay you for following me to that wretched mill and doing what you did. You saved my bacon. Not so long ago, you'd have saved my neck.'

Pat Gorman began to chuckle. He looked sideways at Lord Renfield with an expression of amused, affectionate disbelief.

'Oh, Major,' he said, 'I was never there at all. I never visited the place while you were there.'

'What do you mean? I don't understand—'

'Somebody I know told me what you said to the police — the account you gave to them about what happened to you at that place, Greycote. He made some notes and gave them to me. Then I sent another man I know — a man who likes to wear loud suits — to visit you in prison. He got you to tell him all the details of what you saw and heard at the Old Mill, and then he told me. I got in touch with that barrister and spun him a yarn about how I'd followed you to the Old Mill and saw you leave the place before the shot rang out. Everybody believed me, even you! But I was never there, Major. Not until just before the trial, when I nipped down there to check that I'd get the details right for my moment of glory in court.'

'You astonish me, Pat! *You were never there?* Well, I don't know what to say. I don't — what can I do to make it up to you?'

Frank's eyes filled with tears, and he slid off the bar stool, hurrying away before he made an ass of himself in front of Gorman. On the bar counter, under his empty beer glass, he had left a fifty-pound note.

EPILOGUE

Mr and Mrs Karl Langer stood on the antique stone bridge that crossed the dry moat of Stanton Old Place, savouring the peace and calm that seemed to pervade the Tudor mansion. It was a hot day for the time of year, and they could smell the perfume of melting linseed exuding from the ancient timbers. Ahead of them stretched the formal gardens, ending in a wall of mellow bricks, separating the grounds from the paddock beyond.

'It's so quiet, Karl,' said Jessica. 'We never knew this kind of peace at Renfield. This is a beautiful house, full of beautiful things. When the Steynforths found out that we were buying it, they left so many lovely furnishings behind. Poor Mummy!'

Karl put an arm round his wife's shoulders and thought, *Poor Mummy, my foot!* But he held his peace, because he, too, had been appalled at Lady Renfield's terrible fate. The family's doctor had assured him that she would have died quickly from smoke inhalation. Well, let her rest.

Jess was right. Stanton Old Place *was* wonderful, and it was *his*. Half a mile away was Stanton New Place, a mere youngster of only three hundred years. What an amazing country!

Yes, Stanton Old Place was *his*. He loved its twisting corridors, its unexpected little staircases, its diamond-paned windows. He loved the long Tudor parlour looking out onto the knot garden, a chamber furnished with items from the fourteenth to the twentieth centuries. He loved the bijou 'great hall', romantically remodelled in the early years of the nineteenth century and bristling with suits of armour. There was a staff of twelve, including the gardeners. Fred and Jean Lewis were in overall control — he as butler, she as housekeeper. They dressed more smartly now, and both had learned to address Frank as 'my lord' when they spoke to him.

'You'll have to get used to America, too, darling,' said Karl, 'particularly New York. It's not like this, but it's not like the cops-and-robbers New York we watch on the television.'

Jessica didn't seem to hear.

'It was a wonderful wedding,' she said. 'I'll never forget it, never. Daddy was so proud! That service in Oldminster Cathedral was quite beautiful. And my dress — that was bespoke from one of the top Paris fashion houses. Do you know what I liked best about it? Being given away by Daddy, and walking up that long centre aisle on his arm.'

'Did you like the bit where we both said "I do"?' asked Karl, mockingly. 'I rather liked that bit! And talking of your father, here he is now, with Jackson, the head groom. He sits a horse well, you know, and he's taken to enjoying a daily canter these days. Your father's a survivor, Jess. He's going to be fine.'

As they entered the stone-flagged entrance hall of the ancient mansion, Karl said, 'And now we need to secure the inheritance for the future, Jess. We need to start thinking of the twenty-second baron.'

'Why, what do you mean?'

'You know perfectly well what I mean, Jessica. So let's search the house for a room that's going to be suitable for a nursery. Let's do it now, while the time's ripe!'

* * *

'With luck,' said Linda Reid, 'we'll open for business in August. Tim's already receiving bookings from some of our American clients who liked to stay with us at Church Eaton.'

Noel Greenspan and Chloe McArthur looked up at the sign in great golden letters fixed above the first-floor windows: *Renfield Hall Hotel and Spa*.

'It'll be a year at least before the golf club opens,' said Linda. 'But it will, of that you may be sure. Come inside.'

They were greeted by the din of hammering, and the whine of electric drills. There were workmen everywhere. Tim Reid appeared. He was in his shirt sleeves, and was holding a sheaf of plans.

'We're driving all the ghosts away, Noel,' he said, 'and giving the old place a new start. Come and see the library.'

The books were still there, but at one end of the room stood a magnificent bar. Many of the old family paintings remained on the panelled walls. Noel thought, *I rather think Lord Renfield would be at home here, as long as they stocked his favourite brandy.*

The oak parlour had been subtly converted into a lounge, with a number of period pieces supplementing the existing antique furniture. Whoever it was that the Reids were employing, they knew how to create the illusion that Renfield Hall was still the residence of a member of the English aristocracy.

'Practically nothing needs to be done to the great salon, or banqueting suite, as I prefer to call it. But come upstairs, there's something there that'll interest you.'

They climbed the great staircase, and found themselves on a deep, spacious landing. Comfortable chairs were dotted about, and small round tables, already fitted with white damask cloths. Tim told them that afternoon tea would be served here.

'I can't quite get my bearings,' said Noel. 'Where are we?'

'This space,' said Tim, 'was once the haunted room — Lady Clarissa's room. It was drenched in blood, and cursed.

When this part of the house was rebuilt after the fire, I had the whole room dismantled and removed, and opened out into this landing. There's no place in the Renfield Hall Hotel and Spa for those memories of death.'

Tim Reid stood on the landing, still clutching his sheaf of plans. He remained quite still for a moment, lost in thought.

'You know,' said Tim, 'it's odd in a way. According to those heralds, or whatever they were, I was the rightful owner of this house. Well, I dispute that, but I do feel, somehow, that I've come home at last!'

THE END

Thank you for reading this book.

If you enjoyed it please leave feedback on Amazon or Goodreads, and if there is anything we missed or you have a question about, then please get in touch. We appreciate you choosing our book.

Founded in 2014 in Shoreditch, London, we at Joffe Books pride ourselves on our history of innovative publishing. We were thrilled to be shortlisted for Independent Publisher of the Year at the British Book Awards.

www.joffebooks.com

We're very grateful to eagle-eyed readers who take the time to contact us. Please send any errors you find to corrections@joffebooks.com. We'll get them fixed ASAP.